MISSING PIECES

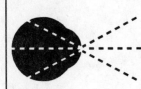

This Large Print Book carries the
Seal of Approval of N.A.V.H.

MISSING PIECES

HEATHER GUDENKAUF

THORNDIKE PRESS
A part of Gale, Cengage Learning

GALE
CENGAGE Learning·

Farmington Hills, Mich • San Francisco • New York • Waterville, Maine
Meriden, Conn • Mason, Ohio • Chicago

GALE
CENGAGE Learning

LIBRARY OF CONGRESS CATALOGING-IN-PUBLICATION DATA

Names: Gudenkauf, Heather, author.
Title: Missing pieces / Heather Gudenkauf.
Description: Large print edition. | Waterville, Maine : Thorndike Press Large Print, 2016. | © 2016 | Series: Thorndike Press large print basic
Identifiers: LCCN 2015046768 | ISBN 9781410486424 (hardback) | ISBN 1410486427 (hardcover)
Subjects: LCSH: Large type books. | BISAC: FICTION / Suspense. | GSAFD: Suspense fiction.
Classification: LCC PS3557.R198 M57 2016 | DDC 813/.54—dc23
LC record available at http://lccn.loc.gov/2015046768

Published in 2016 by arrangement with Harlequin Books S.A.

Printed in the United States of America
1 2 3 4 5 6 7 20 19 18 17 16

For Marianne Merola — my agent,
mentor and friend —
there since the beginning of
this amazing journey

PROLOGUE: 1985

Lydia gazed absentmindedly outside the kitchen window, the bright May sunshine glinting off the dew-glazed sweet-potato vine that cascaded from the window box just beyond the screen. It was barely seven thirty, and fifteen-year-old Jack and eleven-year-old Amy were already on the bus, making the forty-minute ride to school. Their last day before summer vacation began. She'd have to make a special supper to celebrate the occasion. Waffles topped with strawberries and freshly whipped cream, lemonade garnished with mint snipped from the windowsill herb garden.

Outside, Grey, their pewter-eyed silver Lab, began barking. A relaxed, friendly yapping. Lydia leaned in, scanning the yard for the source of Grey's excitement. From her vantage point, the farmyard was deserted. John's truck was still gone and wouldn't return until after six. The bedsheets that she had forgotten on the clothesline overnight flapped languidly in the mild morning breeze. The gravel road that wound its way up to the main highway was empty, no telltale dust announcing the arrival of a visitor. Someone could have come by way of the old mud road, but few dared to, for fear their tires would become stuck in the mire brought along by the early-summer rain. Lydia cocked her ear toward the window; Grey's barking was replaced by the impatient clucks from the henhouse, the Sussexes waiting for their breakfast. Lydia sighed. It had been a long, lonely winter and spring and she was finally beginning to feel better after weeks of nausea and dizziness and a fogginess she could not explain. She looked forward to the hot summer ahead, taking the kids to the swimming pool in town, going on picnics, spreading a blanket across the front lawn at dusk and staring up into the navy blue night pinpricked with stars.

She turned from the window, mentally ticking off the items she would need to make the waffles: heavy cream, last summer's strawberries stored in the cellar freezer. In her periphery a shadow slid darkly behind the sheets fluttering on the clothesline. She paused. Slowly she turned back toward the window, trying to make sense of what she had just seen out of the corner of her eye. The linens swirled lazily with the rising breeze. Nothing there. A trick of light.

She moved toward the cellar with slow, determined strides and stopped in front of the closed door. Normally she avoided the dank, stale cellar and she reluctantly reached for the knob, briefly considering scrapping the dinner of waffles and frozen strawberries. There was leftover meat loaf and mashed potatoes in the refrigerator, a plate of brownies on the counter.

Lydia laughed shakily, slightly embarrassed with her skittishness. She had lived on this farm for fifteen years and had never been afraid. Lonely, yes, but never frightened. With a deep breath she twisted the knob, her fingers fumbling for the light switch. A rush of musty air filled her nose. Over the years she tried to remove the damp, fetid smell by placing bowls of vinegar on the floor, sprinkling baking soda and mothballs into the corners and strategically placing the box fan as far as the extension cord could stretch in order to blow fresh air down from the top of the stairs. Nothing worked. With the naked lightbulb above her head doing little to illuminate her way, Lydia carefully moved down the wooden steps, sliding her hand down the iron handrail. Shelves of small, neatly labeled jars of strawberry, rhubarb and raspberry jams, and quart- and gallon-size glass containers of sweet pickles and chutney preserves lined one wall. In the narrow space beneath the stairs was where they kept the twelve-cubic-foot Coldspot deep freezer. John had bought it for her on their seventh anniversary, and while not the most romantic of gifts, she had to admit it was helpful. Whenever she wanted a pound of ground hamburger or the Iowa chops that John liked, all she had to do was go down to the cellar and retrieve whatever she needed.

With effort she lifted the heavy freezer lid and was met with a blast of cold air. Quickly riffling past the wax-paper-wrapped pork loins and the plastic bags filled with blanched kernels of sweet corn, Lydia plunged her hand into the depths of the freezer in search of what she was looking for: a quart-size package of sliced and sugared strawberries from last summer.

The initial push was the slightest of shoves, a nudge, really. Tentative. Almost a caress. A bird, maybe. A wayward wren or sparrow flying down the chimney and into the house and in its frantic state fluttering its wings against her back. That had happened before, birds getting into the house. Jack and Amy would howl with glee at the bird swooping at their heads, desperate to find its way back out into the open air.

But a second blow followed immediately, striking her in the lower ribs. Her breath was knocked from her lungs and she scrambled to steady herself against the deep freeze.

With difficulty she twisted around, needing to see, needing to know who wanted to hurt her.

Oh, it's you, was Lydia's final thought before being struck in the temple, their eyes locking one last time.

1
PRESENT DAY

The call, like many of its kind, had come in the early hours of the morning, waking Jack and Sarah from a dead sleep. Jack's hand had snaked from beneath the covers, fumbling for the phone. He grunted a sleepy hello, listened for a moment, then sat up suddenly alert.

"Is it the girls?" Sarah asked as she turned on the bedside lamp. They had dropped the girls off at the University of Montana just a few weeks earlier and Sarah's worst fear was receiving an early-morning call like this. Jack shook his head and Sarah breathed a sigh of relief.

"It's Julia," Jack said after hanging up, his voice thick with emotion. "She had a fall. I need to go home."

Now, as their airplane ascended into the blue Montana sky, Sarah settled into her seat and gazed down at the expansive landscape below. The mountains, tipped with white, seemed to burst from the trees, while rivers meandered across the earth and deep lakes glittered in the midmorning September sun. Though she had grown up in Larkspur, she never tired of its beauty and she hated leaving, even for just a short time. She and Jack hadn't strayed from Montana in years, saw no need to travel to exotic lands, to ocean coasts or dry deserts. All they needed they found in their home on Larkspur Lake.

She looked over at Jack, who was shifting in his seat, trying to find a comfortable position for his long legs. The crosshatched lines that rested at the corners of his eyes had become more pronounced overnight, and two deep grooves above the bridge of his nose extended to his forehead like a ladder of worry. She had seen this same look on his face when the first of their twin daughters, Elizabeth, was born and had waited a full sixty seconds, an eternity, to take her first breath. Saw the same expression when their other daughter, Emma, took a nasty tumble from her bike and came to them crying, her elbow dangling helplessly at her side. She knew that look. Jack was scared.

She wished there was something that she could say to ease his nerves, but Jack was a reserved man who kept his worries to himself. She reached for his hand and absentmindedly he fiddled with her wedding band, spinning it around and around her finger like a talisman. "When do you think we'll get to Penny Gate?" Sarah asked.

Jack checked his watch and mentally calculated the distance to the small Iowa town where he grew up. "I'd say we'll get there about seven if we go straight to the hospital. Uncle Hal said they stabilized Julia in the emergency room and now she's in the ICU."

"From what you've told me about your aunt, if anyone can pull through such a bad fall, it's Julia. Thank God your sister found her so quickly."

"Yeah, if Amy showed up at the house any later, I don't know if she would still be alive." Jack went silent then, as if lost in thought, focusing intently on the seat in front of him.

Sarah could hear the worry in his voice. What would they find when they arrived in Penny Gate? Would his aunt be awake and grateful to see him or would she succumb to her injuries and not survive the night? "We'll be there soon," Sarah assured him.

"You know, it's been twenty years since I've been home. After the accident, I just couldn't go back there. Hal and Julia took

15

us in and treated us as their own, and I couldn't even be bothered to visit in all these years."

Jack rarely spoke of his life in Penny Gate, of the years before the accident that took the lives of both his parents. He kept those memories well hidden, the only part of himself that was off-limits to Sarah. All she really knew was that on a rainy spring night the year Jack turned fifteen, his mother and father climbed into their rusty old pickup truck and Jack never saw either of them again.

Jack had been her physical therapist, treating Sarah's injured shoulder after her own car accident, and after twelve painful but productive rehab sessions he announced that he had done all he could for her, at least physical-therapy-wise, then promptly asked her out on a date.

She remembered the night Jack told her about the accident as if it was burned in her memory. They had been dating for about a month and spent the weekend kayaking on Deer Lake, three hours north of Minneapolis. It was a warm summer night; the sun was beginning to set, a large gilded orb melting into the lake's horizon. They were in no rush to return to shore and laid their paddles across their laps and drifted languidly across the water.

Sarah, at the front of the kayak, gently waved away mosquitoes that hummed past her ear and asked Jack about the night his parents had died. She wasn't sure why he chose that moment to answer; he had sidestepped her questions so many times before. Perhaps it was because in the rear of the kayak she couldn't see his face. Perhaps it was the remote location; they hadn't seen another boat in hours. The only sound was the gentle slap of water against the side of the kayak. Jack had breathed the details of the story in staccato, short-clipped phrases that seemed to punch the air from his chest: *He was drinking again. I should have stopped her. Stopped him. The roads were wet.*

Sarah wanted to turn and reach for Jack but forced herself to remain facing forward in the kayak, afraid that any movement would cause him to stop talking.

He flipped the truck. Upside down in a cornfield. Killed instantly.

Jack's breath came out in jagged chuffs and Sarah could tell that he was crying. Slowly, carefully, as one might to a skittish animal, she reached behind her and found Jack's hand.

A year later they were married, she quit her job as a reporter and they moved to

17

Larkspur to begin a family. In the past twenty years Sarah had wanted to ask Jack so many questions. Not just about the accident and the years that followed, but about what his life was like before his parents died. Simple questions. Did he look more like his mother or his father? What books did she read to him before bedtime or did she call him by a pet name? Did his father teach him to bait a hook or skip rocks across a pond? But every time she broached the subject, Jack would find a way to avoid the conversation. He wouldn't let her in.

Jack released Sarah's hand and ran his fingers through his gray-flecked hair, a nervous gesture that she knew he would repeat a hundred times before they landed. "I shouldn't have waited so long to come back," he murmured.

Jack jiggled his leg up and down, striking the back of the seat with his knee. The man in front of him turned around and glowered with irritation. Jack didn't notice.

"I'm sure they understand," Sarah said, laying a hand on his leg to still it. But she wondered if Jack's aunt and uncle truly understood how the boy they took into their home could stay away for nearly two decades.

"I should have called her back." Jack's

voice caught and he cleared his throat. "It just slipped my mind and I knew she'd call again in a few days." Jack's aunt, without fail, called the house each Sunday evening to check in and catch up on the events of their week. But the previous Sunday they were out for a walk and had missed Julia's call. She had left a message on their machine, but it was late when they returned home and Jack had forgotten to call back the following day.

When they came home and listened to the message, Sarah had thought she detected a shakiness in Julia's voice, a tremor that made her think of Parkinson's. At the time she had dismissed it, but now she wondered if she should have said something to Jack.

"Do you think that Julia sounded different the last few times she called?" Sarah asked, pulling her cardigan more tightly around herself to stave off the plane's chilly temperature.

Jack narrowed his eyes as if mentally shuffling through recent conversations with his aunt. "I don't think so. What do you mean?"

Sarah hesitated. "I'm not sure. Has Hal said anything about any health concerns?"

"No, but that doesn't mean she hasn't had any problems," Jack admitted. He tilted his head back against the headrest and stared up at the plane's ceiling. "I can't believe they still live in that house," he said, changing the subject. "It's too big for two people. And those steps. They're so steep. I tripped down them all the time when I was a kid. I just can't believe that someone hasn't had a bad fall before now. The place is a death trap."

Jack crossed his arms in front of his chest and burrowed more deeply into his seat. "We used to go to this pond," he said as she slid her hand through his arm and rested her head on his shoulder. The comforting scent of his shaving cream and the starch used to iron his shirt filled her nose. "Aunt Julia would pack these elaborate picnics. Strawberries that we'd spent hours picking and pickled herring on crackers, cheese with names we couldn't pronounce and her homemade bread." Jack's voice sounded far away and Sarah hung on his words. "Then we'd all climb into the back of Uncle Hal's truck and drive down the old mud road to the pond. We'd sit on the bank and fish for hours and would end up with just a few bluegills, a bass if we were lucky. Julia would make a big deal out of each one we caught, though, clapping her hands and jumping up and down."

Sarah thought about the times they had

20

taken Elizabeth and Emma fishing. The girls squealing over the wiggling worms that Jack used to bait their hooks. Their delight at Jack pretending to buckle beneath the weight of their catches.

"Sometimes I can still taste those strawberries." Jack smiled sadly and Sarah squeezed his hand.

"It must be hard going back," Sarah reflected. "Lots of memories."

He nodded tentatively, a ghost of a smile playing on his lips. "Everything seemed so simple then. Easier somehow." Jack turned to the window then and looked out at the far-reaching landscape below. The world was endless from this vantage point, full of infinite wonder and possibility, and Jack drifted off in thought as he took in the view.

"I remember on stormy summer nights," he started, his voice tinged with sadness. "When the power would go out, my mom would scavenge through the cupboards and drawers looking for flashlights." Sarah's breath caught in her chest. Jack never spoke about his parents. Ever.

"Amy and I would grab the clean sheets from the clothesline just before the rain began to fall. Then we'd throw them over the furniture to make forts. We'd pretend the flashlights were our campfire and tell

21

each other stories . . ."

Jack looked as if he was going to say more but instead he rubbed his hand across his mouth as if wiping away the thought. He turned back from the window and leaned his head against the headrest and closed his eyes.

Sarah wanted to press for more, but she knew this fleeting moment of reminiscence was over.

As the airplane carried them away from the life they had made together, she watched Jack doze. Behind his closed eyelids she knew that a thousand secret memories drifted. She wanted him to let her in, to know that he was safe. Safe with her. Maybe she couldn't erase all the sadness and bitterness he was carrying. But she could be there for him and help him through the pain.

Despite the sad circumstances of their trip to Penny Gate, Sarah was looking forward to seeing the town Jack grew up in. She wanted to drive along the roads that he once traveled, to see the bedroom that he once slept in, to spend time with his family, whom she had only gotten to know over the years through phone calls and birthday cards. She thought it might bring her closer to him.

She let Jack rest until the pilot's voice filled the airplane cabin, announcing their impending arrival in Chicago. The fasten-seat-belt light blinked on, and she lightly nudged Jack awake. Down below, the blue expanse of Lake Michigan was edged by miles of skyscrapers. Each drop in altitude was jarring, and Sarah's stomach churned. She reached for Jack's hand and closed her eyes, squeezing his fingers tightly until finally the wheels touched the runway.

They had only fifteen minutes to get to their gate in time to catch their connecting flight to the small airport near Penny Gate, and Sarah scurried to keep up with Jack's long strides as they wove their way through crowds of travelers, her carry-on bag bumping along behind her.

When they arrived at their gate, they joined the line of passengers to board their connecting flight. Jack quickly called Hal for an update on Julia's condition.

"She hasn't woken up yet," he reported grimly when he hung up the phone. "She's back from X-ray and she has a skull fracture, a broken pelvis and both arms are fractured."

Sarah handed her boarding pass to the gate agent. "That's terrible. Does she need surgery?"

"I don't know. Not yet, anyway. They're watching her closely to make sure there isn't any bleeding on her brain."

They were the last of the fifty passengers to board the full flight. Because of their late booking Sarah's seat was three rows behind Jack and across the aisle.

It was just a short thirty-minute flight to the small regional airport near Penny Gate, and as they got closer to their destination, Sarah watched from afar as Jack seemed to grow more and more restless. His foot tapped nervously and he kept checking his watch. Sarah knew that a million thoughts were banging around Jack's head. He hadn't seen his aunt and uncle in twenty years. How would they receive him? With open arms or cold reservation? Jack was returning to the town where he was born and raised but whose roads had taken his parents away from him. Anxiety seemed to radiate from his body and Sarah wanted to go to him, to reassure him that everything was going to be okay, and if it wasn't she would be right there beside him.

Sarah peered out the window as they descended. Jack was right. He had told her that Iowa had a beauty all its own, and the landscape was a patchwork of verdant greens, golden yellows and rich browns.

When they landed, Jack waited for Sarah at the end of the jet bridge. "Are you okay?" Sarah asked with concern. His skin had taken on a sickly hue.

"Just a little airsick," Jack explained as they went in search of a rental car.

The clear sky above them was quickly being replaced by a blanket of leaden clouds and a cold wind pressed at their backs, hurrying them along to the rental car. Jack loaded their bags in the trunk and then opened the passenger's-side door for Sarah. She smiled at the small act of chivalry.

"The hospital is only about half an hour from here," Jack explained as he drove out of the airport parking lot. Jack was silent as he wove his way through busy interstate traffic past an industrial area with tall sturdy buildings, smokestacks and train bridges. Gradually the landscape shifted and factories were replaced with vast fields stretching majestically into the horizon. Farm buildings peppered the landscape: bullet-shaped silos that reached to the sky, barns painted a crisp white or deep crimson, some barely standing, weathered by years of rain, wind and snow. They passed half-harvested fields of alfalfa, striped gold and green, and acres of sun-bleached corn lying in wait for the following day's harvest. Barbed wire pulled tautly across the wooden fence posts that lined the fields like jagged teeth.

It was nearing seven o'clock and the sun was setting behind the sharp line of the horizon, creating a golden halo across the distant fields. A light rain speckled the windshield and Sarah flipped on the car's heater. Though the speed limit was fifty-five, Jack was barely going forty. She watched him covertly from the corner of her eye. His hands gripped the steering wheel, his eyes stared intently ahead. She wondered if he was trying to delay his arrival at the hospital, reluctant to see his aunt so badly injured, or if he simply dreaded returning to his hometown where he faced such painful loss.

The road followed the path of the Gray Fox River and curled through the countryside. Could this have been the highway his parents were driving on the night they died? Maybe one of the recently harvested cornfields was where their car had come to a final rest.

"You seem distracted," she said. "Do you want me to drive?"

Jack glanced down at the speedometer and pressed down on the gas. "No, sorry, I'm fine. Thanks for coming with me. Are you going to get behind on your column?" he asked.

"Don't worry," Sarah said, patting his knee. "I let the paper know I'd be away for a few days. I've got a bunch of responses just in case," Sarah said of the advice column she had been writing for the past seven years. Sarah nodded toward the landscape. "Has it changed much?"

The ditches were lined with rosy thistle and spiky purple prairie clover. In the distance stood dozens of wind turbines, rows of towering structures that seemed to have sprouted incongruously from fields of alfalfa. Their blades were eerily still at the moment, waiting to capture the prairie wind as it swept by.

"Not a bit," Jack observed.

The Sawyer County Hospital was just on the outskirts of Penny Gate, and as they pulled into the parking lot Sarah could see it was a small building constructed of dark brown brick that looked nearly black beneath the ashen sky. Jack eased the car into a parking spot and pulled up on the hand brake. Sarah waited for him to open his door, but he just sat there, looking ahead.

"It's going to be okay," she said, hoping to calm his nerves. They sat quietly for a moment and Sarah wondered what was going through his mind. Was it fear? Sadness? Regret? Probably a combination, she decided, then broke the silence.

"You ready?" she asked.

Jack took a breath and held it awhile before letting it out with a deep sigh. "I think so," he said as he popped open the door and stepped out from the car.

But Sarah wasn't so sure she was ready herself.

2

Side by side, Sarah and Jack made their way across the hospital parking lot, sharp pellets of rain striking their skin. They stepped through the main entrance and were immediately assaulted with the uniquely antiseptic odor of health-care facilities. The hospital was clean but dated. Institutional-green walls were lined with faded Impressionist prints and the carpet was worn and thin. Jack inquired about Julia at the information desk and they were directed to the fifth floor.

Once upstairs Jack hesitated outside the room. "I don't know if I can do this," he said softly, rubbing his eyes. Sarah slid her hand into his and waited. She knew how difficult this was for him, that coming home would release a floodgate of memories and emotions that he had kept locked up inside himself for decades.

Finally, Jack knocked lightly, pushed open

the door and stepped inside.

The room was dim. The lights were off; the shades were drawn. The redolence of death hung in the air, and it was stifling.

Sarah's eyes locked on the tiny elderly woman lying in the hospital bed. Asleep or unconscious, it was difficult to know. Next to her, Sarah heard Jack inhale sharply. Beneath the oxygen mask, Julia's skin was bruised and pale. What appeared to be bits of dried blood clung to her tightly curled white hair, a section shaved away and covered with a thick bandage. She was connected to an IV filled with clear liquid. Both of her arms and hands were casted and her right leg was held immobile in a brace from toe to pelvis. A sense of dread washed over Sarah and she rubbed her arms, trying to scrub away the chill.

"Jesus," Jack murmured, tracing the tips of his fingers over his aunt's right forearm. "All this from a fall?"

The room was drafty and the mechanical hum of the medical equipment filled the air. If it weren't for the heart monitor that Julia was connected to, it would be difficult to know she was still breathing.

On the bedside table was a photograph of Julia and Hal from early in their marriage. Julia was young and hugely pregnant, wearing a smile of pure joy. Hal's eyes were firmly fixed on Julia. They were obviously crazy about each other. Next to Julia's bed was a set of rosary beads and a daily devotional. Someone had tucked a handmade pink-and-yellow postage-stamp quilt around her small, diminished frame. A powdery, rose-petal scent emanated from the old fabric but couldn't quite mask the odor of iodine and illness that permeated the room. Sarah wondered who had placed these comforts from home so lovingly around the hospital room. Hal, she guessed.

"Jack?" came a voice from behind them. Startled, they both turned to find a small woman with dark, curly hair and large green eyes that shone with warmth. Sarah recognized her from Christmas photos exchanged each year and the photographs didn't do her justice. Her heart-shaped face was unlined and pale, a stark contrast to her black curls. Her full lips curved into a disarming smile revealing a deep dimple in her left cheek. She was beautiful.

"Jack," the woman said again, and Sarah sensed a tone of relief in her voice.

"Celia," he said, and smiled, perhaps for the first time since they had arrived in Iowa. The woman stepped forward to wrap her arms around him and Sarah felt as if she

31

had suddenly disappeared into the room's white walls.

"It's so good to see you. I can't believe you're really here," she said into his ear.

Sarah had never met Celia, the woman married to Jack's cousin, Dean. In fact, the last time Jack had gone home to Penny Gate was for Dean and Celia's wedding. Sarah had stayed behind with the twins, who were under a year old at the time. It was a quick trip, just two nights and three days. *Three days in Penny Gate is more than enough,* Jack had said, but looking back, Sarah wondered if Jack was relieved that she opted to stay behind.

Sarah had looked forward to finally meeting Celia in person. They had talked briefly on the phone several times over the years, exchanged Christmas cards. But now she couldn't help but feel intimidated by the woman.

Jack pulled away from their embrace and took a step backward, holding Celia by the forearms to get a better look. "Of course I came."

For the first time Celia seemed to notice Sarah. "Sarah?" she asked, and Jack nodded in affirmation.

"It's so wonderful to finally meet you in person," Celia said, drawing her into a tight hug that felt a little too familiar. "All the nice things Jack has said about you, I feel like I've known you forever." Celia looked around the room. "Where are the girls? Did you bring them?"

"No, no," Sarah said. "They couldn't make it." She was about to explain how the girls were tied up with school when Jack's cousin, Dean, appeared in the doorway and diverted her attention. He was a tall, broad man who wore the weathered look of a tired farmer and a son worn down with worry.

He didn't look like the same recklessly handsome man she had last seen twenty years ago when he was the best man at their wedding. He had gained well over fifty pounds and his thick dark hair had disappeared. His face was scoured and lined by hours spent out in the fields beneath the blazing Iowa sun.

"Jack," Dean said, and the two men embraced with heavy claps on the back. "Thanks for coming." Dean pulled away and swiped at his eyes with the back of one large hand. "I know it means a lot to Mom that you're here. She thinks the world of you."

"I'm so sorry about Julia," Sarah said, and reached out her arms as he pulled her into a hug. "What are the doctors saying?"

Dean shoved his hands into his pockets. "She has a fractured skull and broken bones. Almost too many to count. But she's a strong old bird."

"What happened?" Jack asked, looking down at his aunt. Sarah knew that he was thinking the same thing she was: it was a miracle this elderly wisp of a woman was still alive.

"All we know is that she fell down the stairs sometime early yesterday evening. Amy was the one who found her and called 9-1-1."

"How's your dad doing?" Sarah asked. "I bet he's just sick about it."

"He's doing okay. I don't think he can believe this is happening. He's down in the cafeteria with Amy, getting something to eat."

"I've been trying to get ahold of Amy for weeks," Jack said, "but she never answers her phone."

Dean hesitated before speaking. "That was something I was hoping to talk to you about."

"Why don't we take a walk and get some air," Celia said to Sarah, but Jack shook his head.

"I don't mind if Sarah stays if you don't," Jack said. "Is something wrong?"

"It's about Amy," Dean explained. "Let's go outside."

They moved into the hallway and Jack looked expectantly at his cousin. "Is Amy okay? Did something happen?"

"We're worried about her," Celia said uncomfortably.

"I hate to spring this on you," Dean said, scratching the back of his neck. "And I know this is the last thing you need to hear right now, but Amy's been having a hard time lately."

"Of course she's having a hard time," Jack said with confusion. "Julia's like a mother to her."

"It's more than that," Dean said. "She was acting strange before the fall, too."

"Has she been drinking again?" Jack asked. Sarah thought of Jack's dad and his drinking. Alcoholism ran in families, but Jack drank only socially, never allowing it to impair his thinking.

"I think so, maybe pain pills, too. She lost her job at the motel a few weeks ago."

"She's worked there for over two years. Do you know what happened?"

"She was showing up late, not showing up at all — that's what I heard."

Two nurses dressed in green scrubs brushed passed them and Sarah's eyes fol-

35

lowed them down the depressingly dim corridor. She noticed on the ceiling that a brown spot had bloomed against the white plaster and rainwater dripped rhythmically into a large bucket below. She imagined mold and mildew festering behind the walls.

"Amy walks around like a zombie half the time and she's lost a lot of weight. I just don't want you to be shocked when you see her."

"How's she paying her bills?" Jack asked. "Has she found another job yet?"

"I don't think so, but she's still living in that little rental house on Oleander, so she hasn't been evicted yet. I'm guessing that my mom and dad have been giving her some money to get by." Dean shifted his weight uncomfortably. "They're on a fixed income themselves and don't have a lot of extra cash to spare."

"Hal and Julia shouldn't have to pay Amy's way," Jack said quietly. "She's a grown woman."

"We just thought you'd want to know," Celia said. "I've tried talking to her, but she hasn't been answering my calls, either."

Jack opened his mouth to speak when something down the hallway caught his eye.

"Jack?" Sarah asked, but his eyes were fixed on a point in the distance, down the hall. He didn't answer and Sarah repeated his name, this time more loudly. "What is it?" she asked as she turned and followed his sharp gaze, but all she saw was a doctor standing at the nurse's station taking notes on a chart.

"Nothing," Jack replied, and shook his head. Sarah thought he seemed confused. "It's nothing," he repeated with finality, and turned his attention back to them. "So, you think Amy's been abusing pain pills? Have you talked to her about it?"

"My mom has. I know she was worried about her and they argued about it a few days before the fall."

"Thanks for letting me know. I'll try and talk to her before we go back home."

"Here comes Hal now," Celia said.

An elderly man wearing work boots and a frayed tan barn jacket approached. Though he was nearly six feet tall and broad-shouldered, he was a smaller, softer version of Dean. His bald head was speckled with age spots and sun damage, and his weary, deeply lined face lit up when he saw them. "Jack," he said warmly. Behind thick glasses, his eyes glistened with emotion and worry. "Thank you so much for coming."

"Uncle Hal," Jack said, reaching for the older man. They clung to each other for a long time and Jack closed his eyes as he settled comfortably into their embrace. "I'm so sorry," he whispered.

Hal pulled away, smiling through tears. He took Jack's face in his hands. "You know when she wakes up she's going to give you hell for taking so long to come back home."

Dean snickered and suddenly the tone felt lighter. Easier. "He's right, you know. I can hear her when she wakes up. 'You mean all I had to do is fall down a flight of stairs to get that boy to come home?' " Dean's voice rose an octave as he mimicked Julia's voice.

"That sounds about right," Jack said, giving a small laugh. "You remember Sarah, don't you?"

"You haven't changed a bit," Hal said as he embraced her. "Thanks for coming."

Sarah watched as her husband fell into the comfortable banter of a family catching up after so many years of lost time. She was surprised by how easy it was, not even a hint of the devastation that had befallen them all that time ago. Jack and Hal interacted like a father and son, and Sarah could see the mutual love and respect in their eyes. She was so enrapt by this unseen side of Jack that she almost didn't notice the small frail woman who had seemed to arrive from out of nowhere.

38

"Amy," Celia said, "look who's here."

Amy's brown eyes were flat and expressionless, and Sarah thought she looked even thinner than the last time she had seen her. Her pale skin was pulled tightly against her bones and seemed paper-thin. Almost translucent. Her hair was bleached a nearly colorless blond and was pulled back into a lank ponytail. Sarah could understand why Dean and Celia were so concerned about her. She looked sickly.

"I wasn't sure you'd come," Amy said almost accusingly. She hesitated and then wrapped her reedlike arms around her brother. At first taken aback, Jack returned the embrace.

The last time they had seen Amy was four years earlier. She had called out of the blue all the way from Spokane, Washington. From what Sarah could gather, Amy had traveled there with a man and it ended badly. Jack made the drive to collect her and six hours later Amy arrived in Larkspur, haggard, bruised and hungover.

Sarah never quite understood the dynamic between Amy and Jack. She knew Amy had had a hard life and didn't think she ever quite forgave Jack for going away to college and leaving her behind in Penny Gate. He didn't talk to or see his sister very often, but when he did it was usually in conjunction with some major catastrophe, usually of Amy's own making: a job lost unfairly, a poisonous relationship with a man, a brush with the law. After the phone calls Jack would hang up drained and distracted.

Jack murmured in Amy's ear, too quietly for Sarah to hear, but she could tell by the way Amy's demeanor seemed to soften that Jack had said something to ease her. She nodded and wiped her eyes, leaving behind black streaks of mascara beneath her eyes.

Sarah was suddenly overwhelmed at the sight of Jack comforting Amy. Blinking back tears, she could almost picture them as children, Jack the protective older brother, always looking after his fragile little sister. "Amy, it's so good to see you," Sarah said, taking a hesitant step toward her sister-in-law. "It's been way too long."

"Hi," Amy said hoarsely, surprising Sarah by giving her a hug. The odor of cigarette smoke clung to Amy's clothes and Sarah could feel the sharp point of each rib. Sarah carefully returned the embrace, afraid of squeezing too tightly against Amy's thin frame. "Thanks for coming."

"Of course." Sarah reached into her purse and pulled out a small package of tissues and offered them to Amy.

"Amy, did you get something to eat?" Celia asked.

Amy nodded and Celia gave her a pointed look.

"I did," Amy said with annoyance. "You can even ask Hal."

"She did eat," Hal confirmed. "Not much, but then neither did I."

"You need to take care of yourself," Celia pressed. "Why don't you stay at our house tonight? Get a good night's sleep."

"No, I think I'll stay here tonight," Amy replied, hitching her thumb toward the hospital room. "I'm going to check on Julia." She hugged Jack again. "You don't know how glad I am that you're here." She wrapped her arms around her midsection as if warding off the cold and moved past them down the hallway toward Julia's room.

"She's taking this really hard," Hal said, looking fondly after his niece. "But she's been great. She's been glued to Julia's side almost the entire time."

"Amy loves Julia more than anyone else in the world," Jack said.

"Is she the one who decorated Julia's room with all the photos and things from home?" Sarah asked.

"No, Celia did that," Hal responded, rub-

41

bing his hand absentmindedly across his head.

"That's really nice," Sarah said. "When Julia wakes up she'll have some comforts of home nearby." She was not only beautiful, Sarah observed, but Celia was thoughtful, too. It was obvious she made it a priority to take care of everyone in the Quinlan family.

To confirm Sarah's observation, Celia started gathering up empty coffee cups and stray napkins. "Hal," she said, "didn't you have your hat earlier?"

Hal's hands went to his bare head. "I think I left it down in the cafeteria."

"I'll go get it," Jack offered. "I could use a cup of coffee, anyway."

"I'll go with you," Sarah said, not wanting to be left alone. Jack's family was nice enough, but she hardly knew them, and she was eager to avoid the grim scene inside the dark hospital room. The drawn shades, the stuffy air, the pneumatic hum of the oxygen machine. It was practically suffocating.

Sarah and Jack made their way to the elevators. "Amy doesn't look good," Jack commented. "I'm worried about her."

"She's the one who found Julia after she fell, right? That must have been very traumatic."

"Yeah, but there's something else." Jack

42

pressed the elevator's down button, and then again and again, as if the elevator couldn't come quickly enough. He searched for the right words. "Something in her eyes," he added.

"You should talk to her," Sarah said. She caught a flurry of movement out of the corner of her eye. A doctor was hurrying down the corridor, her long white coat flowing behind her. Sarah's first thought was Julia had taken a turn for the worse and held her breath until the doctor turned in the opposite direction of Julia's room.

The elevator door finally opened and they stepped inside. The doors closed and Sarah leaned against Jack.

"I don't know. I probably should, but I'm sure it won't make a difference."

The old elevator creaked and groaned and was excruciatingly slow in its descent, stopping at each floor, though no one was there to get in. Sarah figured whoever was waiting gave up and used the stairs instead.

"I think she'd listen to you, Jack. She seemed so glad to see you."

Sarah's thoughts suddenly went back to their earlier conversation about Amy. She recalled how Jack had become distracted by something he had seen down the hallway.

"What did you see earlier?" Sarah asked.

"When we were in the hallway talking to Dean and Celia?"

Jack pushed the first-floor button again as if it could speed up their descent. "I'm not sure what you mean," he said, feigning ignorance.

"Come on, Jack, tell me," Sarah pressed.

"It was nothing," Jack insisted. The elevator finally arrived at their floor and the doors opened to an empty, quiet hallway. It was cold and eerie, and Sarah couldn't help but wonder if they kept the morgue down here, as well. Jack turned right, following the sign directing them to the cafeteria, and Sarah quickened her pace to keep up with him.

"Jack, you looked like you'd seen a ghost."

Jack stopped abruptly. "Cut it out, Sarah. I didn't see anything," he said, but Sarah looked at him expectantly. "Okay. Fine. For a second I thought I saw my dad."

"Your dad?" she questioned in confusion. He was the last person she expected Jack to mention. "That's impossible."

"I don't know. It's not like I got a clear look at whoever it was."

"I know it's not easy being back here. I'm sure it's bringing up a lot of old memories."

They entered the cafeteria, where the dim recessed lighting and a low ceiling made the room feel downright dismal. The smell of overboiled broccoli and strongly brewed coffee filled Sarah's nose. The room was empty except for a woman in a white apron and a hairnet perched behind a cash register, flicking through a magazine, and a man sitting alone at a table, staring out a rain-spattered window into the black night, his food untouched in front of him.

Sarah's eyes searched the room and landed on a table in the far corner. "There," she said, pointing. They walked past the cashier, who didn't look up from her magazine, and made their way toward the back of the cafeteria.

"God, he still wears this old thing." Jack smiled as he bent over and picked up the hat from the worn green linoleum. "I think Amy got this for Hal for Christmas, like, twenty-five years ago."

"It must mean a lot to him," Sarah said.

Jack grew quiet.

"Hey." Sarah nudged him gently. "It's okay. Everything's going to be fine."

"I just can't shake the feeling that I saw my dad," Jack said. "You must think I'm nuts."

"Of course not," Sarah replied, trying to comfort him, though she couldn't help but feel a little uneasy. "Last month I thought I saw my grandpa at the grocery store and he died when I was seven."

"Yeah, but I bet you'd be happy to get the chance to see your grandpa again. I can't say I feel the same way about my dad. I won't ever be able to forgive him."

"Never?" Sarah asked. "You'll never be able to forgive him?"

"Would you be able to forgive your dad if he killed your mother?" Jack asked pointedly as he motioned to leave the cafeteria. Sarah followed as Jack bypassed the elevator and pushed open a heavy metal door that led to the stairs. The stairwell was windowless and weakly lit by dusty fluorescent bulbs. Cobwebs swung precariously in the corners where drab cement block walls met the ceiling and Sarah quickened her pace.

"I don't know," Sarah answered honestly. "I'd like to think I'd be forgiving, especially if it was an accident."

Their footsteps reverberated on the metal stairs as they wound their way upward. Sarah almost preferred the rickety old elevator to the confines of this dingy, damp stairwell. She felt relief when Jack pushed open the door to the fifth floor. They were both slightly winded from the climb.

"You must be a better person than I am,"

Jack said somewhat breathlessly, and Sarah decided it was best to end the conversation there.

When they returned to the waiting area, Hal was sitting by himself, staring up blankly at a television set affixed to the wall.

"Found your hat," Jack said, handing it to his uncle. Hal set it on his bald head and adjusted it into place.

"No coffee?" Hal asked, noting their empty hands, and Sarah realized they were so distracted they had completely forgotten to get the coffee. She instantly longed for the rush of caffeine.

"Coffee looked like sludge," Jack replied, and Sarah wondered why he didn't just tell Hal the truth. "Where is everyone?"

"Amy's still with Julia, and Dean and Celia went to see if they could find out what time the doctor is doing rounds tomorrow."

"I'll go see if Amy needs a break," Jack said. He gave Sarah a peck on the cheek and she smiled warmly as he turned and exited the waiting area, leaving her alone with Hal.

Sarah sat down in one of the stiff-backed chairs next to Hal. Purple rings of exhaustion circled Hal's eyes and were magnified by the thick lenses of his glasses.

"I shouldn't have left her home alone," he

said, sliding his thumb and forefinger beneath his glasses and rubbing his eyes. "Her balance hasn't been very good lately. She's been stumbling a lot."

Sarah thought again about the phone message that Julia had left on their machine and the tremble in her voice.

From across the corridor Sarah watched as Jack entered Julia's room. Moments later, Amy emerged handling a pack of cigarettes as she moved toward the elevator.

"I wish she'd give those things up," Hal said.

"It must have been terrible for Amy to find Julia after her fall."

"She found Julia at the bottom of the steps and called an ambulance right away. Then called me."

"That probably saved her life."

"I think so, but a social worker came to talk to me this afternoon. Have you ever heard of that? I mean, after an accident?"

"A social worker?" Sarah repeated. "Why?"

"She was asking all these questions about Julia's accident. I wasn't even at the house when she fell. I was in town. She asked if there were any problems in the family, any reason Julia wouldn't feel safe."

"They probably have to ask those kinds of

questions when there's an accident in the home," Sarah said, though she wasn't quite so sure and didn't want to let on to Hal that it worried her. "What did you say?"

"I told her what I just told you. That she's been stumbling a lot lately. I mean, hell, so have I. We're getting older.

"The social worker said someone reported that the fall might not have been an accident, after all. Why would someone say such an awful thing?" he asked incredulously, rubbing the sharp gray stubble on his chin, his blue eyes clouded with worry.

"What did Dean and Amy say? Did the social worker talk to them, too?"

"Just to me, I think. I haven't told anyone. I didn't want to bother them with it." He shifted in his seat, pulled out a white, linen handkerchief from his pocket and smoothed it with his blunt fingers. "Do you think we should be concerned?"

"I think you should tell them. Tell Jack. They can help you talk to the social worker," Sarah advised, and Hal said that he would.

"It really helps having family here," he said, and crossed one leg over his knee, his heavy brown work boot weathered with age and toil. "I know Jack doesn't like coming back here."

"He wanted to come. We wanted to be

here for you and Julia." Sarah reached out and patted Hal's knee and he covered Sarah's hand with his own.

"Well, I can't tell you how much it helps," he said, and cleared his throat. For a moment Sarah wondered if she should seize the opportunity to ask Hal about Jack, about the ghost of his father he thought he saw earlier. But instead she allowed silence to fall between them.

For the next hour Sarah sat in the waiting room while Jack's family took turns sitting with Julia. Hal was the last and after what felt like aeons he finally emerged from the room, haggard and weary.

"I think we're all tired," Dean said, pushing himself up from his seat with difficulty. "Maybe we should all go home and get some rest. The nurses will call if there's any change."

"What if she wakes up?" Hal asked, twisting his hat in his hands. "She'll be scared if she wakes up and no one is here."

"Everyone can stay at our house," Dean said. "We're close enough to the hospital that we can get here quickly if she wakes up. Jack, you and Sarah are welcome to stay with us. We've got the room."

Jack rubbed the shadow of bristle that had

grown on his chin. "I don't think that's the best idea, Dean."

"No shit," Amy muttered from her seat.

"Be quiet, Amy," Dean said, tossing a magazine onto the coffee table. It slid across the surface and fluttered to the floor.

"Fuck you, Dean," Amy snapped.

"Whoa, settle down," Celia interjected.

"Amy," Jack pleaded. "Please don't."

"Really, Jack?" Amy's tone softened, the anger replaced with hurt. "You think that coming back here after twenty years is going to make everything okay?"

"None of this is good for Julia and that's who we need to be worrying about," Jack said. "Hal, why don't you stay at Dean and Celia's tonight? Sarah and I will get a hotel room."

"What's the matter, Jack?" Amy asked archly. "You don't want to spend a night in the house of horrors?"

"Amy, just shut the hell up." Dean's face flushed with anger.

"What do you mean, house of horrors?" Sarah asked before she could stop herself. Up until then she had uncomfortably watched the tense exchange in silence. She didn't really know Jack's family, didn't understand their dynamics, and it was clear that it was better for her to stay out of it.

"Never mind," Jack said sharply, and Hal lowered his face into his hands.

"Please don't fight. Not here."

"You're right," Jack said. "You should get some sleep. We can take you back to your house."

"Stay with me," Hal insisted. "It's silly for you to stay in a hotel. I want to sleep in my own bed, but I can't stand the thought of going home to an empty house. Please stay."

"Sure, Hal," Jack said soothingly. "We'll stay at your house." To Dean he said, "Thanks for the offer, but it would be strange staying in the old house."

Why would it be strange? Sarah wondered. And what did Amy mean by "house of horrors"? It brought to Sarah's mind an image of chain saws and rubber knives, a silly Halloween gag. And yet the words lingered in her thoughts. Was Amy just being dramatic, like Jack said she always was, or was there more to it than that? And why had Jack brushed her off when she asked about it?

She wanted to believe that he'd meant nothing by it, that he was merely trying to keep his family from combusting. But she had a sinking feeling that there was more to it than that. Jack was keeping something from her.

3

The automatic doors that led out to the parking lot slid open with an airy hum. A steady rain was falling and the lights that edged the parking lot illuminated the wet pavement, giving it a glossy, slick sheen. Fat raindrops sent ripples through standing puddles and the temperature had dropped ten degrees since they arrived in Penny Gate.

As Sarah and Jack walked through the quiet parking lot toward their rental car, Sarah wrapped her coat tightly around herself, chilled to the bone, the icy rain drenching her hair. Confusion and questions bounced around in her mind like a Ping-Pong ball. Sarah waited until they were out of Hal's earshot before speaking.

"Jack, what did Amy mean by 'house of horrors'?"

Jack slid his hands into his pockets and Sarah tried to keep up, the slap of their footfalls echoing throughout the nearly deserted parking lot. "I really don't want to talk about this right now."

She tried to keep any accusation from her voice, any irritation. She wanted to give Jack the benefit of the doubt, but she could hear the reproach in her voice. Jack sped up as if trying to avoid her.

"Jack, wait," she said, snagging his sleeve to try to get him to slow down, and he shook her away.

By the time they reached the car, both of them were soaked, their hair flattened, raindrops dripping from their noses. Jack unlocked the doors and they climbed in. He placed the key in the ignition, and Sarah reached over and put her hand over his. "Jack, talk to me. Please."

Jack pulled his hand away and sat back in his seat. "There isn't anything to say. You know Amy. She's exhausted, Aunt Julia is hurt and Amy's scared. Everything becomes one big drama and she lashes out."

Jack turned the key and the car rumbled to life. Sarah knew she only had Jack to herself for just a moment longer.

"I'm not trying to fight with you," Sarah said quietly, trembling as much from Jack's loud indignation as from the cold. "I'm just trying to understand."

"I know." Jack lowered his voice. "Hal's waiting. Can we just talk about this later?" he asked, but before she could respond, Jack had backed up the car and pulled out of the spot. Their conversation would have to wait.

He drove the car to the front of the hospital entrance where Hal was waiting for them.

"You remember how to get to the house?" Hal asked.

"Of course," Jack answered. "How could I forget?"

As they pulled away from the hospital and back onto the highway, darkness enveloped them. They drove in silence, each of them lost in their own thoughts. Sarah's mind drifted to Julia, the image of her limp body hooked up to all those tubes and wires. She couldn't imagine what Hal was going through, what it was like to be so close to losing a spouse. Could she live without Jack if she had to? She shook off the thought.

They drove past an expansive field, and Jack pointed into the dark. "I worked in that field for eight summers," Jack recalled.

"I remember," Hal said with a nostalgic laugh. "I had to drag you out of bed each morning."

"That was hard work," Jack said. He held up one hand, putting it on display. "I think

I still have calluses."

Sarah sat back and looked out the window. The countryside seemed to have gone to sleep. Farmhouses were dark and still, and hulking equipment lay dormant in the fields. No other cars were on the road, and the rain continued to beat steadily on the roof of the car. The rhythmic swish of the windshield wipers was hypnotic and Sarah found her eyes growing heavy.

Jack slowed the car and carefully turned onto a gravel road. The rain had washed away much of the loose rock and the car bumped and bucked through the deep gouges in the road. Sarah grabbed the dashboard to steady herself. Walls of corn rose ten feet above the ground, surrounding them on both sides, a narrow tunnel nearly obscuring the sky. Sarah peered into the dark shadows between the stalks, wondering what might be lurking in the night.

Finally the tight passage opened up into a wide expanse, revealing the sharp-angled silhouette of a farmhouse, the sloped curves of a barn crowned with a weather vane and two dome-shaped grain bins. The house was still and dark. There was no warm glow from a porch light, no lamp burning from behind a pulled shade to welcome them home. Jack parked in the driveway and sat for a moment, hands on the wheel, staring at the house with an unreadable expression. Sarah knew he was shutting down.

"Do you remember where we keep the key?" Hal asked, breaking the silence.

"Of course," Jack forced a smile as he popped the trunk. "I used it many times when I had to sneak inside in the middle of the night."

Sarah was reluctant to leave the warmth of the car, but she stepped out into the chilly night while Jack retrieved their luggage from the trunk. She shut the car door, the interior light was extinguished and they were once again plunged into blackness. Sarah immediately recognized the loamy scent of black earth and livestock in the air. The porch swing creaked on its chains and soft warbling wafted up from a nearby chicken coop.

Jack jogged ahead and rooted around the wrought-iron light affixed to the porch. "See, told you I didn't forget," he said, raising the key.

Jack nudged the door open with his shoulder and ushered Sarah and Hal inside. The entryway was dark and smelled of lemon wood polish. Hal flipped a switch illuminating the room in a soft light. "Jesus, it looks exactly the same," Jack marveled. "You didn't change a thing." He dropped their bags by the steps.

A lumpy, misshapen brown-and-black plaid sofa lined one wall; above it hung a Norman Rockwell print depicting a haggard farmer holding a bird in his hands. On another wall was a crucifix with palm leaves tucked behind it. An oblong coffee table, covered with a lace cloth, held a neat stack of *Farm Journal* magazines and a white dish filled with butterscotch candy. An oversize gold armchair sat facing a console television set, the only relatively new piece of furniture in the room. "Same sofa, same lamps, same pictures."

Hal leaned heavily against the walnut post at the bottom of the steps. Suddenly he seemed miles away.

"Hal, is everything okay?" Jack asked.

"It's nothing," Hal said, clutching his hat against his chest. "It's just that . . ." His voice trailed off as he glanced down at the floor, and Sarah realized that this was the spot where Julia had landed after her fall down the steps. It must be haunting, she thought, to stand in the same place where something so tragic had happened. Would Hal ever be able to walk through this room without picturing his critically injured wife splayed on the floor? She couldn't help but wonder then who cleaned up Julia's blood after the fall. She imagined Hal on hands and knees, dipping an old rag in a bucket of soapy water and wiping away the sticky, congealed blood. Sarah shivered at the morbid thought.

"I think I'll go on to bed if you don't mind," Hal said, his face heavy with exhaustion. "Help yourself to anything you need. You know where your old room is."

"I remember," Jack said, embracing his uncle tightly.

"Get some rest," Sarah said. She rubbed his arm sympathetically. "We'll see you in the morning."

Sarah watched as Hal slowly and carefully made his way up the steps, then she turned to Jack. His attention was focused on a wall covered with framed photographs, and she watched his expression transform as his eyes traveled from picture to picture.

"Oh, wow," he murmured, and Sarah joined him in front of the wall. "Me and Dean. I was about fourteen here." The photo showed a young Jack, tan and lean, his eyes fixed on a spot just beyond the photographer, an easy smile on his face, a smile that seemed to share a secret with whomever he was looking at. Dean, also slim and bronzed by the sun, was grinning widely into the camera and had his arm thrown carelessly around Jack's neck.

"What were you doing?" Sarah asked. She had never seen a picture of Jack that young. He said it was taken the summer before his parents died. No wonder he looked so happy, so carefree.

"We were walking beans for my dad. God, I hated that job, but we earned good money. Six hours of bending over and weeding acres of soybeans." Jack grimaced at the memory.

"You look like you're having fun," Sarah said.

"Dean made it fun. He was always screwing around, throwing clumps of dirt, picking up snakes. He'd sneak wine coolers into our water bottles and we'd be half-hammered by the time we were finished for the day. It's a miracle that we got any work done."

Jack examined the wall and pointed to another photo. "There's Amy. When she was ten, I think. She was such a cute kid." Sarah could see what he meant. The girl in the photo had eyes that sparkled brightly and a disarming smile, nothing like the pale, withered woman she had seen earlier that evening. "She was a good sport, too. She never ratted on Dean and me when we got ourselves into trouble. She could keep a secret."

"She seems so different now," Sarah observed. "How did she go from that sweet little girl to being so angry and guarded? Was it your parents' accident?"

"Amy was a lot younger than I was when they died." Jack ran his finger along the top of the picture frame, wiping away a thin layer of dust. She felt Jack bristle beside her. "Of course it changed her. It changed both of us."

Sarah knew she was broaching dangerous territory and returned her gaze to the wall. "Who's that?" she asked, nodding toward a small black-and-white photo of a young man in a military uniform. He looked somberly at the camera but his eyes snapped with mischief.

Jack shoved his hands into his pockets and leaned in to get a better look. "It's my dad."

"Wow," Sarah said. Jack and his father looked so much alike it was uncanny. If not for the navy uniform and a tear-shaped birthmark on his father's cheek, she would have thought the man in the picture was Jack. "You look so much like him."

Jack opened his mouth as if he was going to argue the point but didn't speak.

"Is there a picture of your mom here?"

Sarah asked, scanning the wall in hopes of finally catching a glimpse of her.

"I don't see one," Jack said as he reached into his pocket and pulled out his phone. "Do you think it's too late to call the girls?"

Sarah looked at her watch and shrugged. "They usually stay up late. I'm sure it's fine," she said, and Jack sat on the couch and began dialing.

While Jack spoke with the girls, Sarah joined him on the couch. She took off her shoes and rubbed her feet, the exhaustion of the day finally hitting her. Jack engaged in his comfortable father-daughter banter, and for the first time that day he seemed relaxed.

Jack handed Sarah the phone and returned to the wall of photos. As she spoke with her daughters, she watched as Jack scanned the pictures with a smile she could only interpret as nostalgic. The memories weren't all bad, she thought; he'd had a lot of good times here, as well.

She listened as Emma recounted her day, keeping her eyes fixed on Jack. His gaze moved high and low across the wall until suddenly something caught his attention in the far corner of the wall. From the couch she couldn't see what he was looking at, but clearly it hit a nerve. He leaned into the wall more closely and she noticed the expression on his face grow serious. He looked over at Sarah and realized she was looking at him and quickly turned his attention to their luggage.

"You ready to go upstairs?" he asked after she ended the call and hung up. "I'm exhausted."

Sarah looked at the grandfather clock standing in the corner. It was only nine o'clock. "You're not hungry? You haven't eaten anything since breakfast."

"No, but help yourself to whatever you can find in the cupboards." Jack embraced Sarah and kissed her on the lips. "Thanks again for being here. I know things got a little tense earlier at the hospital."

Sarah leaned into his arms, the heat from his body warming her cold limbs. "It was tense," she echoed. "And that whole argument in the waiting room between Dean and Amy. Dean got so upset when Amy mentioned the house of horrors. Did something happen in Dean and Celia's house?"

"I told you Amy was just stirring up trouble. It's nothing," Jack said shortly, pulling away from her. He took a suitcase in each hand and started toward the stairs.

"It's not nothing," Sarah pressed, and grabbed the handle of the suitcase to keep

Jack from fleeing. "Just tell me why?" Sarah didn't know what she expected Jack to say. Would he tell her some creepy urban legend about the house? Maybe a terrible crime was committed there a hundred years ago, but would that be enough to keep him from staying at the house? She didn't know Jack to be skittish about anything.

Jack looked up at the ceiling and shook his head. "Dean and Celia live in the house that Amy and I grew up in before our parents died." He tugged the suitcase away from Sarah. "Is that enough of an explanation for you? Can I please go to bed now?"

This was sometimes how it was with Jack. She knew that his wall was up and the conversation was over, and she watched in stunned silence as he hefted the suitcases and lugged them up the steps with difficulty.

She was exhausted, too. Her eyes were gritty with lack of sleep and her mind was spinning from the extreme emotions of the day. Why did Dean and Celia live on the farm where Amy and Jack grew up? And why was it such a big deal? More importantly, why couldn't he talk to her about it? And there was still the niggling question as to why Amy called it the house of horrors?

She went to the photographs and studied the wall where Jack had been fixated earlier.

There was a picture of children splashing in a small wading pool, an old sepia photo of a stern-looking couple in wedding garb and a picture of two women smiling happily into the camera. Sarah stood on tiptoe to get a better look. One of the women was clearly Jack's aunt Julia, thirty years younger. Could the other woman be his mother? She scrutinized the woman's face, searching for any hint of resemblance to Jack or Amy. Maybe in the shape of their eyes, the tilt of their heads. It was difficult to tell.

Obviously, she wasn't going to be able to ask Jack about the photo. At least not tonight. There was no way that she'd be able to sleep anytime soon. She looked around the room. She didn't want to turn on the television and disturb Hal or Jack, and she had forgotten to pack a book to read. She realized it had been over a day since she'd last checked her work email, so she grabbed her laptop and made her way to the kitchen.

Sarah's job as an advice columnist for the *Midwest Messenger,* a prominent newspaper in Montana, was an opportunity that had come to her unexpectedly seven years ago when a former colleague and the paper's editor, Gabe Downing, contacted her out of the blue. Sarah had once been a hard-news reporter, the kind that traveled all over the world to places like Bangkok and Eastern Turkey, covering major international news stories. But she'd made the difficult decision to leave after the girls were born, and she adapted to her new life as a stay-at-home mother.

When the offer to write for the *Messenger*'s popular Dear Astrid advice column arose, it felt like a step down. She'd once covered wars and political upheavals, and now she'd be telling people how to confront a difficult neighbor or ask a girl on a date. But by then the girls were much more independent and, with college tuition looming, Sarah decided to swallow her pride and take the job. She'd be helping people, she convinced herself. And now, seven years later, here she was.

Only a handful of people knew Astrid's true identity: Sarah's editor, Gabe; Jack, of course; and her mother and sister. Not even Emma and Elizabeth knew. Not that it was some big secret, but it never came up. They knew their mother wrote for a newspaper but were too immersed in their own lives to pay much attention.

Sarah preferred the anonymity. Most of the letters were from regular everyday people looking for an unbiased opinion, a fresh perspective. They were often amusing, sometimes sad. Heartfelt. But some of the letters were odd. Downright disturbing. Dark, needy letters describing base desires either contemplated or completed. Some were overtly violent. So graphic that she'd have to alert the police in whatever city the letter was postmarked from.

As Sarah set up the laptop on the kitchen table, she sensed Julia's presence. Small touches that reminded Sarah of her own mother. A vase filled with cut flowers on the table, small ceramic birds resting on the windowsill, a half-eaten chocolate cake beneath a glass cover. The kitchen was dated but clean. The linoleum floor was swept and scrubbed, and the faint scent of cinnamon and anise hung in the air, as if ingrained in the fabric of the yellow gingham curtains hanging over the window. The only thing that seemed out of place was the stack of dirty dishes soaking in the sink. Julia must have fallen before she had the chance to wash them.

A ceramic container with hand-painted roosters rested on a brown laminate countertop, and Sarah imagined Jack as a teenager, reaching into the canister for freshly baked cookies, still warm from Julia's oven, doing his homework at the kitchen table. Sarah lifted the lid of the canister and, sure enough, it was brimming with peanut-butter cookies. Sarah's stomach growled, and she helped herself to a cookie.

Sarah turned on the computer and waited for the system to boot up. She pulled up her email and began going through letters. There was one from a man struggling with the decision of whether to place his aging father in a nursing home and one from a teenage girl fed up with her parents' incessant arguing. It was funny, she thought, how she managed to come up with just the right words to help complete strangers, but when it came to her own husband, sometimes nothing she said seemed to come out right.

She finished up the last of the new letters and shut her laptop when Hal shuffled into the kitchen, barefoot and bleary-eyed.

Sarah stood. "Is everything okay?" she asked. "Did the hospital call?"

"No, everything's fine." Hal waved his hand dismissively and Sarah lowered herself back into her chair as he sat down next to her. "I couldn't sleep so I decided to get up. You can't sleep, either?"

"Just catching up on a little work." Sarah nodded toward her laptop. "Jack was showing me the pictures in the living room earlier. It was nice seeing him as a kid. I'd love a copy of the one of him with Dean."

Hal smiled. "I know exactly which one you're talking about. Jack, Dean and Celia would walk beans all day and then come back to the house with sunburns. Celia's hands would be full of blisters." Hal shook his head. "I don't know how many times I told her to wear gloves."

"Celia worked on the farm with Jack and Dean?" Sarah asked. Celia didn't seem like the farmhand sort.

"She held her own. Lasted two summers longer than Dean did."

"I would have thought Dean working on the farm was just a given," Sarah said.

Hal laughed. "Well, now he does. I knew he'd come back to it. It's in our blood. But at the time, Dean thought farmwork was beneath him. He worked at some restaurant in Cedar City. The rest of the time he was with that girlfriend of his. What was her name?" Hal looked up at the ceiling as if he'd find the answer there. "Kelly? Cassie? I don't remember."

"He wasn't dating Celia back then?"

"No, Jack was," Hal replied, and raised an eyebrow. "You didn't know that? I swear, after Jack came to live with us, Celia spent more time at our house than her own."

Sarah's stomach flipped. How could Jack have never told her that he dated Celia? She searched her memory and was certain he'd never mentioned even a high school girlfriend, let alone that his former girlfriend was now married to his cousin. Of course she had asked him about former girlfriends, but he had shrugged it off. *There was no one special until I met you,* he'd say, and she believed him. She had no reason not to.

Hal seemed to sense her disquiet and quickly changed the subject. "I know that Julia has a box of pictures of Jack when he was a baby. I'll dig them out and you can take some back with you."

"Thanks," Sarah said, her mind still on Jack and Celia. How long had they dated? Why had they parted ways? Was it a bad breakup, and who had broken up with whom? Why hadn't Jack told her? Sarah caught Hal looking at her with concern and she tried to shake the thoughts from her head.

"All you Quinlan men look alike," Sarah observed, returning to the photographs. "You and Jack's dad have the same eyes. It's uncanny."

Hal picked up the saltshaker from the center of the table and held it in his thick fingers. "It's funny. People always said that John and I looked like brothers, even though there was no relation. But you're right.

Jack's the spitting image of his dad."

Sarah was confused. "You and Jack's dad weren't brothers? But Jack's last name is Quinlan and so is yours . . ."

"John was my brother-in-law. He was Julia's brother, not mine. After Jack and Amy came to live with us, they took our last name. Their family name is Tierney," he said, and again Sarah was stunned. Why would Jack go to the trouble of changing his name? And Amy, too? She could understand it if Jack and Amy were very young, but Jack was fifteen years old when his parents died. Nearly an adult. Did he really hate his father so much? She tried to put herself in his place. What if her father had been drinking and caused an accident that resulted in her parents' deaths? Would she change her last name and pretend they never existed? And would she keep it a secret from her husband? She didn't think so. In fact, no matter how painful, she would want to share this part of herself with her husband.

In a matter of minutes, it felt as if her whole life had been upended. Between the revelation about Jack and Celia, and now this lie about his last name, Sarah wondered what else Jack might be keeping. She wasn't sure she wanted to know.

"I wouldn't worry, Sarah," Hal said, sensing her concern, and suddenly Sarah felt guilty. Hal's wife was in the hospital with critical injuries and *he* was the one comforting *her.* "Jack has always kept things pretty close to the vest. He's always found it really hard to talk about his mom and dad."

"I know, but I guess I just don't understand why he wouldn't tell me something like that."

"Be patient with him. It was a painful time," Hal said, and patted her hand. Sarah noticed his nails were thick with cracks streaked with black from years of working the land. "I think I'm going to try and get some sleep, and so should you. You've had a long day."

"I'll go up in a few minutes," Sarah promised. "And, Hal, doctors can do so much these days. Jack says that Julia is one of the strongest women he's ever known. If anyone can get through this she will."

Hal gave her a halfhearted smile as if he wanted to believe her. "Good night," he said wearily, getting to his feet and squeezing her shoulder as he moved past her and left the kitchen.

Sarah glanced at the clock on the wall. Twelve thirty. Her eyes burned from fatigue and her shoulders ached. She should go up to bed, be with her husband. But her mind was buzzing with questions and she knew that sleep wasn't going to come anytime soon. Why hadn't he ever told her that he'd changed his name? Sarah felt as if she had unearthed a relic from Jack's past, a broken shard of who he once was. It's just a name, she reminded herself. It doesn't mean anything. But it wasn't so much about the name. It was the fact that he had lied to her about it.

And why hadn't he ever told her that he and Celia had dated? Did he think she would judge him? Did he think she would be jealous of Celia, a woman he hadn't seen in twenty years? And why had he been dodging her questions all day?

Through the window a sliver of moon appeared and a thin light spilled into the kitchen. The thrum of rain on the roof ceased and the only sounds were the creaks and groans of an old house at night. The unfamiliar settling and sighing of a house she did not know. Sarah suddenly felt cold and exposed, and despite her irritation with Jack she didn't want to be alone. The questions could wait until morning.

She picked up her laptop, moved to the living room and paused at the wall filled with family pictures, her eyes landing once again on the photo of Jack's father in his military uniform and then on the picture of the two women. Though Jack looked so much like his father, upon a second look Sarah was sure that the woman in the photo with Julia was Jack's mother.

She crept up the steep stairs and tentatively opened a door to make sure that it was the correct room and was relieved to see their suitcases lined up against one wall. Too tired to change into her pajamas, she peeled off her pants and climbed into bed next to Jack. He didn't even stir.

Coming here Sarah realized just how little she knew about her husband's life before they met. She didn't know the name of his first-grade teacher, what his birthday parties were like, if he went to church. She hadn't even known his real last name.

In the dark, she shivered beneath the blankets and listened to the slow, even breaths of her husband, felt the rise and fall of his chest. Sarah thought back to when Jack had asked her to marry him. How thoroughly certain she was that they belonged together, that every minute of her life, every experience, had led her to him. She thought they were soul mates, fated for each other. Now, she couldn't help but question their life together. Had it all been based on lies?

Hurt prickled behind her eyes and she pressed her face into Jack's slumbering form. *Who are you really?* she wanted to ask him. He knew the best and the worst of her, and she thought she knew the same about him.

4

Before she even opened her eyes, Sarah felt warm sunshine on her face. The sheets still had the crispness of laundry hung on a line, and for a moment she basked in the tranquillity of morning, allowing herself to forget for a moment the chaos and uncertainty of the day before.

She wanted to talk to Jack privately before they left for the hospital, about what she had learned from Hal last night, about why he had lied to her for all these years and about why he now seemed to be evading her. She lifted her head and turned to the side, but the space next to her was empty.

Stiff jointed and achy, she climbed out of bed and looked around the bedroom that Jack slept in as a teenager. She was hoping to find some clues, some insights into his childhood, into the life he led before he met her. There were no athletic trophies on the bookshelf and no bulletin board plastered with photos and mementos. She picked up a few random books from the bookshelf and riffled through the pages. There were no carnation corsages pressed between the pages, no concert stubs or baseball tickets. Of course, it had been over twenty-five years since Jack had lived here. Julia and Hal had most likely redecorated years ago and used this as a room for guests.

A small oak desk sat in the corner of the room and she pulled out the drawers, each empty except for a few stray paper clips and ballpoint pens. Instead of clothing, the tall dresser held neatly folded tablecloths and bed linens. She opened the closet door to find it empty except for two heavy winter coats hanging from the metal bar and a shoe box with Jack's name on it on the top shelf. Jack pushed open the door. "How'd you sleep?" he asked.

Startled, she closed the closet door and turned to face him. "Okay," she answered. But she hadn't slept well at all. For what felt like hours she had lain next to him in the dark, tossing and turning, her mind racing with questions, restless about how to confront Jack. Where would she even start, and how would Jack react?

She searched for the words, knowing she had to be careful or Jack would shut her down in an instant. "Last night, Hal told me your real last name is Tierney," she blurted, unable to mask the accusation in her voice. "Is that true?"

Jack looked at her blankly. "You knew that," he said. "I told you that after we started dating."

Sarah shook her head. She would remember if Jack had told her. "No, you didn't."

"Of course I did. You must have forgotten."

"Jack," she said more firmly, and he sighed in frustration.

"You already know this, Sarah. After Amy and I went to live with Hal and Julia, we had our name legally changed to Quinlan. I was fifteen, Amy was eleven. Hal and Julia became our legal guardians and they were all the family we had left in the world. It just seemed easier."

Maybe she was overreacting about the name change, but that still didn't explain why he had kept it from her.

"Hal also told me that you and Celia dated in high school. Why didn't you tell me these things? Why the secrecy?"

"Sarah, there are no secrets!" Jack exclaimed, his face reddening. "Celia and I hung out when we were young. Hell, I hung out with a lot of people. It's a small town."

Jack grabbed his watch from the dresser. "I really can't deal with this right now. Why can't you just drop it?"

"I'm not trying to fight with you," Sarah said quietly. "I'm just trying to understand."

Jack sat down on the bed and rubbed his eyes. "I don't want to fight, either. I'm sorry if I didn't tell you. I really thought I had. And me and Celia, it was nothing, just kid stuff." He reached for her hand and she reluctantly took it. His skin felt warm, re-assuring. "Hal's downstairs waiting to go to the hospital. Are you ready?"

They drove to the hospital separately, with Hal and Jack in the truck and Sarah follow-ing behind, alone, in the rental car. The rain-washed fields glittered with moisture and puffy white clouds moved leisurely across the blue sky. It was a beautiful morn-ing, but still Sarah felt uneasy, off balance. The highway was lined with wooden tele-phone poles that reminded Sarah of cruci-fixes where sharp-eyed hawks and hook-beaked shrikes perched in wait.

Jack was confident he had told her about changing his last name, but she racked her memory. No, she would have remembered if he told her, she was sure of it. As for Celia, what had Hal said? That they were inseparable? That certainly sounded like more than just *hanging out.* She was so engrossed in her thoughts she lost sight of Hal's truck and pressed on the accelerator in hopes of catching up.

When Sarah finally pulled into the parking lot, she could see Jack and Hal already entering the hospital. She knew that Hal was anxious to check on Julia and she felt childish for being disappointed that they hadn't waited for her.

Sarah waited for the excruciatingly slow elevator and when she stepped out onto the fifth-floor landing Jack and Hal were nowhere to be seen. Sarah caught sight of Celia, hands full, heading down the hall toward Julia's room, and Sarah hurried to catch up with her.

"Good morning," Sarah said breathlessly as she pushed Julia's door open for Celia.

"Good morning," Celia said, looking well rested and refreshed. Sarah saw Celia with new eyes now that she knew she and Jack were once an item. She was beautiful. Slim and fit. Her black curls were pulled back from her face and she was perfectly put together in sharply creased khakis and a neatly pressed blouse. Sarah looked down and was dismayed to see that her long-sleeve T-shirt and jeans were hopelessly rumpled from being stored in her suitcase.

Celia came bearing fresh-cut purple asters from her garden. "The last of the season," she said as she set the vase on Julia's windowsill. Amy was curled up in a chair next to Julia's bed, looking even more diminished than the day before. She stiffened as Celia leaned over Julia's bed and adjusted her pillow.

"How was Julia's night?" Sarah asked. The room was eerily quiet, and she sensed a palpable tension between Celia and Amy. She hoped Jack and Hal would arrive soon.

Amy rubbed her eyes with the sleeve of her sweatshirt. "She hasn't woken up yet, but the nurse said her vitals are stable."

"That's good news," Celia said. "Now maybe you can go home and get some rest."

"I'm fine," Amy said shortly. She stood and stretched. "Where are Hal and Jack?"

"They peeked in on Julia for a few minutes and then the doctor wanted to go over a few of Julia's tests with them," Celia explained. "When's the last time you've eaten? Why don't you go down to the cafeteria and get something?"

"Jesus, Celia, I said I'm fine," Amy answered, crossing her arms in front of her just as a high-pitched beeping erupted from Julia's heart monitor.

"What's happening?" Amy asked fearfully

as all eyes swung toward Julia. Julia's body went rigid, her face contorting into a tight grimace. The heavy hospital bed rocked with her spasms and Julia's eyes opened and rolled back into her head so that only the whites showed.

"Go get someone," Sarah yelled, frantically reaching for the nurse's call button. Celia hurried from the room in search of help.

"Do something!" Amy beseeched, her eyes wide and panicked.

Moments later, Celia raced into the room with two nurses. Jack, Hal and Dean were close behind. "What's happening?" Hal shouted in horror as Julia convulsed in the bed. Jack reached for Sarah's hand and squeezed it tightly.

"She's having a seizure," one of the nurses said as they expertly rolled Julia onto her side. She produced a syringe and injected it directly into Julia's IV. Her body shuddered violently.

"What is that? What did you do?" Amy cried.

"Lorazepam," a nurse said, her voice caught in the frenzy of the beeping machines and Julia's moans. "To stop the seizure."

"Why is she making that noise?" Hal asked helplessly. "Is she in pain?"

"It isn't working," Amy yelled, pushing her way to Julia's bedside. She bumped the vase of flowers and it cartwheeled and shattered as it struck the floor. Shards of glass flew everywhere and a puddle of water formed on the floor next to Sarah's feet.

Sarah sidled back into a corner, trying to stay out of the way as Jack tried to pull Amy from Julia's bedside where she was grasping for Julia and getting in the way of the nurses. "Let them do their work," he urged.

"It's not working. The medicine isn't helping," Amy cried. "Please make it stop," she begged as Julia continued to writhe in her bed, a foul odor rising from the sheets. Amy clapped a hand over her nose and mouth.

The seconds ticked by like hours. The nurse grabbed another syringe and injected it into the IV. How long could this last? Sarah wondered.

Slowly, Julia's body relaxed, her face smoothed and her hands uncurled, but the heart machine continued to beep rapidly.

"What's wrong?" Amy asked the nurses who were standing over Julia, watching her carefully. "Why is it still making that sound? Don't just stand there, do something!"

"She has a do-not-resuscitate order," Dean said under his breath, so softly that Sarah was sure she was the only one who heard him.

"*Do* something," Amy pressed, her voice rising as she spiraled into hysteria. She clutched onto the nurse's sleeve violently, begging her not to let her aunt die.

"She's DNR," Dean repeated, this time more loudly.

"What does that mean?" Amy cried as she leaned into Jack, tears streaming down her face. "Why aren't they helping her? Make them help her."

"They can't. She doesn't want any heroic measures keeping her alive," Dean explained.

The heart monitor blipped frenetically and Amy pressed her hands to her ears as if trying to block out the sound. Gradually, Julia's chest stopped moving and the beeps stretched into one continuous, mournful cry.

"No!" Amy cried as she pulled away from Jack and lunged toward the bed. "Please don't leave me," she begged, pressing her lips against Julia's warm cheek. Amy lowered her head and her brokenhearted keening became entangled with the mechanical scream of the heart monitor until they became one. A nurse reached over and turned off the machine. The only sound in the room was Amy's weeping.

Hal approached his wife's side on unsteady legs and reached for her hand. A dry sob came from deep within his chest; he leaned over the bedside rail and murmured into Julia's ear.

Sarah watched as Hal went slack with helplessness. She went to his side and reached for his hand. His fingers were ice-cold.

Dean tried to stifle a cry and Celia buried herself in his chest. Hal slowly lowered himself into a chair, his face a map of disbelief.

A nurse carefully removed the oxygen mask from Julia's face and began to unhook the monitors from her chest. "Stop," Amy yelled, clawing at the nurse's arm again, trying to pull her away from the machines. Her eyes were filled with fury.

"Amy!" Celia exclaimed in horror as the nurse, wide-eyed, tried to shake her off. Celia grabbed Amy's hands and she released the nurse, whose arm was lined with angry red scratches that bloomed with blood.

Sarah watched in disbelief as Amy squirmed from Celia's grasp and shoved past them, out of the room.

"Are you okay?" Celia asked.

"I'm fine," the nurse said, clearly shaken, blotting her bloody arm with a tissue.

"Shouldn't someone go after her?" Sarah asked, heart pounding.

"No, just let her go," Jack said. "Let her cool off."

"Jesus Christ, she's fucking crazy," Dean hissed, his voice tense with anger.

"Please!" Hal interjected. "For God's sake, have some respect for your mother." Everyone froze and a mix of shame and grief washed over them. Hal's head fell heavy in his hands and the room filled with the soft sobs of a man who just lost his wife. "Fifty years," he said mournfully. "We were married fifty years." He looked up from his hands, his eyes wet and bloodshot. "Fifty years and she had to leave me this way?"

The nurse watched from the doorway as Jack's family seemed to collapse under the weight of their own grief. "I'll have to ask you to step out for a few minutes, Mr. Quinlan," she said kindly. "We'll take care of your wife and get the room cleaned up, then you can come back in and take as much time as you need."

The room looked like a war zone. The floor was slick with water and flower petals. Shards of glass from the broken vase crunched beneath their feet. Hal remained by Julia's side until Dean gently took his arm and guided him from the room. Sarah bent down and picked up the handmade quilt that had fallen to the floor. She folded it neatly and draped it over the back of a chair.

Jack paused at Julia's bedside and looked down at the woman who had welcomed him into her home after his parents had died. He whispered into her ear and lightly brushed her cheek with his fingers.

"I'm sorry, sir," the nurse said. "We have to ask you all to step out, please."

Sarah held her hand out to Jack. Together they stepped into the hallway and Sarah pulled him into her arms. "It's going to be okay," she murmured. She felt Jack's heart thrumming against his chest.

Jack released Sarah and went to his uncle. "She loved you," Hal said, taking Jack's hands in his own. "You and Amy, just like you were her own. You know that, don't you?"

"I know," Jack replied, his voice hoarse with emotion. "She always believed in me. No matter what."

Sarah embraced Hal. "Is there anyone I can call for you?"

"I know who to call," Celia interjected in a way that struck Sarah as oddly aggressive.

"What about Amy?" Sarah asked. "Do you think someone should go check on her?"

"I think it's probably best to just let her be for a while," Celia answered. "Let her catch her breath."

Sarah wrapped her arms around Jack's waist, and he rested his chin on top of her head. "Did you know Julia had a do-not-resuscitate order?" she asked.

"No. And Amy must have not known, either. I've never seen her act like that before."

"I should call the girls, let them know what's going on."

"No, not yet."

"I could make arrangements to have them fly here?" Sarah offered.

"No," Jack said quickly.

Sarah pulled back and looked up at him. "But . . ."

"Sarah," he said in exasperation. "I said no."

Sarah didn't understand Jack's reluctance to bring the girls to Penny Gate. They should be here with them. That's what families did; they were there to support one another when times were difficult.

The tension between them was broken by the sound of determined footsteps. They shifted their gaze down the long corridor, where a woman in a long white doctor's coat and a man who appeared to be a

88

security guard were approaching with quick, long strides.

"This can't be good," Jack said in a low voice. "Can you find Amy?"

Sarah hesitated, glancing at Jack with uncertainty.

"Sarah, please just go!"

She started down the hallway, hurt by Jack's harsh tone. When she reached the end of the hallway, she turned to see the doctor and security guard confront Jack in the doorway of Julia's room. He held up his hands in placation, as if trying to calm them.

The nurses must have alerted security about Amy's outburst and they were coming to . . . what? Escort Amy from the building? Detain her until the police came to arrest her? Sarah quickened her pace, though she wasn't sure what she would say to Amy if she found her. Should she tell her to run, to get out of there as quickly as possible? Or should she try to convince her to come back upstairs to talk things through?

Once again she bypassed the elevator and raced down the stairs and through the lobby. The automatic doors slid open and Sarah saw Amy shivering on a bench just outside the hospital entrance. A brisk wind had swept the clear skies away and replaced them with dark clouds heavy with rain. Amy had stopped crying and was blankly staring upward, a cigarette pressed to her lips. She had one arm wrapped protectively around her waist, the same way that Jack always did.

"Amy." Sarah cautiously approached her sister-in-law. "I'm so sorry about Julia. Are you okay?"

"I can't believe she's gone." Amy swiped at her nose with the back of one hand. "I can't believe she's really dead." She pressed the heels of her hands against her bloodshot eyes. "I really freaked out up there. Did I hurt that nurse?"

"Just a few scratches." Sarah sat down on the bench. "She's fine. But everyone's worried about you."

"I bet Dean went ape shit." She gave a short bark of laughter and then started to cry again.

Sarah wasn't sure what to say. She barely knew Amy, but what she did know was that she was volatile and unpredictable. But this was Jack's sister and she also knew that Amy loved her aunt and was grieving terribly. Sarah slid closer to her and put an arm around Amy's thin shoulders. "Do you want to come back inside?" she asked once Amy's cries subsided. "I bet if you apologize to the nurse, she'll forget the whole thing."

"I can't go back in there," Amy said, taking a shaky drag on her cigarette. "Not now, anyway." She gave the cigarette a tap and watched the long ash fall to the concrete below. In her other hand she held what looked to be a round silver charm. The kind you might find on a bracelet or on a necklace.

Amy caught Sarah looking and held it out for her to see. Engraved on one side was a cross and on the other was the word *faith.* "It was lying next to Aunt Julia when I found her. I was going to hold on to it until she woke up and then give it back to her." She shook her head. "I don't think I can face them." She looked up toward Julia's room. "It's all my fault."

"What do you mean it's your fault?" Sarah asked.

Amy didn't answer. She dropped the cigarette to the ground and squeezed the charm tightly in her palm. "Amy," Sarah prodded. "What do you mean?"

"I don't know. Maybe if I had gotten there fifteen minutes earlier . . ."

"You can't think that way about it. You'll drive yourself crazy," Sarah said. "Just think about what could have happened if you hadn't shown up when you did."

Amy shrugged, unconvinced. "When are

you leaving town?"

"We'll stay for the funeral, of course, but will probably need to go home soon after."

Amy nodded and lit another cigarette. "That's probably a good idea. People who stay around here too long either die or go crazy. Jack had the right idea. He left Penny Gate as soon as he could and didn't look back. If my mom would have just left . . ." Amy trailed off.

"You can't blame the accident on your mom's decision to stay in Penny Gate," Sarah said. "There's no way to know what would have been different."

" 'The accident'?" Amy gave a skeptical snort. "Is that what Jack is calling it these days?" She stood, took a deep pull on the cigarette and blew a stream of smoke out of the corner of her mouth. "You need to talk to your husband," Amy said as she started to walk away. "You know Jack. Always full of secrets."

Sarah's stomach clenched. What else hadn't Jack told her? She watched as Amy walked away, her gaunt frame hunched against the sharp wind. She considered chasing after her but to what end?

Maybe she had been overreacting about Jack's name, and even about Celia. But Jack

was definitely keeping something from her.
Something important.

5

The accident? Is that what Jack's calling it these days?

Amy's cryptic comment tumbled in Sarah's mind. Tears pricked at her eyes as she ticked off the half-truths and lies that Jack had told her. She was tired of all the secrecy, the avoidance. Yes, Jack was reserved, private. But she had thought they had both known the important parts of each other's lives.

She pulled out her phone and entered *Jack Tierney* into the search engine. Three hundred and eighty-one thousand results.

She plugged in two more words, *Penny Gate,* and it narrowed the search. Sarah clicked on the first link, a newspaper article headlined Penny Gate Woman Found Bludgeoned. Her eyes skittered down the page. *The body of Lydia Tierney, thirty-six, was discovered yesterday afternoon in her rural Penny Gate home.* Before Sarah could read any further, Jack approached.

"Sarah?" he asked, and she nearly dropped her phone. "What are you doing?"

Heart thumping, she quickly slid her phone into her purse. "I was talking to Amy. She just left," she said. Jack's eyes were red-rimmed and seemed to hold immeasurable sadness.

Jack sat down next to her, his leg pressing against hers. "They posted a security guard outside Julia's room and made us leave," he said. "They said that an autopsy has been ordered."

"Why?" Sarah asked in confusion. "I thought it was an accident."

"They wouldn't tell us much of anything." Jack rubbed his forehead in frustration. "Just that Julia's injuries weren't entirely consistent with an accidental fall down the stairs."

"What does that mean? Like someone *pushed* her down the steps?" Sarah asked. "Who would do that?"

"I don't know." Jack closed his eyes and brought his hands to his face, forming a tent with his fingers. "It has to be some kind of mistake."

"A home invasion?" Sarah wondered out loud.

"That's the only thing I can think of that

makes any sense. But then why wasn't there any mess? Why was nothing taken?"

What was it that Amy had told Sarah earlier? *It's all my fault.* Amy had dismissed it, but now Sarah wondered what she meant. Did Amy know more than she was letting on?

"Hal is a mess," Jack added. "I don't know how he's going to get through this." He reached for Sarah's hand. His skin was cold and damp, and Sarah's first instinct was to pull away, but he held tight. "He can't face going back to the house right now, so we're all going to go back to Dean and Celia's. Do you mind heading there with Celia now? I need to stay here to help with some of the arrangements."

"Whatever you need," she murmured. She knew she had to be there for Jack and his family, but all Sarah really wanted to do was get back to the newspaper article she had discovered.

"I have to talk to Amy. Do you have any idea where she went?"

"She didn't tell me."

Celia emerged from the hospital. Her face was blotchy and her eyes swollen from crying.

"Cel," Jack began, "Sarah will go back to the house with you. We'll be right behind."

Cel. Such a familiar use of her name. Sarah wondered if that was what Jack called her when they were teenagers.

Celia nodded. "Thank you," she said, blinking back tears. "I really don't want to be alone right now."

"Of course. Whatever I can do to help."

"I'll call you later," Jack said, and kissed Sarah on the cheek. His lips were cold and dry.

Sarah and Celia made their way to the hospital parking lot. "I can't believe she's gone," Celia said, her voice breaking with emotion. "One minute she's just lying there and the next she's having a seizure." Celia shivered. "I've never seen anything like it."

Sarah stepped over a large puddle as she climbed into the passenger's side of Celia's truck. "Jack said that the doctor didn't think Julia's fall was an accident. How could she know that?"

"I don't think anyone could know without an autopsy." Celia started the car and then looked over her shoulder as she backed out of the parking spot. "It's got to be a mistake."

Celia offered a steady stream of commentary as she drove. "Our house is about a twenty-five-minute drive from here and Hal's is just fifteen minutes farther. The funny thing is, you can walk through the cornfield right outside our door and end up in Hal's yard in about the same amount of time. The town's a little farther. I can't believe you've never been here before." She looked over at Sarah. "I'm prattling on and on. I think if I don't keep talking I'll start crying again and not be able to stop."

"That's okay," Sarah said. "I was the same way when my dad died. If I kept moving, kept talking, I was okay. The minute things were quiet I fell apart."

"I'm glad that Jack got here in time to see Julia before she died. I think he would have really regretted it, if he hadn't. He's always had such a soft heart."

Sarah tried to ignore the flash of jealousy that sizzled in her chest. It was a long time ago, she told herself. Celia didn't know him, the man he turned out to be. But then again, Sarah realized with a stab of regret, she wasn't sure if she knew him as well as she thought she did, either.

"Hal said you and Jack dated when you were younger," Sarah said, trying to keep her voice light. Conversational.

"Well, yeah." Celia flashed a hint of a smile. "But that was ages ago. We went to school together. Jack and I were in the same class. Dean graduated four years before us.

I got to know Dean through Jack. Didn't Jack tell you that he and I dated through most of high school?"

"Well, yes," Sarah fumbled. "Sorry, I didn't make the connection."

"That's Jack for you, a man of few words." Celia shook her head. "After Jack left for college I mooned around after him, hung around Julia and Hal's house like a little lost puppy." She gave a halfhearted laugh at the memory. "One evening, Julia had me over for dinner and Dean had just moved back to the farm. I hadn't seen him in a few years and it was like the sun came out. A couple of years later we got married, and the rest is history."

Celia turned onto a narrow two-lane highway that ribboned through the countryside, speeding past gold-and-green patchworks of cornstalks and soybeans, punctuated by an occasional farmhouse. Cattle gnawed languidly on grass, their tails flicking at unseen insects, their soft eyes barely glancing as they passed. It was beautiful, Sarah had to admit.

Once again, the sky had cleared and Sarah knew what Jack meant when he said the weather in Iowa changed on a dime. The air was clean and crisp like freshly starched laundry and the sky was a brilliant shade of blue that reminded Sarah of a time when the girls were four and Elizabeth described the sky as "so blue it hurts." A blue so big and beautiful that it causes your heart to ache.

The thought made her miss her daughters more than she thought was possible.

Celia parked the truck and Sarah took in the view of the farmhouse and outbuildings that made up the Quinlan farm. Patches of the house were scraped clean of the paint that had once covered it, and the roof was badly in need of new shingles. The front porch was in disrepair, the steps leaning dangerously to the left. The barn and machine shed weren't in much better shape. Long stalks of grass and weeds grew wildly, scorched and dry like hay from the hot Iowa sun. The property clearly hadn't been well maintained over the years. The place looked like it was right out of a scary movie, and it made Sarah think about Amy's "house of horrors" comment and the article she found earlier about the death of Jack's mother. What other dark secrets was this house keeping?

"The outside isn't all that much to look at, but the inside is great. Dean hopes to start working on the exterior next spring."

Sarah smiled but didn't respond. She

wondered what Jack would think about the deterioration of his childhood home.

"Come. I'll show you around," Celia said as they stepped from the Bronco. "I know I need to start making phone calls, but I can't bear to tell people the news about Julia yet. I feel like if I can put off telling them I can almost make myself believe she really hasn't died." Celia closed her eyes for a moment and took a deep breath. "But first things first," she said, clapping her hands together. "I'll get you a pair of boots. What are you, a size seven?"

"Eight, but really these are fine," Sarah insisted.

"Oh, no. They don't call them shit-kickers for nothing. Believe me, you'll want to put on a pair of boots." Celia walked off toward the house and Sarah surveyed the farmyard. A soft wind spun the blades of a tall galvanized-metal windmill that sat among the swaying switchgrass. There were three outbuildings: a midsize A-frame barn, a large prairie barn with a low-hanging, sloped roof, and a small shed.

The farmyard was overgrown and weedy in some spots, and brown and bald in others. Poking up from the weeds were riots of color just beginning to brown at the edges: purple and white aster, rose-colored sedum and cheery goldenrod. Tired browned remnants of once-spritely hollyhock slumped among the glossy green leaves of the bushes nestled against the foundation of the largest barn. The door to a small shed was open, revealing a cluttered array of farm tools and cracked clay pots. Well away from the barn was a pile of partially charred remains of what appeared to be an odd pyre of dried leaves, barn board and broken furniture.

Everything felt too still, too quiet. It was unsettling and Sarah raised her face to meet the warmth of the sun while blackflies buzzed around her face.

Celia came back carrying a pair of green rubber boots and handed them to Sarah. They walked the final fifty yards to the midsize barn, and Celia wrenched open the door. "This is where we keep our meager little zoo." They stepped into the dimly lit barn. The musty smell of hay filled her nose and bits of dust and straw danced in the streams of light that seeped through the narrow windows. Rusty farm equipment that clearly hadn't been used in years leaned against the rough wooden walls. "We have lots of old stuff that was here before we moved in. As for the house, we've tried to restore as much as we could. The floors are original and some of the furniture has been in Julia's family for generations. I have boxes of Jack's mom's embroidery work from over the years. I couldn't bring myself to get rid of them. I tried to give them to Amy, but she doesn't want any. I thought about packing some things away for Jack, but he doesn't seem very interested, either."

"You've talked to him about it?" Sarah asked with surprise.

"Sure, over the years. I don't want to push it, but I wanted him to know that he's welcome to much of what's in the house. After Lydia died, Julia packed everything away. Most of it's down in the basement."

Three small goats clambered over to them, their large, protruding black eyes wide with curiosity. Sarah knelt down into the soft straw and rubbed their coarse black-and-white coats. "Can I ask you a question?" Sarah asked tentatively.

"Sure, go ahead," Celia said, gently nudging one of the goats away.

"I found a news article that said that a woman was bludgeoned to death in the house that Jack grew up in." Sarah tipped her head in the direction of the house.

Celia froze for a moment, then bent down to pick up a large tabby cat that was circling her ankles. "You didn't know?" she asked.

She shook her head.

"Don't you think you should talk to Jack about this?" The cat purred loudly, a content rumble, as Celia stroked her back.

That was the problem, wasn't it? Sarah thought. Everyone was telling her to talk to her husband about the strange, mysterious things that none of them could speak of. But Jack wasn't talking, either.

Sarah stood and brushed straw from the front of her pants. An old, long-dormant need was growing inside her. She hadn't felt this way since she was a young journalist on the trail of an intriguing news story. The need to uncover the facts that more often than not became an obsession to know the truth. This was different, though. The stakes were much higher in this case. This was her husband's life. Her life.

"I know you're right," Sarah said. "But losing Julia has been such a shock for him. I don't want to probe and make him relive the past. Not now."

Celia bit her lip as if trying to decide what to do. Finally she nodded. "I'll tell you what I can." Celia paused again. "For the record, I'm uncomfortable talking to you about Jack's parents, but I understand why you need to know. I just can't believe he never told you about this before." Another jolt of jealousy coursed through Sarah. Celia knew things about her husband that Sarah probably never would. "What is it you'd like to know?" Celia asked.

Sarah knew that Jack would be arriving at the house at any moment and she needed to gather as much information from Celia as quickly as she could.

"How did Jack's mom die?" she asked, inwardly wincing at the bluntness of her words.

"She was murdered," Celia said uncomfortably.

"Bludgeoned to death?" Sarah asked, thinking of the newspaper headline.

Celia nodded. "Jack was the one who discovered her body," she said. "It was horrible."

"Who did it?" Sarah asked, her heart pounding.

"At the beginning, no one knew. At first everyone thought it might have been a stranger, someone looking for a house to rob and accidentally came upon Lydia." The cat squirmed, Celia released her and she landed soundlessly on the barn floor. "Jack's dad disappeared before anyone could even question him. No sign of him anywhere. There was a statewide manhunt — his picture was all over the news. But he never surfaced." Celia shook her head at the memory. "It was bad enough that Jack came home and found his mom bludgeoned to death, but then to learn that it was his father who did it . . ." Celia shuddered.

No wonder Amy called this place a house of horrors. A cold sweat broke out on her forehead. She didn't know if she should cry for Jack or be angry with him for keeping this from her. A million more questions flittered through her mind.

"Sarah." Celia's voice floated in front of her. "Are you okay?"

"I'm fine," she murmured.

"I know this is a shock to you." Celia watched her carefully.

"They never caught him?" Sarah asked numbly. "Jack's dad?"

"No." Celia shook her head. "It's like he disappeared off the face of the earth. You know, there was a time when Jack couldn't say enough nice things about his dad. At school, it was always *my dad said this* or *my dad did this.* The house was built board by board by his great-grandfather. When we were kids I told him how I wanted to move away from here, go to college, see the world. He said he never wanted to leave — everything he could ever want was right here.

"That all changed after the murder. Jack spent the next three years trying to figure

106

out how to get out of Penny Gate." She smiled wistfully. "Kind of funny, isn't it?"

"What?" Sarah couldn't find anything humorous in what she had learned about Jack in the past twenty-four hours.

"Growing up, all Jack wanted to do was stay in Penny Gate, live in this house, farm this land. I thought we were going to get married, have a house filled with kids. Instead, he left, met you and now he only comes back for weddings and funerals."

Get married? Sarah thought. Jack had never even mentioned they had dated, let alone were serious enough for marriage. An ember of doubt ignited in Sarah's chest.

"I guess everything works out the way it's supposed to. Not the death of his mom, of course," she quickly clarified. "But there was a time I would have given anything to be Mrs. Jack Tierney. Now I can't imagine having a different life and I'm sure Jack feels the same way. After all he's been through, though, I'm shocked he ended up getting married and having a family. He must really trust you."

Sarah murmured her agreement but knew it wasn't true. Jack clearly hadn't trusted her at all.

"Where?" Sarah asked. "Where did it happen?" Did she die on the floor in front of

the stone fireplace? Did Jack find her life-
less body on the kitchen floor or upstairs in
her bedroom? She imagined Lydia's corpse
in the barn, surrounded by the shrill squeal
of goats. She suddenly had the urge to run
from the dim barn.

"Sarah, I . . ." Celia said with uncertainty.

"Where?" Sarah pushed. "Please tell me."

"In the basement," Celia said.

Sarah was consumed with a morbid desire
for Celia to show her the basement. Maybe
if she saw the place where Jack's life was ir-
revocably changed, some of this — any of it
— would make sense. But before she could
press any further, they were interrupted by
a shout from outside the barn.

"It's Dean," Celia said. "We're in here,"
she called back.

Sarah's mind was still reeling. She took a
moment to collect herself, then followed
Celia outside to where Dean, Jack and Hal
were waiting, grim faced.

"What's going on?" Celia asked.

"The sheriff stopped by the hospital. We
thought he came to offer sympathies." Dean
folded his arms across his chest. "Instead,
he was there to talk to the doctors and
nurses about Mom."

Celia shoved her hands into her pockets.
While the sun shone brightly, the wind had

picked up, whipping her black curls around her face. "What did they say?" Celia asked.

"Let's go inside and talk," Dean invited, and together they moved toward the house. Sarah kept stealing glances at Jack. He had lied to her for the past twenty years about his mother's death. Why?

Celia led Sarah up the porch steps. "Be careful," she warned. "It's liable to collapse on us." Sarah warily tested the first step with her foot. It creaked precariously but held, and she kept going.

Celia pushed open the door, and despite the weathered exterior and crumbling front porch, the living room was warm and inviting with rich oak floors, and an oversize sofa and love seat situated in front of a large stone fireplace. This was where Jack grew up. He ran across these floors, looked out these windows, and climbed up and down these steps to his childhood bedroom. "I'll make coffee," Celia said, leading them to the kitchen.

Jack's face, Sarah noticed, was a pasty white. His hands were jammed in his pockets and his eyes were pinned to the lace curtains above the kitchen window. She realized that this was probably the first time Jack had stepped foot in this house in decades.

"I've known Sheriff Gilmore for years." Hal was indignant. "I can't believe he seriously thinks that one of us could have hurt Julia."

Jack's gaze went to the kitchen counter where Celia had tossed a dish towel hand embroidered with fall leaves.

"I don't think he really does," Celia said diplomatically. "But he has to investigate. It's his job."

"I'd just like to know who reported such nonsense," Hal said, annoyed.

Jack walked over to the kitchen counter and picked up the dish towel to examine the intricate stitching.

"It must have been the doctors or nurses who reported it." Dean paced the kitchen. "What a nightmare."

"Has anyone talked to Amy?" Celia asked. "Where did she run off to?"

Jack brought the dish towel to his nose and Sarah realized the embroidered dish towel was once his mother's.

Jack lowered the towel from his face and his eyes went to the basement door. He seemed to be in a trance.

"Jack? Are you okay?" Sarah asked with concern. She could see the small muscle in his jaw working. "Jack? What's the matter?"

Before he could respond, he rushed past

Sarah and out of the kitchen. Sarah followed him as he raced down the hallway and into the bathroom. He slammed the door and she heard his knees striking the tile floor and then the retching. The sound of deep, heaving spasms spilled out from beneath the bathroom door.

"Jack, are you all right?" Sarah rapped on the door and pressed her face against the cold wood. "What's wrong?" she called.

But Sarah knew perfectly well what was wrong. There were too many memories here. Too much pain. Long-buried secrets. She couldn't help but think it was a bad idea for them to come back to Penny Gate. They should have stayed home in Larkspur and let the family handle Julia on their own. It was all too much — for Jack, and for her — and yet she feared that this was only the beginning.

6

"Jack," Sarah called through the door again. "Are you okay?" The door opened and Jack emerged, sallow faced. "What's going on?"

"It's been a terrible day. I'm sure it's just the stress," Celia said as she handed Jack a glass of water.

Sarah bit back a sharp response. Sarah knew her husband, or at least thought she did. Returning to this house, to where his mother had died, had been murdered, that's what had made him so violently ill.

Jack took a sip of water. "I'm better now, really."

"Let's go sit down," Celia said, leading them all to the living room. Sarah noticed that Jack kept his eyes down as if purposefully trying to avoid catching sight of anything else that might trigger a memory.

"Has anyone heard from Amy?" Jack asked, settling into an armchair. Celia patted the love seat where she took a seat, inviting Sarah to join her.

"No, but she's the one who found Mom," Dean said. "I'd like to talk to her and I know the sheriff does, too."

"They had their differences, but surely Amy wouldn't do anything to hurt Julia," Celia insisted.

Dean held up his hands. "Maybe, maybe not. But you have to admit the way she was acting today was downright strange. Christ, she practically attacked the nurse."

"I've never seen her act that way," Jack said. "She's done some crazy things but . . ."

"That's not fair," Celia interjected. "Of course Amy is upset. Julia was the only mother that Amy has known since she was eleven."

Jack pinched the bridge of his nose as if trying to ward off a headache. "I'll keep trying to call her. I'm sure she'll show up."

"So what happens next?" Sarah asked.

"The sheriff says he wants to talk to each of us," Dean explained. "In the meantime —" Dean's words snagged in his throat "— they'll do the autopsy."

"Well, I'd like to talk to Gilmore here and now," Hal said defiantly. "I might just call him up myself right this minute. I want to know if he really thinks one of us hurt Julia. He knows us. He knows no one in the family is capable of this!"

"Look," Jack said. "We obviously need to get to the bottom of this, but right now, we need to focus on Aunt Julia."

"Jack's right," Celia added. "We still need to call everyone and start making funeral arrangements. I can stop at Saint Finnian's and meet with Father Gordon if you'd like, Hal," Celia offered.

He nodded, his eyes brimming with tears again, and he swiped them away.

"What can I do?" Sarah asked, knowing she had very little to offer. She didn't know Julia well, didn't know her friends or community.

"I guess we'll need clothes for the wake and funeral," Jack said, holding out the keys to the rental car. "Could you take care of that while we talk to the funeral home? Maybe run into Cedar City to pick up a few things?"

"Sure," she said, grateful for the chance to extract herself from the heavy sadness that had settled over the house.

Once to the car, Sarah realized that she had left her purse in the Bronco. She trudged through the tall, wet grass, the ground spongy beneath her feet, to the vehicle that Celia had parked near the outbuildings. Sarah opened the passenger's-side door, retrieved her purse and just as she was shutting the door, heard indistinct voices. No words were intelligible, but the tone was earnest. Without thinking, Sarah crouched down next to the Bronco so that she was just able to peek through the windows but remain unnoticed by the source of the heated conversation.

Dean and Celia were moving toward the smaller of the two barns. Dean's mouth was moving rapidly, and he gesticulated wildly. Celia, walking a few paces in front of him, stared straight ahead, her expression set in defiance. With one large hand, Dean grabbed Celia's arm to stop her, his thick fingers encircling her forearm. A squawk of pain erupted from Celia. She tried to wrench free, but he held tight. Sarah opened her mouth to call out, to intervene, when Celia's hand shot out and connected with Dean's cheek with a resounding crack. Taken off guard, Dean dropped Celia's arm and she made a dash back toward the house. Even from her distant vantage point, Sarah could see the rage on Dean's face, as well as the fear that overcame Celia once she realized what she had just done.

Sarah crouched down behind the Bronco, her heart beating madly against her chest. She tried to hold completely still, hoping that Dean wouldn't look her way.

What was that all about? she wondered, trying to steady her breathing. She thought back to the conversation in the house. Had Celia said something that would anger Dean? Celia had defended Amy when Dean suggested that she might know more about Julia's fall than she had let on, but was that enough to enrage him?

Maybe Celia had told Dean that Sarah had been asking questions about Jack's parents and their deaths. Maybe he was angry that Celia would share such private family matters with Sarah. But that didn't seem to be a good enough reason to evoke such violence, either.

Cautiously, Sarah peeked around the Bronco. Dean had moved toward a mud-splattered pickup truck, climbed in and roared away. Once he was out of sight, Sarah hurried toward the rental car, grateful that Dean had chosen to leave in his truck rather than the Bronco. She didn't know what she would have done if he had caught her cowering behind his wife's vehicle.

Once in the car, she drove quickly away, eager to leave the farm and all its violence, past and present, behind her. The way Dean had manhandled Celia left her feeling uneasy. He outweighed Celia by nearly one hundred and fifty pounds. He could have snapped her arm in two. Even more surprising, however, was Celia's reaction. She had slapped Dean squarely on the cheek with no indecisiveness, no hesitation. The regret came after the blow had met its mark. But the question was, was Celia sorry that she had hurt her husband, or was she sorry that she'd have to face Dean's wrath for fighting back?

She should tell someone. But who? She could tell Jack, but at the moment she had her own questions for Jack about his own secrets. And somehow she knew that he would just tell her to mind her own business. Dean and Celia could handle their own marital spats without the two of them butting in. Besides, she was ashamed to admit, what if she told Jack and he went to comfort Celia? Would Sarah be inadvertently pushing her husband into the arms of his first love? She tried to shake the thought away.

She began to second-guess herself. What had she seen, really? She couldn't hear what Dean and Celia had been saying; she didn't know how hard Dean had actually grabbed Celia's arm. Neither of them looked any worse for wear. *Coward,* a small voice inside her head scolded.

Right now, there was nothing she could do, and there were important preparations for Julia's funeral that needed tending to. All of this would have to wait.

As she drove to Cedar City, the largest nearby town, her heartbeat returned to a normal cadence.

Sarah mentally ticked off the days in her head. Hopefully Julia's autopsy would only take a few days and then her remains would be released. There would be a wake, the funeral and maybe a few days to help Hal put Julia's affairs in order. Five days, a week at the most.

She pulled into a strip mall that included a clothing store where she was able to find some clothes for them to wear to the wake and the funeral. She then stopped into a big-box store and quickly ran through the store aisles, tossing some basic items that she and Jack would need for their extended stay in Penny Gate into her cart. She paid for her purchases, stowed them in the trunk of the car and collapsed into the front seat. A few minutes outside of town she tried to call Jack to see where she should meet him — at Hal's or Dean's. No answer.

She rubbed her eyes and checked the clock. It was only five thirty, but she felt as if it could be midnight. Her head ached with too much caffeine or maybe not enough.

Consulting the rental car's GPS, she began the drive back to Penny Gate. She wasn't quite ready to head back to Dean's, and she decided to go in search of coffee. She pulled into an empty parking spot in front of a small redbrick building with a faded sign that read The Penny Café.

As she opened the café door a bell tinkled announcing her arrival and Sarah felt as if she had stepped back into the 1950s. She walked across the grimy black-and-white checkered floor to a counter that was surprisingly clean. Sarah sat down on an orange stool, careful not to catch her sweater on the torn vinyl. She read the offerings printed neatly on a large chalkboard, then ordered a cinnamon latte.

While Sarah waited, she pulled out her phone. She was eager to get back to the article about Jack's mother she had found earlier, but when the screen lit up she saw that she had new emails. She was sure there was nothing urgent, but she opened up the mail app just to make sure.

She clicked and the email popped open.

Dear Astrid,
  Three blind mice.
  A beautiful spring morning.
  Laundry on the line.
  Strawberries.
  See how they run?

Sarah shook her head. Nonsense. She deleted the message and quickly scanned through her other emails. To think that so many people looked to her for advice when sometimes she felt as though she had no answers and in fact could use some advice of her own.

"I've got my own problems," she murmured with a sigh.

A gray-haired man sitting on the stool next to her turned in her direction. "Penny for your thoughts," he said.

"What?" Sarah asked, startled by the intrusion.

"You said you have your own problems. I'm no therapist, but I'm a darn good listener."

A sharp quip formed on her tongue, but she swallowed her words. The man was well into his seventies with deep-set, wary eyes, closely cropped silver hair with a matching mustache tucked below a prominent nose, pocked and purple veined. He wore a dun-colored sheriff's uniform and held a matching hat in his thin fingers.

"S-sorry," Sarah stammered. "I didn't realize I was talking out loud."

"Been known to do it myself. Verne Gilmore," the man said, and held out his hand.

"Sarah Quinlan," Sarah replied. She set her phone on the counter and took his hand. It was warm and rough. The waitress set Sarah's latte in front of her.

"Refill, Sheriff?" asked the waitress, a young woman with a nose ring and a sleek red ponytail. She tilted the coffeepot over his empty cup.

Gilmore looked down at Sarah's latte. "You know, I think I'll have what she's having. Always wanted to try one." The waitress raised one penciled-on eyebrow and walked away. "I know a lot of Quinlans, but I haven't had the pleasure of meeting you." He looked at her expectantly.

For some reason, Sarah felt defensive. "I'm married to Jack Quinlan," she said, stirring her latte with a cinnamon stick. "He used to live here."

Gilmore nodded. "I saw Jack just a little while ago at the hospital. I'm sad to hear that his aunt Julia passed away. She was a nice woman."

"Yes, she was," Sarah agreed. "But Jack said that the doctor doesn't think Julia died because of the fall. Why?"

"That's what we're trying to find out," the sheriff said neutrally. "In fact, I've been trying to get ahold of Amy. Any idea as to where she is?"

"No, but she was very upset when I saw her earlier. She probably just needs a little time to herself."

The waitress set the latte in front of the sheriff and he took a cautious sip. "Not bad," he said, white foam clinging to his mustache.

"That'll be four fifty." The waitress held out her hand.

"Really?" Gilmore asked. "For this? It's all foam and air." The waitress smiled mischievously at him, hand still outstretched. Gilmore sighed and reached into his pocket for his billfold and slapped a five-dollar bill into her hand.

He had to be around the same age as Hal and Julia, and Sarah wondered if he had been with the sheriff's department when Jack's mother died. "So you knew Jack when he was growing up?" she asked.

"Sure did. Knew the whole family. Must be hard for Jack to come back home. Lots of memories."

"Jack doesn't really like to talk about it," Sarah admitted.

"Understandable." Gilmore pulled a napkin from the dispenser and wiped it across his mouth.

"I wish he would. Talk about it, I mean." Sarah fiddled uncomfortably with her cup. "We've been married for twenty years, but it's like everything is before and after, you know? Before his parents died and after. He doesn't talk much about the before and definitely not about what actually happened to his mother or father." Gilmore was quiet and Sarah winced inwardly. She felt her face redden, embarrassed that she was revealing so much about her private life to a complete stranger.

The sheriff waited until the curious waitress moved away from them. "What is it you'd like to know?"

"I know Jack's mom died in the house he grew up in and I know his father was a suspect. Beyond that, I don't know anything."

"Jack never told you what happened?" The sheriff narrowed his eyes, trying to unsuccessfully mask his surprise. Sarah didn't answer. "Well, in the end it was all pretty straightforward. The husband did it. I'm not sure what more I can tell you about it."

Gilmore blew into his coffee before taking another sip.

"But why?" Sarah asked. "What was so bad that he had to kill her?"

Gilmore shrugged. "Sometimes the reason is cut-and-dried. An affair or greed. Sometimes the motive isn't so easy to identify and this was one of those cases. We don't know for sure why John Tierney killed his wife. It looks like he just snapped."

The sheriff looked at his watch. "Well, duty calls. It was nice meeting you, Mrs. Quinlan. I'll be calling on the family in the next day or so. If you talk to Amy, tell her to check in with me. I want to follow up on some questions about Julia's fall."

"Nice to meet you, too," Sarah said.

He turned to a woman sitting on the other side of him. "See you at the office, Margaret." Gilmore propped his hat back on his head and walked away.

"You're Jack's wife?" the woman asked from across the empty stool.

"Pardon me?" Sarah asked, still thinking about the sheriff's inadequate response to her question.

The woman scooted over to the stool next to Sarah. "I couldn't help overhearing your conversation with the sheriff. I'm Margaret Dooley, one of the dispatchers at the sheriff's department." She was a stout woman of around fifty with red hair.

Sarah nodded and took a sip of her coffee. She was just about to excuse herself, anxious to get back to the articles on her phone, but Margaret continued. "Did I hear you say that you're Jack Quinlan's wife?" Margaret fingered the reading glasses that she wore on a chain around her neck. "I used to babysit for Jack and Amy when they were little."

"Really?" Sarah asked.

"Really," Margaret said with a pleasant smile. "I wasn't all that much older than Jack. He must have been six and I was twelve. Amy was just a baby, maybe two."

"What were they like?" Sarah leaned toward Margaret, eager to know more. "God, I would have liked to have known Jack back then."

"They were nice kids. Easiest dollar fifty an hour I ever made. All Jack wanted to do was play outside and Amy would follow him around like a puppy. She was the sweetest little thing."

Sarah laughed at the thought of Jack and Amy running through the tall grass together as children. Laughing and carefree, no knowledge of what one day would befall their family.

"You really don't know what happened to Jack's mom?"

"It's embarrassing to admit," Sarah said, "but I don't know the details. For some reason he's been less than forthcoming with me." Sarah didn't know why she was pouring her heart out to this stranger, but it felt right, and a weight seemed to lift from her chest.

"He's probably just trying to protect you," Margaret said, and pushed her empty plate aside. She checked the chunky gold watch on her wrist. "I've got some time before I have to go into work. We could talk."

The two moved to a corner booth for privacy. "I'm sorry to hear about Julia," Margaret said soberly, her eyes filled with sympathy. "She was a nice woman."

"Thanks. I'll tell Jack you said so. It was all very sudden. I wish I would have gotten to know her better."

"You don't know anything about what happened to Jack's parents?" Margaret asked.

Sarah shook her head. "Believe me, I've tried talking to Jack about it. I've gotten nowhere. It's like hitting a brick wall. All I know is that Jack's mom died in the house he grew up in, that Jack found her and that his dad was wanted for questioning. That's

126

it. That's all I know."

Margaret looked over her shoulder, and when she was sure that no one was lurking she leaned forward in the booth, the stack of brightly colored bangles on her wrist clanking together as she propped her elbows on the tabletop. "I couldn't believe it when I heard that. There'd never been a murder in Penny Gate before. We were all shocked. My mother and Lydia Tierney were best friends. Let me tell you, she was absolutely devastated. Cried for weeks. She still isn't over it."

Sarah fought the urge to hurry Margaret along in her story. She had an almost feverish gleam in her eyes and Sarah got the feeling that she enjoyed being the center of attention, of having a rapt audience.

"Jack came home from school one day and found his mother down in their cellar beaten to death. They searched high and low for Jack's dad but never found him. They found his truck sitting in a cornfield, but there was no sign of John Tierney. There was even a statewide manhunt. It was as if he just disappeared off the face of the earth."

"But why?" Sarah asked, wanting more details. "Why did he do it?"

"That's the million-dollar question," Margaret said, tapping one manicured nail against the table to emphasize her point. "No one was sure why John would kill Lydia. They were a nice couple. I never saw any problems between them and I babysat for them for years."

"But what do you think?" Sarah pressed. "Do you think he did it?"

Margaret shrugged. "It sure looks that way. Why else would he have run away? Besides, you know small towns. Everyone had a theory as to why he would have killed her. Lydia was having an affair, John was having an affair, they were having money problems."

"So that's it?" Sarah asked. "Case closed?" This made Sarah immeasurably sad and even more bewildered by Jack's secrecy. Why did he feel as though he needed to make up some big story about his parents dying in a car accident? Did he think she was too fragile and couldn't handle the truth? Did he think she would judge him, not want to marry him because his father was a murderer?

"Well, not officially closed. They never made an arrest. What little evidence they had pointed to John Tierney. But they did check out other suspects — vagrants in the area, an escapee from a work-release program in Cedar City. And, if you can believe it —" Margaret leaned in even closer toward Sarah and whispered "— Jack was even the top suspect for a time."

"Jack?" Sarah asked. Jack was the last person in the world she could imagine as a murder suspect. She thought about how loving he was with the girls, how gentle he was with his physical therapy patients. It made absolutely no sense. "Why would Jack be a suspect?"

Seeing the stricken look on Sarah's face, Margaret backpedaled. "No, no. He was the one who found her. The person who finds the victim is always a suspect." All of Margaret's earlier relish in sharing the details of Penny Gate's most famous murder had disappeared. "I really didn't mean to upset you. Of course I don't think Jack murdered his mother. That's ridiculous. Now I wish I hadn't said anything."

"No, no," Sarah said, trying to muster an encouraging smile. "I really appreciate that you would even talk to me. I want to know what happened. I *need* to know," she added with force.

Margaret glanced down at her watch wistfully. "I do have to get to work. I wish we could talk more, though. I have so many great stories about Jack and Amy growing up."

"I'd love to hear more about Jack and Amy as kids, and I'm sure Jack would get a kick out of seeing his babysitter again," Sarah said, though she wasn't quite sure if this was true. It seemed that Jack had done everything in his power to avoid reminders of his past.

"I'm so sorry to hear about Julia." Margaret jotted a phone number on a napkin and slid it to Sarah. "Call me or just stop by the sheriff's department." Sarah watched as Margaret paused to greet the other café patrons on the way out the door, her buoyant laughter echoing through the room.

Sarah lingered over her coffee, not wanting to return to Dean and Celia's home. She couldn't face Jack, who now seemed like a complete stranger to her. And she didn't want to take part in idle chitchat with Dean and Celia after seeing their violent encounter.

Sarah's phone vibrated and reluctantly she answered.

"Sarah," Jack said. His once-familiar voice now seemed different, laced with worry. "We still haven't been able to get ahold of Amy and I'm starting to get worried. How close are you to coming back to Dean's farm?"

"Actually, I'm in Penny Gate. I stopped at a coffee shop and ran into the sheriff. He said he needed to talk to Amy, too."

It was nearing supper time, and the café was quickly filling and growing loud with chatter.

"Do you think you could do a favor for me since you're in town?" Jack asked.

"Sure," Sarah said, expecting Jack to ask her to stop at the florist or the funeral home to help with arrangements for Julia's funeral.

"Can you swing by Amy's house and see if she's there? We've been calling and calling, and she's not picking up. I'm getting a little worried about her."

"Do you think something's wrong?" Sarah stood and wove around small round tables, acutely aware of the curious glances people were giving her. She was a stranger in a small town.

"I'm not sure," Jack admitted. "It's probably nothing. Amy's probably upset and not answering her phone. I'd feel better if someone would check on her. I can drive into town, but it would take me twenty minutes. Would you mind?"

"Okay," she said grudgingly. She wasn't sure how Amy would react when she found the sister-in-law she barely knew pounding on her front door. "What's her address?" Sarah asked, stepping outside and digging into her purse for a pen and scrap of paper.

"She lives on Oleander. It's just two blocks off Main." Sarah heard the murmur of a female voice in the background. "Celia says it's on the corner. The only blue house on the street." Of course Celia was right there, Sarah thought to herself.

"Okay," Sarah said, shoving the pen and paper back into her purse. "I'll call you after I get there." She hung up the phone, wondering if Celia had told Jack about Dean grabbing her wrist, about slapping him. She imagined Celia crying on Jack's shoulder, an intimate moment where she would look up at him with her big doe eyes and all the memories of their past together would come rushing back. Sarah cringed and wiped the vision from her mind.

She considered walking the two blocks to Amy's house. It was a nice evening. Cool but pleasant. But for some reason she felt an almost inexplicable urgency, a need to move quickly. She climbed into the rental car and found Oleander Street in less than a minute.

Sarah parked in front of the shabby robin's-egg-blue house dwarfed by an ancient buckeye tree. Spiny hulls and glossy brown nuts covered the patchy lawn. Sarah paused to pick up one of the buckeyes and rolled the smooth golf-ball-size seed between her fingers, recalling from her childhood that they were meant to be good luck. She would need it, she thought to herself.

She followed the cracked, uneven pavement up three steps to the front door and knocked. She waited a moment and tried again. Still no response. She turned away from the door and surveyed the street. It was dead quiet.

Sarah walked around the property. She looked for a car, but there was no garage, and although there were several vehicles parked along the curb, any one of them could have belonged to Amy.

"I saw her come home earlier," came a voice from out of nowhere, startling Sarah. She turned to find a wizened old woman dressed in a floral housecoat and tennis shoes.

"She's not answering her door," Sarah explained. "Is her car here?"

"Who's wants to know?" the woman asked, looking at her suspiciously from behind grimy trifocals.

"I'm Amy's sister-in-law, Sarah Quinlan. We've been having trouble getting ahold of her, and we're getting a little worried." Sarah held out her hand in greeting.

"You got some ID?" the woman asked, ignoring Sarah's outstretched fingers.

"Yes, of course." Sarah dug through her purse until she found her driver's license and then handed it to the woman. The woman flicked her eyes back and forth between the license and Sarah's face until she seemed satisfied.

"I'm Cora Berry," she introduced herself, and handed the ID back to Sarah. "That's Amy's car there." The woman pointed to a two-door red hatchback with a dented front fender parked beneath the buckeye tree.

"I wonder why she's not answering the door?" Sarah said.

"My guess is that she probably doesn't want to talk to you," the woman said archly.

Sarah retreated down the steps and sidled between the overgrown boxwood hedges that edged the home's foundation. Using her hands to block the glare of the evening sun she pressed her face against the front window and peered through the narrow opening between the drawn curtains. Gradually the contents of the sparsely furnished room came into focus as her eyes became accustomed to the dim interior.

Directly in Sarah's field of vision was a

flimsy particleboard cabinet that supported an old box television airing what appeared to be a local news program. Sarah's eyes landed on a wooden coffee table that was covered with the detritus of someone who lived alone: a bottle of vodka, dirty cereal bowls, an overflowing ashtray, an orange prescription bottle tipped on its side. To the right of the coffee table, positioned at an angle, was a grungy taupe sofa draped with a large blanket crocheted in greens and blues.

Cora crowded in next to Sarah. With effort she lifted her heels and placed her hands on the windowsill. Sarah saw that they were speckled with age spots and gnarled by arthritis. "I could have sworn she was home," Cora said more to herself than to Sarah.

"The TV's on and her car is here," Sarah observed. "Maybe she's in the bedroom taking a nap or maybe she's taking a shower."

Cora pressed her nose to the window to get a better look. "What's that?" she asked.

"Where?" Sarah tried to follow Cora's line of vision but saw nothing out of the ordinary.

"There, on the couch."

Sarah squinted, trying to get a better look. "Oh," she said with surprise. What she had thought were the lumpy cushions of an old sofa was, Sarah realized, a small, slight figure covered in a blanket. "Is she sleeping?" Sarah asked.

"I don't know," Cora said doubtfully. "She's not moving." From their vantage, Sarah could see what looked to be the pale skin of Amy's foot peeking out from beneath the blanket. "Amy," Cora said loudly, pounding on the window with surprising strength. "Amy, wake up!"

She didn't stir. Sarah stared intently at the form, hoping to see the rise and fall of her back, any evidence of breathing. Nothing. Sarah joined Cora in rapping on the window and calling Amy's name. A neighbor peeked out to see what all the ruckus was.

"I'm going to see if the door's unlocked," Cora said breathlessly, lowering her feet to the ground. Sarah continued to peer through the window, once again noting the vodka and pill bottle on the coffee table. Had Amy, in her grief over Julia's death, her guilt over not finding her sooner, decided to swallow a combination of drugs and alcohol? But to what end?

Cora jiggled the doorknob. "It's locked."

"I'm calling 9-1-1," Sarah said, already reaching into her pocket for her phone.

"My sister-in-law isn't moving," she said

when the emergency dispatcher answered the phone. "I'm outside and I can't get in, but I can see her." She tried not to panic as the woman on the line asked her a series of questions.

"I've got help on the way," the woman said calmly. Her voice remained calm and businesslike. "What's your sister-in-law's name, ma'am?"

"Amy Quinlan," Sarah said, keeping her eyes on Amy, hoping, praying, for some sign of life.

"Is this Sarah Quinlan?" the voice asked.

"Yes. Yes, it is," Sarah said, confused as to how the 9-1-1 dispatcher would know this. "My husband asked me to come check on his sister."

"Sarah, this is Margaret Dooley," the dispatcher said. "I've got an ambulance and sheriff's car on the way. Can you still see Amy?"

"Yes, I can see her."

"Tell me what you see."

"She's lying on the couch, covered in a blanket. There's a bottle of vodka and an empty pill bottle on the table next to her." Sarah's voice cracked with emotion and tears blurred her vision.

"What else do you see?" Margaret urged. Sarah swiped at the tears, trying to stay focused. What if Amy was dead? she wondered.

A thin, nearly invisible wisp of smoke rose from the pile of cigarette butts in the ashtray on Amy's coffee table. "I see a cigarette. A burning cigarette," Sarah relayed with relief. The fact that the cigarette was still smoldering gave her hope that Amy hadn't been unconscious for too long.

In the near distance Sarah heard the wail of sirens. "They're here," Sarah said as she turned from the window and hurried out from behind the shrubs, her shirt catching on the sharp branches.

"I'm going to hang up now, Sarah," Margaret explained. "Call me if you need anything, you hear? You've got my number."

"I will, thank you," Sarah said gratefully as a sheriff's vehicle turned the corner and came to a stop in front of the house. By now, most of the neighbors were outside and standing together in small clusters, with arms crossed and wearing worried expressions.

A young sheriff's deputy leaped from the car. "Where is she?" he asked.

"Inside," Sarah said, and pointed to the front door. "It's locked. We can see her through the window, but she won't wake up." She wished he would hurry up and get inside.

The deputy, thickly built with a short marine haircut, tried the doorknob. "I'll have to force my way in."

"Where's the ambulance?" Sarah asked. "Margaret said that an ambulance was coming."

"It's on its way," he promised. "Now stand back." Sarah and Cora stepped aside as the deputy gave the door a tentative shove, causing it to shudder on its hinges. He planted his feet and brought his hands in front of him, then threw his shoulder into the door. It swung open with such force that it bounced off the interior wall and flew back toward the deputy, who put out a protective hand to stop it from striking him in the face. The sound of another siren filled the air. The ambulance was near.

In seconds they were inside the house and Sarah was immediately assaulted with the unmistakable smell of vomit. The deputy pulled away the blanket to reveal Amy's still form. She was lying on her back, her face turned and pressed against the couch cushions, which were soaked in vomit. Her skin was pale, almost translucent. One arm was tucked beneath her body, the other dangled limply at her side, her knuckles grazing the floor.

"Is she breathing?" Sarah asked.

The deputy placed two fingers against the nape of Amy's neck. "I think I found a pulse."

"Oh, thank God," Sarah said with relief.

The EMTs rushed into the room, and Sarah and Cora stepped aside so they could attend to Amy. The deputy canvassed the room. It looked as if Amy had been packing up her meager possessions. Dean had mentioned that she had recently lost her job. Maybe as a result Amy had lost her home, as well. A jumble of boxes filled with DVDs, books, magazines and knickknacks sat in a corner.

"Looks like it could have been an overdose," the deputy observed, picking up the empty prescription bottle from the coffee table. "Diazepam. Valium," he clarified. "Do you know any reason why she would want to hurt herself?"

Sarah didn't know where to begin. Amy had just lost her aunt, possibly to murder. She was jobless and according to her cousin, a drug addict. And, Sarah thought, on top of it all, Amy's mother had been murdered by her father. It was easy to see how all these could contribute to a suicide attempt.

"I'm not sure," Sarah finally said. "I think you'll need to talk to her family."

The deputy narrowed his eyes at her. "I thought you were family."

"I am," Sarah blustered. "Technically. But Amy's my sister-in-law." The deputy had already started to move away from her, his attention on Cora, who was bending over, staring intently into one of the boxes piled in the corner.

"Ma'am, is everything okay?" he asked.

Cora looked up at them with a puzzled expression. "I think it's blood," she said, pointing toward the box. "And maybe hair."

Sarah and the deputy joined Cora to see what she had found.

"She's coming around," said one of the EMTs. "She's waking up."

Sarah turned from the box toward Amy, but the EMTs were surrounding her in tight formation, making it impossible for Sarah to see Amy's face.

She turned back toward the box, where she discovered a plastic grocery bag, whose edges were speckled with what appeared to be dried blood. Inside the bag was some kind of tool. A metal hook with a short shank attached to a wormwood handle.

"Don't touch anything," the deputy ordered.

"What is it?" Sarah asked, her stomach flipping dangerously. The smell of vomit mixed with cigarette smoke and the perspiration of many gathered in a small space left her feeling vaguely nauseated.

"What the hell?" came a slurred, groggy voice. Sarah turned. Amy slid her legs from the sofa and sat upright, swaying unsteadily as she got her bearings. Eyes half-closed and unfocused, she swatted ineffectually at the EMT who was trying to take her blood pressure. "Get off me," she said, pulling at the Velcro cuff on her arm.

"Ma'am, stay seated," the EMT ordered. "We need to make sure you're okay."

"Amy," Sarah began, "you weren't answering your phone. I came here to check on you and found you unconscious. We got scared and called an ambulance."

"You let them in?" Amy abruptly stood, then wobbled, grabbing on to the nearest EMT to steady herself. She glanced at the front door, which was wide-open and hanging from one hinge. "You had no right," she said with indignation. "You can't just break into someone's house."

"Amy." Sarah reached out for her hand. "Please sit down. Let them check you over."

Amy slapped her away. "Get out. All of you, get out of my house. Now."

"Are you refusing treatment, ma'am?" an EMT asked.

"Damn right, I am," she said, bringing one shaky hand to her head and recoiling at the matted, wet mess she found. "I have the flu. That's all. I didn't make it to the bathroom." Amy's lips trembled as her outrage shifted to embarrassment. "Go, please," she added softly.

"I'm afraid I can't do that, ma'am," the deputy said. He snapped latex gloves over his hands. He lifted the box that contained the plastic bag and hooked metal object with a wooden handle, and tilted it toward Amy so she could view the contents. "We need to talk about what's in this box."

7

When the EMTs left and the crowd of neighbors dispersed and went home, Sarah and the sheriff's deputy remained. Sarah realized she hadn't called Jack like she told him she would and he must have been worried sick.

"I'm going to need to ask you some questions, Amy," said the deputy.

"I want you to leave," Amy said shortly. "Both of you. And I don't have to talk to you," she said to the deputy. "I'm sick and all I want to do is take a shower and go to bed."

"I'm afraid that you're going to have to talk to me," the deputy said, his patience beginning to grow short.

Amy narrowed her eyes as she looked in the box. "Is that blood?" she asked in disgust.

Sarah came up behind Amy and peered over her shoulder into the box and her hand flew to her mouth. The metal hook was covered with a rusty-colored substance that looked very much like dried blood.

"And hair," the deputy added, nodding toward the long, silvery filaments that clung to the hook.

"That isn't mine," Amy insisted.

"Well, it's been found on your property," the deputy said. "So unless you can tell me where it came from and how it got here, you've got a problem."

Amy's eyes darted back and forth between the deputy and Sarah. "It isn't mine," she repeated more forcefully.

"Amy, let me call Jack or Dean," Sarah said earnestly. "Don't say anything else."

Amy shot her a look that told Sarah she didn't want or need her help.

"Okay, then," the deputy said, pulling out his phone. "I'm declaring this house a crime scene. You," he said, pointing at Sarah, "need to leave the premises immediately. And you," he said to Amy, who finally had the sense to look nervous, "need to take a seat."

"Amy, don't say anything until you get a lawyer," Sarah advised. "Do you understand?"

"I don't need a lawyer," Amy said defiantly as the deputy ushered Sarah out of the house through the damaged front door.

Sarah pulled out her phone and saw that she had several missed calls from Jack. She pressed the call button and he picked up on the first ring.

"Sarah," he said, relief flooding his voice. "I was getting worried. What's going on?"

Sarah wasn't sure where to begin. "Amy's fine. Sort of. She's alive."

"Alive?" Jack exclaimed. "What happened?"

Sarah paced along the curb in front of Amy's house, careful to stay off the property. "She's not hurt and she's at the house. But a sheriff's deputy is questioning her."

"Why? What for?" Jack asked in confusion. "Sarah, what the hell is going on?"

"I'm trying to tell you," Sarah cried impatiently. "All I know is that the deputy found some kind of tool covered with dried blood and hair in a box in Amy's living room. He's declared the house a crime scene."

Two more law-enforcement vehicles turned onto Amy's street. Behind the wheel of one of them was Sheriff Gilmore. "Jack, I think Amy needs a lawyer. You need to come right away."

Jack arrived at Amy's house but the deputy wouldn't let him inside. The house was a crime scene and Amy was being questioned.

Sarah and Jack sat in the rental car and waited. After an hour and a half, Sheriff Gilmore had the decency, Sarah thought, to come out to talk to them. He hunched over the side of the car, leaning his arms on the open window. "Amy says she doesn't want a lawyer," he said.

"Can't you make her get one?" Jack asked.

"We're not in the business of getting lawyers for the people we interview," Gilmore said with amusement. "Just doesn't work that way."

"I mean," Jack said in irritation, "Amy was drunk. Can she even be considered competent to answer questions in that state?"

"Amy may have been drinking and imbibing in certain pharmaceuticals, but as Sarah here can also attest to, most of it ended up on the sofa."

"This isn't funny, Sheriff," Jack said in a low voice.

"I never meant to give you the impression that I thought this is funny. In fact, this is dead serious, Jack. A bloody bale hook was found in there —" Gilmore pointed to the house "— and your sister just happened to be the one who found her at the bottom of the stairs. Your sister is free to ask for an attorney at any time but she has already told

147

us she doesn't want one."

Though the sky had darkened, curious neighbors flipped on their outdoor lights and milled around on their lawns and front steps once they realized the earlier drama was going on long after they thought it was over. "I want to see her," Jack insisted.

The sheriff lowered his voice so that only Sarah and Jack could hear him. "Your aunt is on her way to an autopsy in Des Moines. Your sister's home is being searched and she is going to be questioned. She is now a suspect in the murder of your aunt. That's how serious I am taking this."

"After all that she's been through, what we've been through, you think Amy would kill Julia? She loved her more than anyone," Jack insisted.

"I just go where the evidence takes me. And right now it's led me to your sister." He stood upright and tapped the roof of the car with an open hand. "You can head on home now. Nothing more is going to happen here tonight."

"Is she under arrest, then?" A muscle in Jack's cheek twitched.

"No, but we're taking her down to the sheriff's department for more formal questioning. You can talk to her tomorrow."

"I want to see her now. You can't keep me

from talking to her if she's not under arrest." Jack opened the car door and approached the sheriff until they were nearly nose to nose.

"The hell I can't," Gilmore said, holding his ground. Sarah watched Jack step past him and trot up to the house with the sheriff close behind. Though Gilmore was an elderly man, he moved lithely and with quick, purposeful steps.

"Amy, don't say a word," Jack was advising by the time Sarah had caught up with the both of them.

"Jack, don't make me have to take you in, too, for interfering," Gilmore warned.

"Stop, Jack," Sarah said, inserting herself between Jack and Gilmore. The last thing they needed was for both Amy and Jack to be taken away in handcuffs.

Jack held his hands up in supplication. "I'm not interfering with anything. I'm just making sure that Amy knows that she doesn't have to speak to you without an attorney present."

"I don't need a lawyer. I swear I didn't hurt Julia," Amy cried, stopping in front of Jack as the deputy led her by the arm from the house.

"I know, Amy," Jack said. "I know. We'll get you a lawyer. Just don't say anything until we find someone." Amy nodded and was whisked away by the deputy and into his cruiser.

"Bastard," Jack whispered.

"At least he came out and talked to us," Sarah observed. "That's something."

Jack gave a breathy snort. "You give him too much credit. Gilmore doesn't have a whole lot of love for my family."

Together they walked back to their cars and Jack opened the door to Hal's truck. "Let's just go back to Hal's. We'll get a lawyer for Amy and check on her in the morning."

Sarah followed Jack along the winding roads that led back to the farm, all the while feeling as though she'd entered an alternate universe the minute she arrived in Penny Gate.

Sarah thought back to what Jack had asked the sheriff. *After all that she's been through, what we've been through, you think Amy would kill Julia?* This was the closest to a revelation Jack had ever made about his past. At least, the only true one. Sarah knew her next conversation with Jack was critical. He had lied to her for the past twenty years. And not just small, inconsequential untruths, but epic lies that had shaken if not irreparably damaged their marriage.

By the time they reached the farm the sun had set. Hal, even in his grief, was thoughtful enough to leave the porch light on for them, but the rest of the house was dark.

Jack unlocked and opened the front door. He flipped on a table lamp and waited until Sarah crossed the threshold and closed the door behind her, locking and chaining the door.

"What a day," Jack said, releasing a long breath. "Maybe when I wake up in the morning it will all have just been a nightmare."

"Jack, we need to talk," Sarah said in a calm but firm voice.

"Come on, Sarah, the last thing I want to do is talk right now. My aunt died today, my sister . . ." he began, but Sarah stopped him by holding up one hand.

"I love you, Jack, but if you don't sit down and talk to me right now, I'm going to be on the very next flight back to Larkspur."

Sarah expected him to protest, to scoff and wave her off, but he didn't. He must have heard something new in her voice. She wasn't going to be dismissed. She wasn't bluffing.

"Okay," he said guardedly. "I'm listening."

Sarah settled onto the sofa and Jack chose the chair across from her. Though she had

151

planned what she was going to say to Jack on the drive back from Amy's, she found herself struggling for the right words. "You get one chance here, Jack." Her voice trembled despite her resolve to see this conversation to the end.

"Sarah . . ." Jack said earnestly, leaning forward.

"No." Sarah shook her head. "Let me talk first."

Jack sat back in his chair, arms folded across his chest.

"Here's what I've learned in the past twenty-four hours, from people I barely even know. Your real name is Tierney, not Quinlan. And I know you dated Celia. Seriously enough to consider marriage." Jack looked like he was going to protest, but Sarah silenced him with a warning look. He huffed and shook his head in annoyance. "I'm not done," Sarah continued. "I know your mom and dad didn't die in a car accident. And I know that your dad killed her and disappeared and hasn't been seen since." Sarah paused, expecting Jack to protest, to try and explain away his lies. But he didn't.

His expression softened and he rose from the chair and joined Sarah on the sofa.

"I'm so sorry," he murmured. "I messed up."

"No, Jack," Sarah said angrily, her eyes burning with hot tears. "Messing up is forgetting a birthday or anniversary. This is so much worse."

"I know, I know." Jack reached for her hand, but she pulled away. There was no way, she thought, that she was going to let Jack off so easily. "Please look at me," he pleaded. Unwillingly, Sarah met his eyes. "Before I met you, I never thought I would get married and have kids. I never let anyone in. I didn't get close to anyone."

"But you didn't let me in," Sarah protested. "You made up this entire fictional history for yourself. How much could you have really loved me if you couldn't tell me the truth about your parents?"

"I *did* love you. I *do* love you. More than anything. That's exactly why I didn't tell you."

"That makes absolutely no sense." Sarah pressed the heels of her hands against her eyes.

"Sarah, would you have seriously considered marrying me if you knew that my dad murdered my mother and that he could still be out there?"

"You really think that little of me? You

think that I'm so shallow that I couldn't see past all the things that I love about you because of something your father did?"

Jack shrugged helplessly. "I was afraid of losing you. If I could go back and change it, I would. I would have told you everything."

"Is there anything else?" Sarah asked. "Anything you're not telling me?"

"No, nothing," Jack assured her. "I swear."

"I mean it, Jack, if there's anything else I need to know, tell me now."

"Sarah, I promise you, there's nothing else." He pulled Sarah close to him and this time Sarah didn't pull away. She wanted to melt into his arms, but something didn't allow her to surrender fully.

"I'm going up to bed," she told him tiredly as she broke the embrace.

"I'll be up in a few minutes," Jack told her. He brushed his fingers against her cheek. "I love you, Sarah," he murmured, and kissed her softly on the lips.

"I love you, too," she answered, not quite able to meet his eyes. She trudged up the stairs to the bedroom that Jack had slept in when he was fifteen years old. She was struck at how only twenty-four hours in Penny Gate had aged her husband. What was it Amy had said about the town when they were at the hospital? *People who stay around here too long either die or go crazy.*

Sarah crawled into bed, willing her brain to still itself. So many emotions were pummeling her: anger, fear, confusion. On some level she wanted so badly to return to the blind trust she once had in Jack, but she now knew that unshakable confidence was gone forever. Had he really just been a young man who was afraid of losing Sarah because of the actions of his father? Sarah wasn't fully convinced.

8

Sarah awoke early the next morning disoriented, not sure where she was. She thought she heard something, a light knocking, but she wasn't sure from where it was coming. Beside her Jack slept. She rolled over in bed and reached for her phone, checking to see if either of the girls had called or left a text. They hadn't. She clicked on her mail icon and immediately an email from someone named Seller85 stood out from the rest with an odd subject line: "Two blind mice." She touched the email to open it.

Dear Astrid,
  Two blind mice.
  Iron
  Cold and Hard.
  A whore in a yellow dress.
  See how they run?

She recalled the similar email she had

received yesterday. *Three blind mice,* she remembered it had read. It was odd, she thought, but she was used to getting bizarre emails from readers. She deleted the email, thinking that she'd certainly received worse.

The tapping resumed, a hollow metronome that would pause for a moment and then continue.

"Jack," she whispered. He was sleeping so soundly, so peacefully, splayed on his stomach, his breath rising in slow, even intervals.

Now she eased from the bed, careful not to wake him, quickly dressed and closed the bedroom door behind her with a soft click. The door to Hal's bedroom was also shut. It was still dark out and the house had that quiet, settled feeling before the hum of the day began.

The knocking continued as she made her way down the steps. Someone was at the front door. She checked the clock on the living room wall. Barely 6:00 a.m. Who could be here at this time of day? She flipped on the porch light and peeked through the small glass pane in the door. It was Sheriff Gilmore and two other men dressed in deputy uniforms.

Sarah opened the door and saw the grave look on Gilmore's face. Sarah felt the breath squeeze from her lungs. "Is it Amy?" she asked. "Is she okay?" Two stone-faced deputies flanked Gilmore. Sarah recognized one as the deputy who had been at Amy's home the day before.

"Amy is being questioned in connection with the murder of her aunt. So no, I can't say that things are fine. I'm afraid we're here on not-so-pleasant business. I need to talk to Hal and Jack. May we come in?" Gilmore removed his hat.

Sarah glanced behind her to the still-darkened house. "Can't you come back a little later? Hal and Jack are still sleeping. They're exhausted."

"I'm afraid not," Gilmore said, and Sarah became increasingly alarmed. He held up a piece of paper. "We've got a warrant."

"I think you better wait out on the porch. I'll go upstairs and get Hal and Jack." Gilmore didn't argue, but Sarah also knew that the sheriff and his men weren't planning on going anywhere.

Sarah turned on the living room lamps before she headed upstairs. The light warmed the room and made Gilmore's unsettling visit seem more ominous. Suddenly, she knew exactly why Gilmore was here at this early hour and she hated him for it.

Her mind was racing. Foul play was

suspected in the death of Julia, an object covered with what looked like blood had been found at Amy's and now Amy was being questioned. Had more evidence been discovered? Surely it was too soon for Julia's autopsy to be completed. Had Amy confessed to something? Sarah took the steps two at a time and stumbled, falling to one knee at the top of the landing. "Dammit," she mumbled in embarrassment, and as she pushed herself to her feet, her eyes landed on the spot where the dark oak trim met the plastered wall.

She saw a small spatter of brown dots that looked like blood.

Sarah thought about what Amy had said about Julia being attacked before falling down the stairs. Or was it Jack who had said this? She couldn't remember. She bent down and ran her fingers along the hardwood floor, looking for any clue into what happened to Julia on these stairs. There was one deep gouge about three inches long and two inches wide, but it was an old house, an old floor. The gash could have been there for years. Her eyes traveled upward from the baseboard to the wall. Tiny, dark spots freckled the plaster. She moved even closer. It definitely could be blood, she thought.

She decided to wake Jack first. "Jack,

Jack," she said, and prodded him gently. His eyes fluttered open and landed sleepily on her. "Everything's okay," she began, not wanting to alarm him. "The sheriff is downstairs. He wants to talk to you and Hal. He has a warrant."

"Sheriff Gilmore?" Jack asked blearily. "Here? What time is it?"

"Six," Sarah said, handing Jack his pants. "He has two deputies with him."

Jack immediately became alert and sat upright. "Let me handle this. Let Hal sleep. He doesn't need to deal with this today."

"He told me to get Hal."

"Dammit," Jack muttered. "Why can't we grieve in peace? Can you wake him up?"

"Jack." She grabbed his elbow. "There's blood on the stairs."

"What?" he asked as he pulled on a pair of jeans.

"At the top of the steps and on the wall. I think there's blood."

Jack stuffed his shirt into his pants. "Is it noticeable?"

"No, there's just a little bit, if that's what it even is." Sarah hugged her arms close to her.

"Don't say anything to Gilmore," he said shortly.

"But what if it has something to do with

Julia's fall?" Sarah asked.

"It's probably nothing. Did he say anything about Amy?"

Sarah shook her head. "Just that she's okay."

"Go ahead and wake Hal," he said firmly. "And don't say anything about the blood on the steps."

Sarah watched him leave the room. Didn't he want to know what had happened to his aunt? Was it more important to protect the person who might have hurt her, even if it was Amy?

She heard Jack greet the sheriff and walked quickly to Hal's room. He was sleeping soundly, one arm flung to the empty side of the bed as if he fell asleep reaching for his wife.

"Hal," Sarah said as she roused him. "Sheriff Gilmore is here. I think he wants to search the house."

"What? Why?" Hal sat up and turned on the lamp on his bedside table. He reached for his glasses and slid them onto his face, magnifying his red and swollen eyes.

"They must be investigating Julia's fall. He wants you to come downstairs."

He swung his bare legs over the side of the bed. They were thin and lined with spidery purple veins. His large, round stomach hung heavily over the elastic band of his boxer shorts and his hands clutched the mattress on either side of him as if to help keep him upright. "Does it have something to do with what they found at Amy's house? Do they really think she could have hurt Julia?"

"I don't know," Sarah finally said out loud. "Do you think Amy could have hurt her?" she dared to ask.

Hal stood, and the hardwood floor creaked beneath his bare feet. "Of course not," he said emphatically, and Sarah wondered if he was trying to convince himself as much as Sarah.

While Hal dressed, Sarah went to the bathroom to quickly wash her face and brush her teeth. She turned on the tap, scrubbed her hands under the hot water and looked at herself in the vanity over the sink. She looked the way she felt, which was downright haggard. The trip and lack of sound sleep had left her skin dry and her lips cracked. Her hair, usually smooth and shiny, was dull and frizzed, and she futilely tried to pat it down with her fingers.

She glanced around in search of a hand towel and in the corner noticed a wicker basket lined with Spanish moss and filled with what Sarah could only describe as old farm tools. A small pulley, a rusty hand trowel, a worn leather tape measure and several other items that Sarah couldn't identify. One spot stood glaringly empty, as if one of the tools had been removed. Sarah flashed on the bloody object found in Amy's home. Wouldn't it have fit perfectly within the empty space? What if Amy, in a fit of rage, pulled the bale hook from the basket and attacked Julia at the top of the steps?

She tried to push the thoughts away. Don't borrow trouble, she told herself. Her imagination was working overtime. The autopsy results on Julia were still pending and the supposed weapon found at Amy's home was probably not connected to her death at all.

Sarah called Dean to let him know what was happening. She hadn't seen him since she had witnessed the violent incident with Celia, but she knew Hal would appreciate having his son there.

By the time she came back downstairs, Gilmore and the deputies were standing in the living room with Jack and Hal. Hal was staring down at a piece of paper, and Jack looked fired up and ready to pounce. "I can't believe this is happening," he said in bewilderment.

"I'm going to have to ask you all to leave

while we execute the search," Gilmore explained, ignoring Hal's statement. "It shouldn't take very long. We also need to ask each of you some questions. Why don't I meet you all down at the sheriff's department and we'll talk. I know you've got some hard days in front of you. That's why we thought it was best to come early and let you get on with your business."

"I don't understand," Hal said as he sank into a chair.

"We can't go into the specifics, but as you know, we have reason to suspect that Julia's death was not an accident. We need to conduct a thorough investigation. We'll be out of here as quickly as possible."

Jack pointed a finger at Gilmore, a crimson flush creeping up his neck. "You've had it in for my family since my mom died."

"Just doing my job, Jack," Gilmore said mildly. "Just like I did thirty years ago."

"What parts of the property are you going to search?" Sarah asked, hoping to diffuse the tension between Jack and the sheriff. "Just the house?"

"The house and the three outbuildings," Gilmore answered. "Like I said, the quicker my people can get to work, the quicker you can go about your business." Hal rose from his chair and together they moved outside.

The sun hadn't yet risen and the farmyard was quiet. In the distance a deep rumble rolled down toward them, and Dean and Celia's pickup came into view. They came to a stop behind the two sheriff's vehicles parked in the grass just off to the side of the dirt lane. They were followed by a white van emblazoned with the words *Sawyer County Crime Scene Unit* across the side. Dean and Celia stepped from the truck and came rushing toward them.

"What the hell is going on?" Dean asked, his words clearly focused at the sheriff. "Can't you have some fucking decency and leave my family alone? We're grieving, for God's sake!"

"Settle down, Dean," Sheriff Gilmore said calmly. "I know this is upsetting, but we're trying to get to the truth behind your mother's death. I know you all want to be able to lay Julia to rest knowing that the person who did this is held responsible."

"Everyone knows who did this just as well as I do," Dean spluttered. "Amy and Mom had an argument. Amy found her at the bottom of the stairs. Amy's in jail. Why come here upsetting my dad more than you already have? You've got Amy."

"My goal isn't to upset anyone," Gilmore said, his voice still amicable, but there was a

165

new shrewdness in his eyes. "Now what's this about an argument?"

Dean pressed his lips together, hesitating before speaking. "Amy and Julia had an argument right before the accident. My mom called last week and said that Amy was very upset."

"Did she say what Amy was riled up about?" Gilmore asked.

Dean sucked in his breath. "What doesn't Amy get riled up about?"

"Dean," Celia chided gently.

"Well." Dean adjusted the seed hat on his head. "We all know Amy. She gets a bee up her ass about every other day. She gets mad, she yells, throws a few things, runs off for a couple of days and then comes back like nothing happened."

"Amy's had a hard life," Jack said in defense of Amy, and Celia stroked his arm sympathetically. Sarah bristled at the display of intimacy.

"Come on, Jack," Dean said plaintively. "Everyone's had hard times. We all care about Amy, but she can be a little out there sometimes."

"What was the argument about?" Gilmore asked, getting the conversation back on track.

"You know my mom never said a bad

word against anyone, but she said that Amy came over, started yelling at her about not getting what was due to her. Amy accused them of cheating Jack and her out of what was rightfully theirs."

"Cheated us? Out of what?" Jack asked in confusion. He turned to Hal. "You've got to know I've never thought that. You always treated us like your own kids. I know what you and Julia sacrificed for me and Amy."

"Why don't we all drive over to my office and we'll talk things through," the sheriff suggested. "My deputies can handle the search here."

"Can't this wait?" Celia began, but Hal held up a hand.

"No, let's do this. You're right," he said. "There's no good time for this, so let's get it over with. We'll meet you at your office."

Gilmore gave a nearby deputy a set of instructions, ordered him to call if he ran into any snags and dismissed him before climbing into his vehicle.

Sarah, Jack and Hal loaded into the rental car, and Dean and Celia followed behind them. They sat in silence as they drove, the air in the car thick with the weight of their sadness. In merely a few days, their entire world had been turned upside down. This should have been a time of reflection and fond remembrance, and instead Jack's family was at the center of a murder investigation.

They drove through Penny Gate, past Saint Finnian's, the church where Julia's funeral was to be held, and past the cemetery. The town seemed to still be mostly asleep. A boy with a canvas delivery bag hanging over his shoulder was sleepily tossing rolled newspapers toward doorsteps, and an elderly couple walked their dog. For now they were oblivious to the murder investigation. Sarah sympathized with them — in just a few hours their quaint, small town would be shaken with the gossip that one of their own had been possibly brutally murdered.

Jack turned down a street lined with maple and oak trees emblazoned in full fall colors. When they finally arrived at the sheriff's office, Sarah thought the modest two-leveled building looked more like a schoolhouse than a place where murder suspects were interrogated and booked. Jack pulled into a parking spot and Dean maneuvered his truck in the space next to him. Together they made their way through the main entrance.

Gilmore had arrived before any of them and was waiting by the front counter. Sarah looked around for Margaret Dooley, but she was nowhere to be seen. Instead, a young female deputy was sitting behind the counter, talking on the phone while jotting down notes.

Gilmore greeted them with a grim smile. "Help yourself to some coffee." He pointed to a table where a coffeemaker bubbled and steamed.

"Is Amy here?" Jack asked. His hair, Sarah noticed, was sticking up at odd angles, and his shirt was rumpled and only partly tucked in. In fact, all of them looked half put together. Except for Celia, of course, who managed to make yoga pants and an oversize tunic look lovely.

Gilmore, on the other hand, was wide-awake and alert, his uniform starched and wrinkle-free. Sarah realized then that Gilmore knew exactly what he was doing. He had caught them all off guard, showing up at the house at the crack of dawn with his warrant, skillfully luring them away from the house and to his office where he could question them on his own terms.

"We're still asking Amy a few questions," Gilmore explained.

"She's been here all night?" Celia asked incredulously. "Has she been able to get any sleep? Anything to eat? Has she been arrested?"

"Now don't you worry about Amy. I promise we're taking good care of her," Gilmore said, then tapped his palms on the desk in a quick rhythm as if to punctuate the end of the conversation. "Now, why don't we get down to business? Jack, let's start with you?"

"Why Jack?" Sarah asked. "We weren't even in town when Julia fell." Sarah thought, naively, that they were only here for moral support. If either of them warranted questioning, she figured it would be her, since she was the one who was at Amy's house when the bloodstained object was found.

"You might be surprised," Gilmore said.

"This is insane," Dean muttered as Jack and Gilmore disappeared down a hallway.

"Well, we might as well sit down and wait," Celia said, reaching for a foam cup. "Hal, would you like some coffee?"

He shook his head and settled into one of the chairs. "We should be planning Julia's funeral," he fretted. "I haven't even had a chance to go to the funeral home yet. I haven't picked out a casket."

"We'll take care of all that when we're finished here," Celia soothed. "Drink this," she pressed, handing him the coffee cup despite his protestations. "I can't imagine we'll be here for very long. I mean, we don't *know* anything. None of us were even at the house when Julia fell. I'm sure the sheriff will come to the conclusion very quickly that if it wasn't an accident, whoever killed Julia was a stranger. An intruder."

"You keep telling yourself that, Celia," said Dean, glowering from where he stood by the window. "But I guarantee Amy is the one who did this. And if by some miracle Gilmore lets her out of jail, I will strangle her with my bare hands."

"Dean, just sit down and relax," Celia ordered. "Let the sheriff do his job." Despite the violent interaction Sarah had seen between Dean and Celia yesterday, Celia did not seem afraid of her husband.

Forty-five minutes later, Jack emerged from the sheriff's office looking drawn and unnerved. "He asked for you next," he said to Celia, and nervously, she rose to her feet.

For the first time all morning, Sarah noticed a crack in Celia's unflappable veneer. Suddenly she seemed uneasy, and Dean took her in his arms. "You'll be fine," he soothed, then touched his lips to her forehead. Once again, Sarah found herself confused by the dynamic between the two of them. One minute they were grabbing and slapping each other and screaming, and the next they were the picture of a perfect marriage.

Sarah turned her attention to Jack. "What did he ask you?"

"I think I need some air," he said, ignoring her question. "I'm going for a walk." Jack rubbed a hand across his face where rough dark stubble had appeared overnight.

"Wait," Sarah said, getting up and following him to the door. "Don't run off. You don't get to just run off."

"I'm sorry," Jack said, reaching for her hand. His fingers were ice-cold. "It was terrible. He kept asking me about what happened in Julia's hospital room. It was like I was reliving it all over again."

"Why would he want to know about that?" Sarah asked.

Jack shook his head. "I don't know. I thought at first he wanted to know about how upset Amy was when Julia died, how she scratched that nurse, but he kept asking me about Julia. About what physically was happening. When she started having a seizure, how long it lasted? Who was in and out of the room and when."

"What does who was in the room have to do with anything?" Sarah asked in confusion.

"That was what I wondered. But he kept

172

asking." Despite the ambivalence that she'd felt toward Jack since arriving in Penny Gate, she couldn't help feeling sorry for him now. Seeing his aunt die was a terrible thing and she knew that it shook Jack to his core, but she couldn't help wonder if there was more to Gilmore's interrogation than what he was telling her.

"Go for a walk," she urged. "We'll be fine here for now."

Together they moved toward where Dean and Hal were sitting. "I'm going to go out and get some air," Jack said. "I'll be back in a bit."

"What was that all about?" Hal asked as they watched Jack leave, the door slamming behind him. "Do you think I should go after him?"

"Let him be," Dean said before Sarah could explain. "Gilmore probably asked him a bunch of questions about Amy. I'm sure it was hard to admit to Gilmore just how screwed up she is."

"I know Amy's got problems, but why would she hurt Julia?" Sarah asked. "If there was one thing Jack has said about Amy, it's how much she loved Julia."

"Yeah, but what he didn't tell you was that Amy, when she's mad, can get pretty violent. A few years back she pushed a boyfriend into a busy street."

"Dean," Hal interjected. "You know there's a lot more to the story than that."

"Maybe so, but the guy ended up with a broken leg."

"They were arguing . . . he grabbed her arm first," Hal countered.

Dean took a breath. "My point is, when Amy feels threatened, she doesn't just get mad, she gets furious."

"The fellow didn't press charges . . ."

"She pushed him in front of a moving car, Dad." Dean's voice rose sharply.

Fifteen minutes later the sheriff and Celia came into the lobby and, like Jack, Celia looked a bit shell-shocked. Her eyes were red-rimmed as if she had been crying. Sarah dreaded being called next. Though she knew nothing about Julia and didn't have anything to hide, she hoped that the sheriff would pass her by and ask Dean or Hal to come back with him next.

"Sarah," Gilmore said, looking down at her from beneath his heavy brows. Sarah released the breath she was holding, gathered her purse and followed Gilmore down a long corridor. She wondered where Amy was in the building. Was she in one of these rooms being questioned or was she locked away in a cell in the basement? She imagined Amy screaming and crying for help from behind bars, insisting on her innocence and begging to be released. The thought that she was all alone and yet within earshot of her own family was chilling.

Gilmore led Sarah to a partially opened door labeled with a placard that read Verne Gilmore, Sheriff. "Come on in," Gilmore invited, and they stepped into a cluttered office that held a mismatch of furniture — a battered old oak desk, rows of metal-framed file cabinets and a bookshelf that ran the length of one wall.

Atop the bookshelf were three framed photos — a young Gilmore dressed in his deputy's uniform standing next to a beautiful, dark-haired woman, and a family portrait showing Gilmore and the woman with two teenagers. His children, Sarah figured. The third photograph was of three toddlers all piled on Gilmore's lap. A wide smile of joy spread across Gilmore's face. "Cute kids," Sarah observed.

"Thanks," Gilmore said simply. "Please, take a seat." Sarah sat down in a chair and Gilmore perched on the edge of the desk in front of her. Sarah wondered if he did this to tower over those he interviewed. A subtle but very effective intimidation strategy.

"So, Mrs. Quinlan, I'm hoping that Penny

Gate has been treating you well."

Sarah shifted in her seat. "Yes, it's a nice town. Everyone has been very welcoming."

"Good, good, glad to hear that. Shall we get right down to business?" he said, and Sarah nodded. "When did you first learn of Julia's fall?"

"Early Monday morning. Jack and I flew here that same day. We got to the hospital around 7:00 p.m."

"What did your husband tell you about what happened?"

"Julia fell down the stairs and her injuries were severe. Hal said that Amy was the one who found her and called 9-1-1." Sarah watched as Gilmore scratched notes into his small, black notebook. "I'm not sure how Jack and I can help you with this. We weren't even here."

"Yes, but you both were in the room when Julia died," Gilmore said matter-of-factly. "You both could be witnesses."

"To what? A murder? While we were in that hospital room?" Sarah asked.

Gilmore ignored her question and moved on. "How did Hal react?"

"He was visibly upset. He had to watch his wife take her last breath. It was horrible."

"Amy, too?"

176

"Yes, Amy, too. She was beside herself." Sarah squirmed and crossed her legs, thinking back to when Amy had scratched the nurse. Was it out of anger? Sadness? A feeble attempt to get the nurse to turn the machines back on? She wondered if the others had mentioned Amy's behavior in the hospital room. "Everyone was upset. It would have been strange if someone wasn't."

"It's okay, Mrs. Quinlan," Gilmore said mildly. "You don't have to worry. I've already heard about Amy's outburst at the hospital yesterday. One of the nurses told me."

Sarah breathed a sigh of relief. She felt guilty enough as it was for calling 9-1-1 when she found Amy passed out on the couch. It was partly her fault that Amy was sitting in a jail cell, and the last thing she wanted was to make things worse by ratting on Amy for her behavior at the hospital.

Gilmore slid from the top of his desk and went to the large window, turning his back to her as he spoke. "I can understand you not wanting to get caught up in all this family drama, but it's critical that I get all the information I can. Even the smallest detail can be very important."

Sarah scanned Gilmore's desktop. It was neatly arranged with a black leather desk blotter, a stapler, three-hole punch and a tape dispenser. On the corner of the desk sat two file-folder trays. One labeled In, the other Out. One stray folder sat on the edge of Gilmore's otherwise organized desk.

"Now, what about Dean? How did he react?" Gilmore asked, turning back to face her. Sarah averted her eyes from the file baskets, hoping that Gilmore hadn't caught her looking. She opened her mouth to insist once again that each person in the hospital room was crushed when Julia died, but paused. She sifted through the scene: Hal crying, Amy shouting, the vase crashing to the floor, Jack standing by helplessly and Dean — how did he react? *She has a do not resuscitate order,* he had said. What did he tell Amy when she begged for someone to try and save her? *They can't. She doesn't want any heroic measures keeping her alive.* He seemed calm, almost resigned to the fact that his mother was dying. But was that an unreasonable reaction?

Gilmore looked at Sarah, waiting for her response. "He was sad, too," she finally said, looking down at the floor. Gilmore seemed skeptical but didn't press her.

"Were you aware of any conflicts that anyone might have had with Julia? Did Jack mention any family disagreements?"

Dean had mentioned that Amy and Julia had an argument soon before the fall, but that was just hearsay. She didn't know anything about it, and she certainly didn't want to start trouble about something she knew nothing about. "No, nothing that I can speak to."

"Tell me about yesterday. What time did you arrive at the hospital?" Gilmore returned to his spot on the edge of the desk.

"We got there pretty early. I'd say by nine o'clock. It was just a few minutes after we came in the room that Julia started having the seizure."

"Who was in the room before you arrived?"

"When we came in?"

"Yes, was someone already in the room when you arrived yesterday?"

"Yes, Amy was in the room."

"By herself?"

Sarah thought about this for a moment. "Yes. Amy was in the room when Celia and I walked in."

"You don't know if anyone but Amy had been in the room alone with Julia before then?"

Sarah shook her head. "I have no idea. But the night before, on Monday night, everyone took turns sitting with Julia. She was never alone."

"You were in the room alone with Julia at some point?"

"No. I meant everyone in the immediate family." Sarah felt her face grow hot. These are easy questions, she told herself. Why was she so nervous?

"Was Hal ever in the room alone with Julia?"

"Yes." Sarah nodded. "Everyone, except me, spent some time alone with her."

"Who was in the room first with Julia? Alone, I mean."

Sarah tried to think back. Was it Amy? Maybe Celia? There was a small window of time when they were all out in the hallway. She was sure of that. "I can't remember," Sarah said, shaking her head. "Like I said, they all took turns."

"Amy spent the night in Julia's room. Is that correct?" Gilmore asked.

"As far as I know she did. She was there when we left and she was there when we came back the next morning. She said she was planning on spending the night."

"Did you see Amy manipulating any of Julia's medical equipment? Maybe doing something with her IV?" Gilmore asked.

"No, why?" Sarah asked. "Why are you so concerned about what happened in the

180

hospital room?" Gilmore's face gave away nothing. "Do you think Amy did something to her there?" Sarah asked. "If so, I didn't see anything. Except for the seizure. I saw the seizure." Sarah knew she was rambling.

Gilmore scratched his neck and stood. "I think that'll be all. Thank you for coming in. I do appreciate your time." Sarah stayed in her seat, taken aback at how quickly the interview had ended.

Why was Gilmore so worried about who was in the hospital room alone with Julia? Did he think that whoever pushed her down the steps wanted to make sure they finished the job? Gilmore had his sights on Amy. Though she barely knew her sister-in-law, she wasn't sure she could see her murdering Julia. She saw the way Amy was with her aunt; she heard the way Jack described their relationship. It just didn't seem plausible. She thought about how roughly Dean had grabbed Celia's arm. He seemed to be the more volatile one. Or maybe even Celia. The way she had reared back and struck out at Dean seemed so out of character for her.

Another thought crept into her head and she tried to push it away, but still it nagged at her. What about Jack's dad? Jack had mentioned that he thought he saw his father at the hospital. Was it a trick of light or an overwrought imagination? Or did he really see him? Was it so far-fetched to believe that a man who could kill his wife could come back and kill his sister? *Yes,* Sarah scolded herself, *it is far-fetched.*

Sarah looked up and found the sheriff observing her curiously. "Was there something else?" he asked.

Sarah bit her lip, not sure if she should bring up the subject, but decided she might not get another chance. "I know that Jack's mother was murdered. I also know that Jack's father was the prime suspect. What I don't know is whatever happened to him."

The sheriff tightened his grip on the pen he held in his hand, his gaze on her intensified. "You've talked to your husband about this?"

"He's told me the basics. The rest Hal and Celia filled in for me. I also found some articles online."

"Ahh." He tapped his fingertips together. "Then I don't quite understand what you need from me."

"I just want to know if he's dead," Sarah said more loudly than she intended. She glanced toward the door and lowered her voice. "From the article I read . . ."

"On the internet . . ." Gilmore interrupted.

"It said that John Tierney was missing. I just want to know if he was ever caught or arrested or if he's dead."

"And the internet didn't give you the answer?"

Sarah shook her head. "I didn't get that far."

Gilmore sighed heavily and rubbed his neck. "Well, since it's a matter of public record, I guess there's no reason that I can't tell you. I have no idea whether John Tierney is alive or dead. Every few years or so, someone calls in a sighting, but it never amounts to anything. You want my best guess? I think he's probably dead and buried somewhere by now."

"What about the rest of the case file? For all intents and purposes, it's a closed case. Am I able to take a look at it?"

"Mrs. Quinlan, I must say, I'm a little confused here. I ask you to come in to answer some questions about the death of your husband's aunt and all of a sudden we're having a conversation about the murder of his mother. Why in the world would you want to look at the case file?" Gilmore asked, tilting his head as if seeing her in a new light.

Sarah knew she sounded a bit crazy. The sheriff was right — what kind of person would want to leaf through the details of a crime of the mother-in-law they'd never even met? "I just want some answers," Sarah said, knowing that this wasn't a convincing argument in her favor.

"I'm afraid I can't help you there," Gilmore said, moving toward the door. "Murder cases are never truly closed. And since John Tierney has never been charged and convicted, technically it's still open. Come on, I'll walk you back to the lobby."

"What about the Freedom of Information Act? Don't I have the right to review the case files?"

Gilmore's earlier patience was quickly being replaced by irritation. "True, but that requires a lot of forms to fill out. Then the paperwork has to be processed. By the time that happens you'll be long gone. Plus, the case isn't officially closed, just suspended. You wouldn't have access to all the evidence."

"I'm persistent," Sarah pressed.

"Let me give you a little advice, Mrs. Quinlan." Gilmore set her with a solid gaze, and it was all Sarah could do to look right back at him. "Maybe there's a reason Jack doesn't want you to know what happened to Lydia Tierney. Some things are better left dead and buried. Maybe this is one of them."

"You know," Sarah said firmly, "I'm not some ghoul who's interested in the gory details of a thirty-year-old murder. I just want to help my husband." This wasn't exactly true. At this point, Sarah was more interested in uncovering the truth as to why Jack had been lying to her, but she couldn't exactly tell the sheriff this.

Gilmore regarded her intensely, and Sarah could tell he was debating whether or not to speak further on the matter. Silence filled the room, but Sarah refused to relent. She kept her gaze fixed on him, a trick she'd learned from interviewing subjects during her days as a journalist. Finally, Gilmore spoke.

"John Tierney was the main suspect in the death of his wife, but he disappeared before we could interview him. The sheriff at the time believed that there was enough evidence to close the case. To answer your question, is John Tierney alive or dead? I really can't say, but has he shown his face around here since?" Gilmore folded his arms across his chest. "No way. And the answer is still no. You can't look at the case file. Could you send Dean on back?"

Sarah stood to follow Gilmore and her purse caught the edge of his desk, causing the contents of her purse to scatter and the file folder on the sheriff's desk to flutter to the floor. "Dammit," she muttered, and bent down to gather up the items.

Her eyes landed on the piece of paper that slid from the file folder labeled Julia Quinlan — Toxicology. Three words jumped out at her: *sodium fluoroacetate: positive.*

Gilmore bent over and quickly picked up the file folder and piece of paper, returned them to his desk and leaned over to help Sarah.

"I've got it," she said, shoving the items back into her purse and trying to memorize the words from the toxicology report — *sodium fluoroacetate.* She vaguely remembered coming across them somewhere else, but couldn't quite recall where.

She got to her feet and offered a rushed goodbye to the sheriff. She hurried down the hallway, back to the lobby, eager to process the information she had uncovered. Why would the medical examiner order a toxicology report for Julia, who supposedly died due to a blow to the head? The questions that Gilmore had asked her had very little to do with the events that led up to Julia's fall. Which in hindsight made sense.

Sarah and Jack weren't even in the state when Julia fell, so it was logical for the sheriff to focus on what happened at the hospital after they had arrived.

Sarah had a pesky feeling that something more may have occurred in the hospital room the day Julia died. In her limited worldview based on *Forensic Files* and *Dateline,* toxicology reports usually meant poison. Did Amy poison Julia? It also meant that everyone who had stepped inside Julia's hospital room was a suspect. Including Jack.

9

Sarah returned to the lobby to find Dean flicking through an outdated *Field and Stream* magazine and Hal dozing. Celia was standing, arms crossed, looking out the window. Jack still hadn't returned from his walk.

"The sheriff wants to talk to you next, Dean," Sarah said.

"What did he ask you about?" Dean questioned.

Sarah wasn't sure how she should respond. Whether Gilmore said it out loud or not, they were now all suspects in Julia's death. On the other hand, Gilmore hadn't instructed Sarah to keep the questions he asked her quiet. "He just asked me about what happened at the hospital. He wanted to know if I was aware of any family quarrels. I told him I wasn't."

"But you told him about how crazy Amy was acting at the hospital, right?" Dean asked, glaring up at her.

"I told him that Amy was upset," Sarah explained, taken aback by Dean's irritation with her.

"Upset?" Dean came to his feet and angrily tossed his magazine aside. "Amy wasn't upset, she was out of her mind."

Sarah held back a sharp retort. She tried to remember that Dean had just lost his mother unexpectedly and violently. Of course he wanted everyone to cooperate with the investigation and answer all questions as thoroughly as possible.

"I'll tell him myself," Dean snapped before stalking back to the sheriff's office.

Sarah was anxious to learn more about the drug mentioned in the toxicology report — sodium fluoroacetate. Could Amy really have poisoned her aunt? Sarah knew she should just step back and let the sheriff do his job, but she was tired of all the secrets that were floating around Jack and his family. She felt as if all these secrets had settled into the bones of her marriage, eroding what she knew to be true and good into something almost unrecognizable.

"I'm going to go outside and get some fresh air for a few minutes. Wait for Jack," Sarah told Celia, who nodded distractedly and turned back to the window. Hal was still dozing in his chair, snoring softly.

Sarah pushed through the glass doors that led to the parking lot. The sky was clear and the midmorning sun felt good on her skin. She shielded her eyes from the glare of the rays and surveyed the street for any sign of Jack. He was nowhere to be seen. She settled onto a wrought-iron bench situated beneath a beech tree.

Sarah pulled out her phone, searched *sodium fluoroacetate* and quickly learned it was nasty stuff. The rodenticide, also known as 1080, was outlawed in the late '80s in all but a handful of western states. Sarah felt a chill run through her; 1080 was a term she was familiar with from growing up in Montana. Sarah knew that 1080 was tightly regulated in her home state and only allowed for use in livestock collars that protected sheep and goats from coyotes.

Sarah jumped to where the symptoms of poisoning were listed: vomiting, abdominal pain, seizures, ventricular arrhythmia. Sarah wished she would have gotten a better look at the toxicology report in the sheriff's office. Did the sheriff find the substance at the hospital or at Amy's house?

It was clear to Sarah that this was no longer the case of an elderly woman accidentally falling down the stairs or even a

190

crime where in anger someone caused Julia's fall. This, if the sheriff's suspicions were correct, was cold-blooded murder.

A shadow passed over Sarah and she glanced up from her phone to find Margaret Dooley standing over her. Her bland brown sheriff's department uniform was incongruous with her teased red hair and bright makeup. "Sarah," she said, "what are you doing out here?"

"The sheriff wanted to talk to all of us about Julia. I'm done with my interview and just waiting for everyone else."

Margaret squeezed in next to Sarah on the bench, setting her large leopard-print purse between the two of them. "Is Amy still here?"

"As far as I'm aware. Do you know if she's been formally charged with anything? We haven't been able to talk to her yet and from what I've heard she's refusing a lawyer."

Margaret pursed her lips together and shook her head. "That Amy. She doesn't make things easy for herself, does she?"

"Were Jack and Amy as serious when they were little as they are now?" Sarah asked wistfully.

"Oh, no. They were silly just like all kids. Probably because Mrs. Tierney was so much fun. She was always singing and playing with the kids. I'd come over and she'd be sitting at the kitchen table coloring with them or playing Chutes and Ladders. She'd create these scavenger hunts for them — they'd go outside with a list of things to find, things like a bird's feather or robin egg's shell or spider's web.

"I remember I would sit at her dressing table and try on her makeup and perfume. She had a closet of pretty things. Most of the time she wore jeans and tennis shoes, but when she dressed up, she seemed so glamorous. Once a month, Mr. Tierney would take her into Cedar City for dinner and dancing."

"They got along okay?" Sarah asked.

"I guess." Margaret shrugged. "They seemed crazy about each other. I never noticed any problems but . . ." She trailed off.

"What?" Sarah prodded.

"I don't want to talk out of turn, but everybody thought Mrs. Tierney was kind of a flirt. My mother's friends would go on and on about how Lydia would smile at and joke around with their husbands."

"But that doesn't mean anything. Were they jealous?"

"Lydia was so pretty and sweet, and a few of the women didn't like the way their husbands looked at her. My mother and Lydia were great friends. She would get so mad when people started saying that Lydia and her flirting were crossing a line. I'm just saying that maybe some of the other mothers might have thought so.

"Now, Mr. Tierney . . ." Margaret held up an index finger. "He was one handsome man. Jack's the spitting image of him, you know?"

"Yes, I've seen a picture," Sarah murmured, not wanting Margaret to stop talking, eager for any tidbit of information about Jack's past.

"He was so quiet, never said much of anything when there was a crowd around. But when he drove me home after babysitting, though, he was so nice, asked me about school and my friends. Real personable." Margaret gave a girlish giggle. "I was half in love with him." Sarah must have given her a strange look. "Oh, it was nothing like that," she scoffed. "John Tierney was completely in love with his wife. He was just making polite conversation when he drove me home. Nothing untoward in his behavior at all.

"I babysat for the Tierneys until Jack was around eleven, then they didn't really need me anymore. Jack was old enough to watch after himself and Amy. Plus, I got a part-time job at the pharmacy in town. Didn't see so much of the Tierneys after that. Just at church." A sudden breeze swept past and Margaret patted her hair to make sure each lock was still in place.

"It must have been a shock when you heard about Lydia's death and now with what has happened with Julia . . ." Sarah trailed off. It was almost too much to wrap her head around. She had never known anyone who had been murdered and now, all of a sudden, she had learned that two people related to her husband had died violently.

"The whole town was shocked when Lydia died. Up until that time, there hadn't been a murder in Penny Gate for fifty years. My mom was inconsolable. Like I said, she and Lydia were best friends. After the funeral, she didn't get out of bed for a week. Now, with Julia —" Margaret shook her head so that her turquoise earrings swung back and forth "— not too many people know what's going on. It won't take long, though, especially with the sheriff questioning Amy and the search at Hal's farm."

"Margaret," Sarah began cautiously. She knew that this conversation could only go one of two ways: awkward or awful. She was hoping for awkward. "Have you ever seen Lydia's case file?"

"Oh, no," Margaret said, reaching into her purse and pulling out a pack of gum. "I'm just a dispatcher. I'm not supposed to have access to files." She offered a stick to Sarah, who declined. Something in the way that Margaret answered the question prodded Sarah forward. She had the sense that even though Margaret technically wasn't supposed to read any of the case files, it didn't stop her when her curiosity got the better of her. She had the feeling that Margaret read every case file she could get her hands on.

"I just feel like if I have a chance to read the police reports, maybe see the case file, I'll understand what Jack has gone through. If I'm able to answer my own questions, then maybe I won't feel the need to have Jack tell me himself and dredge up all kinds of bad memories. What do you think? Can you help me?"

Margaret chewed thoughtfully on her gum. "You could just put in a request at the courthouse."

Sarah shook her head. "I'll be gone by the time the paperwork goes through and the sheriff doesn't seem particularly enthusiastic in helping me out on this. And like you said,

195

the case is closed. They already know who did it."

From their brief conversations, Sarah could tell that Margaret was fond of Jack and Amy. But even more than that, Sarah thought that Margaret might be a little lonely, and secretly helping Sarah with her covert operation might add a little excitement to her life.

Margaret leaned in close to Sarah and lowered her voice. "You know I could get in trouble. Maybe even lose my job over this."

Sarah held her breath. She could almost hear Margaret's inner dialogue as she wrestled with her decision. Sarah would be gone in a few days and when would anyone else, in her lifetime, ask her to sneak into the sheriff's locked files?

"I'll do it," Margaret whispered, almost as if she was talking to herself.

"Thank you, Margaret." Sarah impulsively reached for her hand. "I really appreciate it. You have my number, right?"

The sound of someone clearing his throat caught them off guard and both women's heads swung forward.

"Ladies," Sheriff Gilmore said.

Margaret rose from the bench, snatching up her purse. "Hello, Verne, I'm just heading in." She consulted her watch. "I still have five minutes until I clock in." To Sarah she said, "Nice to see you again, Mrs. Quinlan." She stepped past Gilmore and moved toward the front doors.

"Margaret giving you an earful?" Gilmore asked, taking the seat that Margaret had just occupied.

"She seems very nice," Sarah said diplomatically.

"Well, you want the best gossip, the Dooley women are the ones to consult."

"I don't think anyone's very concerned about town gossip right now," Sarah pointed out. "We're more worried about finding out what happened to Julia and laying her to rest."

Gilmore shook his head regretfully. "You're right, that was insensitive of me."

"Are you finished interviewing everyone?" she asked. "That went quickly."

"Not quite. I still need to visit with Hal. But I do have a request for your presence."

"My presence?" Sarah asked in confusion. "By who? Is it Jack?" He hadn't returned to the sheriff's office as far as she knew unless there was an alternate entrance.

"No, it's Amy," Gilmore said carefully, watching her reaction with his gunpowder-gray eyes.

"Amy wants to talk to me?" Sarah thought

she must have misheard him. "Why?"

"That's the million-dollar question, now isn't it, Mrs. Quinlan? Why would your sister-in-law choose to speak to you and not anyone else? Not to us, not to a lawyer, not even her brother. Just you."

"I don't know," Sarah answered honestly. She couldn't fathom why Amy would want to talk with her unless it was to give her hell for calling for help when Sarah couldn't rouse her from the couch the night before. "You've had her in custody for the past eighteen hours and she hasn't told you anything?"

"Amy's not in custody. She's free to leave at any time. She keeps saying she wants to help us and we've been asking her a lot of questions that she doesn't seem to have any answers to."

"Maybe because she doesn't know the answers," Sarah said.

The sheriff, not looking convinced, stood. "Shall we?"

"Right now?" Sarah's fingers tightened around the metal slats that made up the bench seat.

"She really wants to speak with you. I think it'd be best if we went right now."

Reluctantly, Sarah stood and together they walked back to the main entrance. "Got a call from the medical examiner. He's finished his work and Julia's remains will be transported to the funeral home tomorrow. The family can go on and finalize funeral arrangements."

"What did he say?" Sarah's heart started to gallop as she thought of the covert peek of the report she had gotten in Gilmore's office.

Gilmore fingered his mustache. "Cause of death is pending. Results won't be shared until his final report is ready."

"He must have told you something. What do you think?" she asked.

"I think I'll wait until I see the final report before weighing in on it," Gilmore said cryptically.

Sarah let this sink in as they entered the lobby where Hal, Dean and Celia sat waiting.

"Sheriff, can we wrap things up here?" Dean asked. "We have a lot to do to get ready for my mom's funeral."

"Sure thing. Just let me get Mrs. Quinlan squared away here." He signaled to the female deputy who came to his side. "Tess, please take Mrs. Quinlan down to see Amy. You can put them in the small conference room."

"Why would Amy want to talk to Sarah?"

Hal asked, and then hearing his own bluntness, softened his tone. "I just didn't realize you two were close."

"We're not," Sarah admitted.

"I'm sure that Amy has good reason to want to talk to Sarah," Celia spoke up from her seat. The pale, delicate skin around her eyes was swollen and blotchy, and the sleeves of her sweatshirt were pushed up, revealing a bracelet of bruises ringing her forearm. Sarah suddenly realized what toll Julia's death had taken on her. Celia had been the one to fill Julia's hospital with photos and the quilt from home. She had spoken so fondly of her mother-in-law but never mentioned her own parents or immediate family. Who was she left with? An explosive husband, her husband's flighty cousin, a grief-stricken father-in-law and an ex-boyfriend who lived a thousand miles away.

"Hal, why don't you come on back to my office. I promise I won't keep you long. You either, Dean. I know you have a lot of arrangements to make."

From behind the front counter Margaret spoke up. "Mrs. Quinlan, you'll have to leave your purse here."

"I can hold it for you, Sarah," Celia offered. "We'll wait here for you."

"You don't have to do that," Sarah said. "Just tell me where you're going to be and I'll meet you there."

"We'll probably get something to eat at the Penny Café and then head to the church. We have to settle some funeral arrangements. If you're here longer than we are, I'll give your purse to Margaret to keep behind the counter and we'll text you where we're going."

"Thanks." Sarah handed Celia her purse and followed the deputy down the long hallway, her mind racing in a million different directions. What could Amy possibly have to say to her, and could she really be a murderer? She thought of the ring of bruises on Celia's arm and knew that there were probably more. She thought of Margaret and her promise to get copies of the files from the murder of Jack's mother. It was all too much. *Focus,* she ordered herself. One thing at a time.

The deputy led her down a short flight of stairs and down another corridor with walls painted an institutional green. Sarah wasn't sure what she expected to see in a county jail, but figured that there would be jail cells and a phone where she could talk to Amy through a thick-paned window. She saw none of these.

"You can sit right here. I'll go get Amy and you two can talk," the deputy said, pushing open the door of a small conference room that held a scarred wooden table and two mismatching chairs. Sarah chose the seat facing the door.

There was no two-way mirror that someone on the other side could use to eavesdrop on a conversation, no security camera mounted to the wall recording her every move. So Amy hadn't been arrested or officially charged with any crime. Yet. If she had been, there was no way that Sarah would be allowed to talk to Amy in such a casual, unsecured setting. Why would Amy still be here, then? She would be free to leave. It would seem, then, to Sarah, that Amy was cooperating fully with the sheriff, answering any questions that he had about Julia's death. Would a guilty person do this? Sarah wondered. A guilty person trying to appear innocent might.

A few minutes later the deputy appeared in the doorway with Amy at her side. "I'll be just outside if you need anything," the deputy said, and then shut the door behind her, leaving Sarah and Amy alone. For a brief moment, Sarah wished she had chosen the seat nearest the door in case she needed a quick escape. Amy was, after all, the number-one suspect in a murder. And if the report she got a glimpse of was correct, a particularly ruthless one.

The woman standing in front of her, however, looked incapable of committing such a horrific crime. Thankfully, someone had allowed her to change into unsoiled clothes and wash the vomit from her hair. But still she looked brittle, as if she might shatter at any moment. Her skin was pallid, her lips a bloodless white. Her eyes had a haunted, hunted look.

"Amy, are you all right?" Sarah asked in alarm. "Sit down. Have you gotten any sleep? Anything to eat?"

"I'm not hungry," Amy said hoarsely, and slowly lowered herself into the chair as if her bones ached. "Listen, Sarah." She got right down to business. "I need your help."

"My help?" Sarah narrowed her eyes in confusion. "I'm not sure how I . . ."

"They're going to arrest me for killing Aunt Julia. I know they are." Amy swallowed with effort and her eyes swam with tears. "But I didn't do it. I swear to God, I didn't." Amy's hands trembled and her fingers kept going to her pockets as if searching for something. A cigarette, Sarah figured.

"Do you have a lawyer? Is there someone

I can call for you?"

Amy propped her elbows on the tabletop and lowered her face into her hands. "No, I don't have a lawyer. I haven't been charged. Yet. And there's no way I can afford one."

"I'm sure that Hal or Dean will help pay . . ." Sarah trailed off. Why would Hal or Dean pay for an attorney for Amy if they thought she had killed Julia? "Jack and I can help you," she said before she could stop herself. What if Jack thought Amy was the one who hurt Julia? Would Jack really want to pay for a lawyer to defend the person who had killed the woman who was like a mother to him?

Amy lifted her head. "Dean and Hal won't help me," she said matter-of-factly. "And Dean won't let Celia help me, either. I don't want your money, even if Jack would be willing. He's got his own ghosts to deal with. But I do need your help." Her brown eyes were pleading and filled with what Sarah realized was fear. "I didn't do this to Julia. I loved her. I think I may have loved her even more than my own mother. Julia's been like a mother to me three times longer than my own mom." The tears that had been gathering in Amy's eyes finally spilled.

"What do you mean, Jack has his own ghosts?" Sarah asked, but Amy just shook her head and brushed away the moisture from her cheeks.

"The deputy will be coming back in soon. The sheriff will have a warrant for my arrest, I just know it. I don't have much time. I didn't do this. I didn't kill Julia. That box with that *thing* in it . . ." A shiver of revulsion fluttered across her face. "That wasn't mine. I've never seen it before." Amy moved toward Sarah and lowered her voice to a breathy whisper. "I swear I didn't do it, but I know who did."

Sarah leaned toward Amy so that their noses were nearly touching. "Who?" Sarah asked, transfixed by the fear etched on Amy's face.

"Dean brought a bunch of stuff over the other day. Just after Julia fell. Said they were things that once belonged to my mom. He stuck them in the corner with all the other boxes. He did it. I don't know why, but Dean killed his mother and is trying to make it look like I did it."

"Amy . . ." Sarah began doubtfully.

"Sarah, no one else will believe me." She grabbed Sarah's hands, her thin, bony fingers digging into her skin. "He did it. I know he did. He's got a temper. He's the only one who could have hit her and knocked her down the stairs like that and then blame me for it." There was a knock at the conference room door, but Amy kept her eyes locked on Sarah's. "You believe me, right? You'll help me?"

Sarah didn't. She tried to extract her hands from Amy's grip. "I think we need to get you a lawyer. But whatever you do, Amy, don't say anything more to the sheriff or to anyone else. The best way you can help yourself is to just stay quiet. I'll talk to Jack, and we'll get you a lawyer."

There was another knock on the door. "About finished up in there?" came the deputy's voice.

"Jack won't hang around to help me. He can't wait to get the hell out of here. He's got his own secrets chasing him."

"What does that mean?" Sarah asked as the door opened and the deputy peeked her face around the jamb.

"Hate to interrupt you, but the sheriff would like to talk some more with you, Amy."

Amy released Sarah's hands, leaving behind half-moon indentations on Sarah's skin, her face falling in resignation. "Here we go," she murmured.

"We'll get you a lawyer," Sarah promised as she stood. "We'll do whatever we can to help you." Impulsively, she bent down and hugged Amy; her thin shoulders sharp and unyielding let her know that she didn't believe her.

Sarah followed the deputy from the room. Gilmore, file folder in hand, came down the hallway. Sarah thought she knew what was in that folder — the report from the medical examiner describing the poison. Amy didn't mention anything about poison. But why would she? Amy didn't know that the sheriff was aware of the possibility that Julia had been poisoned.

The sheriff nodded to Sarah as he brushed past her without a word, a look of grim determination on his face. Amy was right. The sheriff was going to arrest her for Julia's murder. Sarah quickened her pace, eager to get back upstairs to find Jack, to tell him what Amy had told her about her suspicions about Dean, about her impending arrest, her need for an attorney. By the time she had climbed the steps and made the journey down the long hallway, she was out of breath and sweating. The lobby was empty except for Margaret and a weary-looking middle-aged woman leaning against the counter.

"Just let me find the form," Margaret told the woman. She went over to a battered file cabinet and with difficulty bent down on one knee to reach the bottom drawer. "We don't get a whole lot of missing-persons reports. Usually the person is found before the first forty-eight hours, but once or twice a year . . ." She yanked on the drawer three times before it opened with a metallic screech.

"Last summer, we had a six-year-old get lost in a cornfield." Margaret glanced up at Sarah. "I'll be right with you, Mrs. Quinlan," she said, her tone impersonal, almost dismissive. She returned her attention to the woman. "It happens more than you think and not just to kids, but elderly folks, too. Usually we find them in just a few hours no worse for wear, but this kiddo . . ." She shook her head at the memory as she fingered through the files. "He was autistic. Afraid of the searchers shouting his name. That boy spent three days in that cornfield. It was near ninety degrees during the daytime and there were thunderstorms at night. Ah, here we go." Margaret held up the form in triumph.

With effort she pushed herself up from the floor and trundled back to where the woman stood at the counter and laid the form in front of her along with a clipboard and a pen.

"Was the boy okay?" the woman asked,

wanting to hear the rest of the story.

"Oh, sure. He ate the corn right from the stalk and drank water from the puddles left behind by the storm. He was just fine — scared his parents half to death, though. You can go ahead and sit over there and fill out the form. Try not to worry. They all show up sooner or later, especially the teenagers."

The woman sniffled and wandered over to the bank of chairs.

"Now, Mrs. Quinlan," Margaret said. "Your husband wanted me to let you know that he and the others were going to get something to eat and then head on over to the church to work on funeral arrangements."

Margaret reached beneath the counter and pulled out Sarah's purse. "Celia gave me your purse before she left, and Jack left the car keys for you and asked you to call him when you were finished talking with Amy."

Sarah was still taken aback by Margaret's standoffish bearing when she spoke again. "I put that recipe you asked for in your purse."

"The recipe?" Sarah asked in confusion.

The young deputy who had escorted Sarah down to see Amy stepped into the lobby. "Is Margaret giving you her recipe for lemon squares? They are the best in town, but don't tell my mom I told you that."

"You're too kind, Tess. Sarah wanted a recipe to make for Julia Quinlan's funeral dinner and I was happy to share. Now if you'll excuse me," Margaret said, nodding to the both of them. "I'll just check on how this lady's doing with that missing-persons report."

"Thank you," Sarah said to Margaret's retreating form, still baffled by her odd behavior. She lifted her purse from the countertop, taken aback by its heft. She peeked inside to find a thick envelope. She looked to Margaret, who gave her a sharp shake of her head, then returned her attention to the woman and her form.

"I hope you like the recipe, Mrs. Quinlan," Margaret said as Sarah pushed her way out the glass doors. "Let me know what you think."

10

The envelope, tucked safely in her purse, weighed heavily on her shoulder and her mind. She couldn't wait to open it and see what was inside, but wasn't sure where she should go to read about the undoing of her husband's family.

She immediately dismissed Hal's house as an option. As far as she knew, they were still conducting a search of the home. The Penny Café or Dean and Celia's house were also out — there was too much of a chance of someone walking in on her while she read.

In the end she decided to drive out into the country and find some lonely out-of-the-way road. She drove outside Penny Gate about ten miles and turned onto a gravel road that appeared to lead to nowhere. No homes, no barns, no other cars, just miles and miles of cornfields. Sarah pulled off to the side of the road in a spot that allowed her to see if any traffic approached both from the front or the rear.

She reached into her purse and retrieved the large envelope. It was bottom heavy and she fingered the contours, trying to figure out what was inside. She pulled out a file folder and opened it to find a thick stack of typed transcripts and set it on the seat next to her. She reached back in and her fingers landed on what was indeed a metallic box. She pulled it out, and found an old Sony Walkman cassette player and earphones. She peeked into the envelope and saw three cassette tapes resting in their protective cases. Sarah tipped the envelope and the tapes tumbled out onto her lap, along with an unopened pack of batteries, courtesy of Margaret, Sarah was sure. Each audiotape was numbered and labeled in small, neat handwriting: *May 30, 1985, Lydia Tierney.* Sarah found the cassette tape number one, picked up the Walkman, pressed the eject button and slid the tape inside.

Sarah slid the earphones over her ears, pushed the play button and nothing happened. She removed the corroded batteries from the Walkman, replaced them with a fresh set and was immediately plunged back in time to the year her husband was fifteen and the day he found his mother's bludgeoned body. The audio was scratchy and slightly muffled. Sarah turned the small wheel on the side of the player, increasing the volume.

Gilmore: *This is Deputy Sheriff Verne Gilmore. Seven thirty-five p.m. on May 30, 1985. Interviewing Jonathan Paul Tierney, known as Jack, fifteen years of age. Jack?*
Jack Tierney: (Inaudible.)
Gilmore: *Speak a little more loudly, son. Right into the recorder here.*
Jack Tierney: *Sorry.*

Sarah gasped at the sound of her husband's voice at fifteen. A little higher pitched, but it was Jack. Her Jack.

Gilmore: *That's okay. I'm going to ask you a few questions about the events of today. We can stop at any time. Just let me know if you need a break, okay?*
Jack: *Okay.*

Gilmore asked Jack a series of simple questions. His address, his age, birthday, the names of his parents and his sister. Jack, his voice initially tight with nervousness, relaxed with Gilmore's gentle, casual probing. He was even able to get Jack to laugh a little, remembering the time when Gilmore, Jack and his father went fishing together and all three ended up falling into the pond.

The questions turned more serious, though Gilmore's tone remained friendly.

Gilmore: *Jack, tell me about this morning.*

Jack: *I got up, helped my dad, ate breakfast, got on the bus like usual.*

Gilmore: *What time was that?*

Jack: *What time I got on the bus?*

Gilmore: *Yes, and the time you got up. First, what time did you get up this morning?*

Jack: *Six thirty.*

Gilmore: *Then what did you do?*

Jack: *I helped my dad for a little bit. Fed the dogs.*

Gilmore: *What did you and your dad talk about?*

Jack: *Nothing really. Said good morning. He told me to feed the dogs.*

Gilmore: *What else?*

Jack: *Nothing. We didn't talk. He went out into the fields.*

Gilmore: *What time was that?*

Jack: *I don't know. Seven or seven fifteen?*

Gilmore: *Which was it, seven or seven fifteen?*

Jack: *I don't know. I'm not sure. Probably seven. I was in a hurry. I still had to shower and eat. I thought I was going to miss the bus.*

Gilmore: *What time did you get on the bus?*

Jack: *Seven thirty.*

Gilmore: *Seven thirty?*

Jack: *Seven twenty-five. Seven twenty-five. The bus always comes then.*

Gilmore kept hammering Jack on the timeline. What time Jack arrived at school, what time he left, what time he arrived at home. He then spent several minutes asking Jack about his mother's actions that morning. What they talked about, if his mother seemed worried or acted out of the ordinary. Sarah choked back tears when Gilmore asked Jack about the interaction he had with his mother just before he and Amy went outside to catch the bus.

Jack: *She said* (Inaudible).

Gilmore: *What was that?*

Jack (crying): *She said, "I love you, Jack, I love you, Amy. Be good."*

Gilmore: *Let's take a break.* (Inaudible.) *It's okay, Jack. It's going to be okay.*

Sarah's intense focus on the tape was suddenly disrupted by the low hisses of a pair of turkey vultures fighting over an animal carcass on the road ahead. Three more soared above, flying in slow, wobbly circles.

Part of her wanted to shove the recorder and tapes back into the envelope and return them to Margaret. It seemed wrong, almost

215

unholy, to be intruding on this very private moment in Jack's life. But there was no turning back now. She had to hear the rest. She took a deep breath, settled back and slid the headphones over her ears.

Gilmore: *You said you got home from school at three o'clock?*

Jack: *Yes, around three.*

Gilmore: *Amy wasn't on the bus?*

Jack: *No, she had 4-H, I think.*

Gilmore: *But the bus stops at your house at three?*

Jack: *Not at my house. Near our house. Down the lane. On the highway. The bus picks up a bunch of kids there in the morning and drops us off after school. We walk the rest of the way home.*

Gilmore: *What kids?*

Jack: *Like Brad Dahl and Terry Oswald.*

Gilmore: *That all? Anyone else?*

Jack: *Amy and Mattie Yoder. Maybe more.*

Gilmore: *Let me know if I got this down right, Jack. Brad Dahl, Terry Oswald, Amy and Mattie?*

Jack: *Yeah, but not Amy. She's at 4-H.* (Inaudible, sound of crying.) *Does Amy know? Where's my dad?*

Gilmore: *You said there might have been more?*

Jack: *Younger kids. I don't know all their names.*

Gilmore: *The bus dropped you all off at three. At the bottom of your lane?*

Jack: *Yes.*

Gilmore: *I want you to think really hard before you answer my next question.*

Jack: *Okay.*

Gilmore: *What time did you get home today?*

Sarah's stomach clenched and she leaned over so that her nose was nearly touching her knees. She could feel it coming. Jack was going to describe what he found when he came home that terrible day.

Gilmore: *What time?*

Jack: (Inaudible.) *Two. I got home at two.*

Again, Jack's voice broke and she heard the sound of sniffling.

Gilmore: *You called the police at 3:05, Jack. You got home at two. What were you doing between 2:00 and 3:05? No lying here, Jack. How did you get home?*

Jack: *My cousin. I cut school. Dean picked me up. He brought me home in his dad's truck.*

Gilmore: *Then what?*

Jack: *I went inside.*

Gilmore: *By yourself?*

217

Jack: *Yes. Dean left. I went inside. I ate a piece of cake, drank some milk.*

Gilmore: *Then what, Jack. I don't want you to leave one thing out.*

Jack: *I had to pee, so I was going to go upstairs to the bathroom, but Grey was sitting by the cellar door.*

Gilmore: *Grey is your dog?*

Jack: *Yes. My mom always makes him go outside when no one is home, so I thought that was kinda weird. I tried to get him to go outside, but he wouldn't get up. He just sat there by the door, shaking and whimpering.*

There was a long pause, just the soft whirring of the tape threading through the recorder. Gilmore was no longer pushing for Jack to answer; he was just waiting to see what Jack would say next. Sarah pressed the back of her hand to her mouth, mentally shouting at Jack to go back, to not open the basement door, but she knew he would. In a matter of seconds, fifteen-year-old Jack would speak the words he hadn't been able to in the thirty years since.

Jack: *I opened the door. Grey ran down the steps. It was too dark to see, so I turned on the light. I called for her. I called, "Mom." But she didn't answer.*

Here Jack's voice became strangled, difficult to understand.

Jack: *I went down the steps.* (Inaudible.)
Gilmore: *I know this is hard, Jack, but it's important that you tell me exactly what you saw.*
Jack: *She was lying on the ground. On her back.* (Sound of crying.) *I kept saying, "Mom, Mom." But she didn't answer.* (Inaudible.) *I walked closer to her. A towel was over her eyes. There was blood and her head looked funny. I knew then. She was dead.* (Sound of crying.)
Gilmore: *Almost done now, Jack. Almost done. That was at what time?*
Jack (shouting): *I don't know. I don't know! My mom was fucking dead. I didn't look at the clock! You . . .* (Inaudible, sound of crying.)
Gilmore: *Dean let you off at your house at two. You ate a snack. How long did it take?*
Jack: *I don't know, five minutes, ten, maybe.*
Gilmore: *You go downstairs at 2:10 and find your mother. Sound right?*
Jack: *Yes.*
Gilmore: *Jack, look at me. Look at me.*

Any fatherly tone that Gilmore had conveyed earlier had dissipated.

Gilmore: *You didn't call the sheriff's depart-*

ment for another fifty-five minutes. What were you doing?

Jack: *I don't know.*

Gilmore: *Jack.*

Jack (shouting): *I don't know!*

Gilmore: *Did you try to revive your mother?*

Jack: *No.*

Gilmore: *Did you touch her?*

Jack: *No!*

Gilmore: *There was a bloody handprint on the cellar door. Was it yours? Did you touch her?*

Jack: *I don't remember.*

Gilmore: *What are we going to find when we fingerprint you, Jack? Will your prints match the prints on the door?*

Jack: (Inaudible.)

Gilmore: *I can't hear you, Jack.*

Jack (shouting): *I don't know! I don't know!* (Sound of crying.)

Gilmore: *What were you doing from 2:10 until you called the sheriff at 3:05?*

Jack: *I threw up. I threw up.* (Inaudible.) *Okay? She was dead! I threw up and I locked myself in the bathroom.* (Sound of crying.)

Gilmore: (Inaudible.) *Okay, Jack. We're done for now. Shhh. It's okay. We're done. We're done.* (Sound of crying.)

After a moment Sarah wiped her eyes and

ejected the cassette from the player and tucked it in the file folder. Her eyes fell on the transcript that accompanied the tape and to a note scrawled in pen across the bottom of the first page. *Reinterview Jack Tierney. Inconsistencies in story. Reports of frequent arguments with mother. Number-one suspect.*

11

Sarah ripped the headphones from her ears and tossed them on the passenger's-side seat. Jack was considered a top suspect in the death of his mother? Why hadn't he told her? Of course he would have some kind of excuse as to why he hadn't mentioned it: *the person who finds the body is always the first suspect, law enforcement always looks at the family first, the deputy didn't like me.*

But Sarah couldn't get past the fact that Jack had promised, had *sworn,* that there was nothing else Sarah needed to know about his past, that there was nothing more worth knowing. More lies and secrets.

The notes scrawled at the bottom of the transcript said that there were inconsistencies in Jack's statements, that there were reports of frequent arguments with his mother. What inconsistencies? What arguments? Didn't every teenager have fights with their parents? God knew she did. What made Jack's dustups with his mom worth noting in the file?

Sarah flipped through the transcripts. There were pages of additional interviews with other family members, friends and townspeople. But this certainly wasn't the bulk of the case file. Margaret must have been only able to get this section for her. Sarah needed to see the rest.

She felt something shift in her mind, in her heart. When she first began to learn of Jack's secrets, she thought they were the closely guarded memories of a traumatized boy who found them too painful or embarrassing to share with even his wife.

But now, Sarah wasn't so sure. The sheer energy that Jack must have expended to keep the secrets hidden and the lies straight in his mind for so many years must have been exhausting. There had to be more that Jack wasn't telling her. *Don't ask the questions if you don't want the answers.* This was something that her editor, Gabe, had told her over and over again during her early years at the *Messenger.* If she didn't want to ask the hard questions, if she didn't want to know the truth, she had no business in being a journalist.

But the stakes were so much higher if she dared to ask the questions that she couldn't quite let take shape. This was her marriage. This was her husband, the father of her daughters. Did she really want to keep asking the hard questions?

She stepped from the car. A westerly wind swept across the countryside, kicking up dust from the gravel road and covering her clothing with a thin, powdery layer. Three fork-tailed, cobalt-blue barn swallows dipped and swooped playfully in the hay field. *Yes,* a quiet voice echoed through her head. She needed to know. Had to know.

She sent a quick text message to Margaret that innocently read, Thanks for the recipe. Would love some more. Can we meet? Jack had sent her texts of his own asking her if she had talked to Amy and for her to please call him.

Amy. Being so immersed in the tape recordings, she almost forgot about Amy sitting at the sheriff's department, probably already charged with first-degree murder.

Almost grudgingly she called Jack. He was a liar and possibly worse. She didn't want to talk with him, didn't want to put on the supportive-wife face because his aunt had died and his sister was in trouble, but she knew she would. It might be the only way she would get the answers she was searching for.

"Sarah," Jack said the moment he answered. "Are you okay? Where are you? We thought you were going to meet us for lunch." He sounded genuinely concerned about her. Was it authentic, she wondered, or was he just that good of a liar?

"I'm fine, but Amy isn't," Sarah said in a rush. "Jack, Sheriff Gilmore is going to arrest her if he hasn't already. You need to get her . . ."

"Whoa, slow down." Jack stopped her. "Where are you? Come back to Dean's and we'll talk."

She didn't want to go back to Dean and Celia's house. She didn't want to see Jack. She was sick of his dysfunctional — and dysfunctional was a kind description — family. She wanted to finish listening to the audiotapes of Gilmore's interviews with the witnesses, and she wanted to connect with Margaret so she could read the rest of the case file. Jack had had his chance, had his opportunity to come clean with her, to tell her the full truth, and he hadn't. He had traded twenty years of marriage for lies.

"Jack, trust me on this. The sheriff has most likely arrested Amy. If there's any part of you that thinks she wasn't the one who killed Julia, you need to get an attorney over there right away."

Jack was quiet on the other end of the line. "You think she did it?" Sarah asked incredulously. "Really?"

"No. I don't know," he amended softly. "I hope not, but I don't think I really know Amy as well as I thought I did."

"About as well as I thought I knew you," Sarah shot back. "Forget it. I'll get her a lawyer if you won't."

Sarah disconnected. She wasn't even sure as to how to go about finding an attorney for Amy. Hell, she wasn't convinced that Amy wasn't guilty. All the evidence seemed to be pointing toward her; even the presence of poison. Amy was the one who had spent the night in Julia's hospital room, who was most likely to have the time to poison her.

She pulled out her phone again and did a quick search of Penny Gate attorneys. Only two names popped up. Arthur Newberry and Dallas Hogan. She settled on Arthur Newberry — at least his name sounded like he was older than twenty-five. She called his office and left a message explaining who she was, why she needed his services and to please return her call as soon as possible. In frustration she tossed the phone back into the car and began to walk down the gravel road, her argument with Jack replaying over and over in her mind.

She heard the rumble of tires from behind her and a cloud of dust rose from the road. Sarah shielded her eyes from the sun to get a better look and realized that she had walked more than a football field away from her car. A large truck emerged from the dust and slowed as it approached.

A wave of uneasiness swept over her. She was all alone, miles from town. The haunting words from the audiotape were still fresh in her mind. She had left her keys and phone in the car.

Two men dressed in camouflage and wearing bright orange vests looked at her from the driver's-side window. "Everything okay here?" the driver asked, his eyes hidden behind a pair of sunglasses, one arm hanging casually outside the window, close enough to grab Sarah if he wanted to. Sarah took a step back from truck and started slowly moving toward her own car.

"Yep, I'm fine," Sarah said, trying to keep her voice light and easy, all the while measuring the distance to her car. Could she outrun them if she had to, or was she better off running into the cornfield and trying to lose them in there?

"We thought you might have had some car trouble," the other man said, revealing a mouth filled with tobacco-stained teeth. "Not many people come out this way. You could have been broken down here and no one could find you for days." Sarah glanced around. He was right. No homes were in sight, no other cars had passed by. Did she hear a taunting, leering tone in his voice? Or was she just spooked after listening to the tapes?

"I'm fine. Just taking a walk." Sarah struggled to maintain eye contact. She didn't want them to know she was afraid.

"All right, then," the driver said, slapping the side of his truck with the palm of his hand. "You take care."

Sarah didn't pause to watch the truck drive away but started walking swiftly back to her own car. Seconds later, she heard the crunch of tires on gravel. She glanced over her shoulder to find the truck following slowly behind her. She quickened her pace and the truck sped up. Sarah sprinted the last twenty yards, flung open the car door and slammed it shut. Once inside she rolled up the windows, locked the doors and grabbed her phone. Slowly the truck rolled by and through the windshield Sarah could see the men having a good laugh over her distress before speeding away. *It's this place,* Sarah thought to herself. Everything about Penny Gate was off.

Breathing heavily, Sarah caught sight of a red-faced, copper-feathered pheasant striding through the cornfield next to her and shook her head. The men were just out bird hunting. Of course they were driving around the off-the-beaten-path gravel roads where the pheasants would be more plentiful. They were jerks, but most likely perfectly harmless; she was the one who was trying to conceal her whereabouts and what she was doing.

Once she caught her breath, she checked her phone in case she'd missed a call from the attorney or Margaret. She saw that Jack had tried to call her twice. She wasn't ready to talk to him just yet.

Sarah checked her emails and sighed at the sheer volume that she eventually would need to get caught up on. As she expected, she had dozens. Most were Dear Astrid letters, a few from friends back in Larkspur and one from Gabe, her editor at the newspaper.

Nothing that a Dear Astrid reader could throw at her seemed more bizarre than what she was living herself. She would have to go back to Dean and Celia's at some point.

She wondered if the search at Hal's home was complete and if the forensic team had found anything.

Another message from Seller85 jumped out at her and she clicked on it expecting more nonsense.

Dear Astrid,
   One blind mouse.
   Blood, crimson and hot
   Pulsing, pouring
   Through my fingers.
   See how they run?

Though Sarah was no stranger to receiving creepy messages and letters, the earlier emails were seemingly innocuous. But this one . . . this one felt a bit different, probably because it was the third email from the same sender in just a few days, she told herself. Trying to push the messages from her mind, she went on to scan through the other Dear Astrid emails. To think that so many people looked to her for support and advice when sometimes she felt as though she had no answers and in fact could use some advice herself. Sarah didn't have the energy to focus on the problems of others when she had such difficult ones of her own. She had plenty of Dear Astrid responses reserved for situations just like this one when she wasn't able to stay on schedule, but she hated getting behind in her work.

Her thoughts kept flipping back to the Seller85 emails. Three from the same sender was downright creepy. On impulse, she dialed Gabe's direct number at the *Messenger.*

"I've been trying to get ahold of you all week," Gabe's warm voice came across the line. "You'd think you were some very busy, important, syndicated advice columnist or something."

"I'm so sorry. It's been crazy."

"Yeah, you use me for my editing skills and then discard me like yesterday's newspaper," Gabe deadpanned.

Sarah didn't know where to start, but decided to give him the basics: she was in Penny Gate, Aunt Julia's death, the suspicion surrounding her death, the weird emails. She recounted each to him one by one.

"They are odd," Gabe admitted. "But you've gotten strange emails before," he reminded her. "What's different about these?"

"I'm not sure. Just a feeling, I guess," Sarah admitted. "Journalistic instinct, maybe."

"Why don't you send them to me. I'll see what I can find out."

"Thanks," Sarah said. "I'm sure it will turn out to be nothing," she added.

"No problem. You're fired, though. I hired a new guy. I hear he returns phone calls."

"You did not," Sarah scoffed.

"Well, I'm thinking about it. I have the memo already written. Seriously, though, I'm so sorry about Jack's aunt. How's he doing?" Gabe asked.

"He's sad. Confused. He's trying to wrap his head around the fact that Amy is being questioned in her death." Sarah hesitated before asking Gabe her next question, but they'd known each other for years. "Gabe, if I tell you something, can you respond to me as a reporter, not as my friend?"

"Sure, what is it?"

"I just found out that Jack's mom and dad didn't die in a car accident like he told me." Sarah went on to explain all that she had learned since she arrived in Penny Gate. When she was finished she was met by a long silence.

Finally he spoke. "As a reporter, I'm intrigued. First, you've got this great guy, Jack, a family man, married for twenty years, who has maintained that his parents died in a car accident. Now you find out that's all been a lie. I'd want to find out what really happened and I wouldn't go to my original source for the answers. He hasn't been reliable. I'd dig deeper."

Sarah took a deep breath. "That's what I think, too."

Gabe's voice took on a softer tone. "But as your friend, I'd say, take care of yourself, Sarah. Watch yourself. And let me know if you get any more emails. If you're spooked, then I am. Be careful."

Sarah thanked him and said goodbye, staring out across the flat landscape. So different than the mountains and valleys of Montana. How she missed Larkspur. As soon as the funeral was over she was going to leave Penny Gate whether Jack was coming with her or not. She should never have come here. It was poisonous.

Her telephone screen lit up with a text from Margaret. Can you meet me at five o'clock at Delia's on Main Street?

She checked the clock on the dashboard. Two fifteen. Where had the day gone? She hadn't eaten anything since the night before and she felt shaky and sick to her stomach. She sent a message back to Margaret letting her know that she would meet her at five.

She reached over to the passenger seat and picked up the headphones again. She was ready to listen to the second audiotape.

Sarah slid the earphones over her head and pushed Play. She listened in rapt attention to all the interviews that Sheriff Gilmore, then a deputy, had conducted during Lydia's murder investigation.

First she listened to Gilmore interview a woman by the name of Victoria Dupree, who identified herself as one of Jack's teachers at the high school. No, Jack wasn't at school the afternoon his mother died. Yes, he did seem to have a bit of a temper, was sullen. She had seen Jack arguing with his mother after parent-teacher conferences. He had knocked the car keys out of his mother's hand and stomped away. No, she didn't know what the argument was about, but probably about Jack's grades. He wasn't doing well in school as of late.

The next interviewee was a farmhand named Randy Loring, who worked for the Tierney family on and off. The first thing he did was establish that he had an ironclad alibi — he was at the hospital with his girlfriend, who was having a baby. He then went on to say that no, he had never seen John and Lydia Tierney argue, nothing more than a few sharp words, anyway. He did, however, see Jack argue with his parents on more than one occasion. Once even

234

violently. Randy described one morning when he drove up to the Tierney farm and found Jack and his father shouting at each other. About what, Randy couldn't say, but Jack had a shovel in his hand, and for a minute there, Randy was sure that Jack was going to hit his father with it. Once Jack saw Randy's truck, he threw the shovel to the ground and stomped away. John Tierney had brushed off the incident, said that Jack was just a restless teenager who resented having to spend all his free time working on the farm when he could be out with that pretty girlfriend of his.

Sarah's stomach dropped. Celia again. She couldn't believe she was hearing her husband described in this way: short-tempered, violent, sullen. Yes, Jack could be withdrawn; she and the girls even would tease him about it. *Dad's going off into his own little world now, so if you need to ask him anything, better do it quick.*

One thing was clear: no one, not one person that was interviewed who knew Lydia and John Tierney, could ever recall a fight, a disagreement or harsh words between them. But apparently one morning John beat Lydia to death and then disappeared.

Gilmore asked each and every person that

he interviewed whether or not they thought John Tierney could have murdered his wife. They all said no except for one person. Dean Quinlan. Dean reported to Gilmore that yes, while Jack and his father argued, it was John who had the nasty temper, was the one who was hard on Jack, the one who got physical. *If anyone killed my aunt Lydia,* Dean said, *it would have been my uncle John. I hate to say it, but unless it was a robber or something, he's the one who did it.*

Why would Dean, Jack's cousin and best friend, be the only one able to envision John as the killer? Did Jack confide in his cousin, telling him about the terrible fights that he had with his father? Had Dean been a witness to the arguments? Or was Dean protecting his best friend by portraying John as overbearing and violent?

Even an eleven-year-old Amy told Gilmore that Jack and their parents fought over *stuff.* When pressed as to what was the stuff they argued over, Amy's answers were short and hesitant. "School. Jack got off the bus but wouldn't always go into school," she said shyly. "Mom would get mad and Jack would yell." Her voice was barely audible. At eleven, there was no sign of Amy's tough facade or cutting remarks. Only one thing in Amy's voice sounded familiar — the bone-aching sadness. Sarah wondered if the loneliness was there before the death of her mother and disappearance of her father or if it was always there, in the fabric of her bones and sinew.

Several of those interviewed, people with names that Sarah didn't recognize, reported that Lydia and Jack fought over Jack's many teenage shenanigans. How he skipped school, how he was drinking and smoking with older kids like his cousin, Dean, the public arguments with his mother and father. The numerous occasions he had run away from home for days at a time. Still, none of this spelled out *murderer*.

The Jack described in the tapes was so different than the one she knew. While Jack retreated into himself now and again, he never ran away like he did when he was a teen and like his father ultimately did. He wasn't a big drinker and certainly didn't smoke. She had difficulty reconciling that they could be the same person, but there it was, right in the tapes. It was clear from Gilmore's questions that Jack was the main suspect, at least initially.

It wasn't until the later interviews dated a few days after the murder that it was clear that John Tierney was missing.

No one interviewed could imagine to

where John Tierney would have run away to. His whole universe was Penny Gate. His grandparents were born here, his father was born here, he was born here, his children were born here. There was nowhere and nothing else that he could possibly have run to.

After the final interview, Sarah hit the stop button and slowly pulled off the headphones and laid her forehead against the steering wheel.

A persistent little thought tried to wheedle its way into her brain. *What if he did it?* the voice asked. *What if Jack killed his mother?* Then what happened to his father? Sarah countered. Could she really have misjudged Jack for so long? Had she been fooled by his quiet reserve, mistaking it for shyness and sensitivity while really it was cold-blooded indifference? Had she all along been married to a monster?

12

Sarah arrived at Delia's, just two doors down from the Penny Café, twenty minutes before Margaret was due to arrive. It was a typical small-town bar. Dim and dated with walls filled with pictures of locals posing with a dark-haired woman whom Sarah assumed was Delia.

Five men and a woman lined the bar, deep in debate over the baseball game that was on the TV above the bar. As she passed by the crowd, the hum of chatter quieted. Three old men, dressed in coveralls and seed hats, hunched over their plates, watched her covertly out of the corners of their eyes as they chewed. She wondered if they knew who she was, and if they had heard about what happened to Julia.

The woman behind the bar had hair dyed an unnatural black with a purple sheen and large brown doe eyes. She looked eerily similar to the woman in the photos and

Sarah wondered if she could be Delia's daughter. "Dinner?" she asked, and Sarah nodded.

"There will be two of us," Sarah said as the waitress led her to the dining room. "Could we have a corner booth?"

"Of course. Are you new to the area?" the waitress asked. "You don't look familiar to me."

"No, I'm visiting family."

"Who's that?" the waitress asked.

"The Quinlans. I'm married to Jack."

"Oh, I remember Jack. I'm Clarice Jantzen," the woman said with a kind smile. "Sheriff Gilmore is my dad. I heard about Julia. I'm so sorry. She was the sweetest lady."

"Thank you," Sarah murmured as she sat, accepting the menu that Clarice offered.

"How's the family doing?" Clarice asked. "I bet Amy's just devastated." Sarah couldn't tell if the woman was prying for gossip or simply making conversation. Sarah nodded tentatively, not comfortable sharing information with this stranger. "What can I bring you to drink?" she asked, taking the hint.

"An iced tea, please," Sarah said as her cell phone vibrated, displaying a number she wasn't familiar with. "Excuse me," she said to Clarice. "But I need to take this." Once Clarice moved out of earshot Sarah answered.

"Mrs. Quinlan?" a young male voice asked.

"Yes?" Sarah responded.

"This is Arthur Newberry. You left me a message regarding representation of your sister-in-law?"

"Yes," Sarah said, taken off guard. The voice on the other end of the line sounded much too young for someone who had attended law school. "Do you think you would be able to help?"

"Yes, of course. I can start right away," he said, barely able to contain his excitement. Sarah wanted to ask him how old he was, but figured that she was fortunate that he had called her back.

Arthur said he would head right over to the sheriff's department. "I'll call you after I talk with Amy. You and I can meet to discuss her case."

From across the room Sarah caught sight of Margaret entering the pub. She thanked Arthur and disconnected.

Sarah stood when Margaret arrived at the table and Clarice approached, her forehead furrowing in confusion. "Hi, Clarice," Margaret said. "I'll have a Bloody Mary. Oh, don't look at me like that, Clarice. I'm not working tonight."

Once Clarice was out of earshot, Sarah leaned forward and whispered, "Did you know that's Gilmore's daughter? Do you really think it's a good idea to be meeting here?"

Margaret waved her red-tipped fingers dismissively. "Of course I know that. I went to high school with Clarice's older sister. I work with her father. We're fine." She picked up her menu.

Sarah opened her own menu. "Do you know if the sheriff arrested Amy?"

Margaret nodded, pursing her lips together tightly. "I don't know many details but I do know he read Amy her rights."

"I figured as much." Sarah dropped her menu to the table. "I got her a lawyer. His name is Arthur Newberry."

"Nice boy," Margaret commented. "Took over his grandfather's practice about a year ago. He'll work hard for Amy."

"Do you think Amy really could have done it?" Sarah asked, unwrapping her silverware from the napkin. "I don't know her well, but I just can't understand it all."

"It's hard for me to believe, too," Margaret agreed. "Amy has always been a lost soul, but a killer?" Margaret shook her head.

"I don't see her knocking Julia in the head, making her fall down the stairs. It's probably all a big mistake. The sheriff will figure it out."

"So that's what the cause of death was? A blow to the head?" Sarah asked, hoping Margaret might offer some information about the possible use of poison.

"As far as I know," Margaret answered. "Why? Have you heard something else?" Margaret looked at her curiously.

"No, I was just wondering. It's all so crazy. I just am having trouble wrapping my head around everything."

Margaret didn't seem to have knowledge of the toxicology report linking the poison to Amy's home or at least she wasn't letting on that she knew anything.

Clarice set their drinks down in front of them. "So how do you two know each other?" she asked after jotting down their dinner orders.

Sarah froze, not expecting this question from their waitress let alone the sheriff's daughter. What possible reason would two virtual strangers have to meet for dinner? Margaret plucked the celery from her Bloody Mary. They couldn't very well tell her that they were colluding to access case files that they had no permission to view.

"Julia Quinlan's funeral dinner. I'm in charge of organizing the desserts." She crunched into the stalk. "I'm making my lemon squares. Do you think you could bring one of your strawberry-rhubarb pies?"

Clarice narrowed her eyes with suspicion, but didn't press further. "Sure, I'll make two," she said as she walked away.

"I listened to the audiotapes. They were . . ." Sarah searched for the right words. "Hard to listen to," she finished. "Thank you for getting them for me."

Margaret patted Sarah's hand. "I know Jack, I know Amy. I knew Lydia and John Tierney. I want to help."

Sarah squeezed her lemon wedge into her iced tea. "I'm embarrassed to admit that I have to rely on someone I barely even know to fill me in on the details of my husband's life." She shook her head ruefully. "I just can't get Jack to talk about it and I don't know why."

Margaret looked at her with sympathy. "You didn't know about any of it? How Lydia died?"

"No." Sarah blinked back sudden tears. It was difficult to admit that her husband couldn't trust her with this information, that he never had.

"It's understandable, I guess." Margaret

244

took a sip of her drink. "Think about it. His mother was beaten to death in the cellar of their home and he discovered her body. I heard that one of the young deputies who responded to the call went inside the house, took one look at Lydia, ran up the stairs and outside and quit. Turned in his badge and gun right on the spot. This horrible thing happened to Jack's family, and when he was finally able to leave Penny Gate, he could put it all behind him. He went off to college, moved to another state, started a new life where no one needed to know what happened in the past."

"I don't know . . ."

"Then —" Margaret held up one finger to show that she wasn't finished "— he met you and he was faced with the choice of telling you about how his father murdered his mother and then disappeared or taking the hard way out."

Sarah gave a short laugh. "The hard way out? How do you figure?"

"Listen, honey," Margaret said kindly. "I know I'm not that much older than you, but I've been married twice. My first husband I divorced because I caught him cheating on me. My second husband died of prostate cancer."

"I'm sorry about that, but I'm still not

quite following you," Sarah admitted, wishing that she had ordered something stronger than iced tea. "How is *not* telling me the hard way out?"

"Now bear with me. My second husband had cancer for six months before he told me. Later he told me that he wanted to try the *active surveillance* —" she lifted her fingers to create air quotes "— treatment option first and didn't want to worry me.

"What I'm saying is, my first husband lied to me because he was a shit. My second husband lied to me because he wanted to protect me and I loved him for it. Now, I'm not saying I wasn't pissed off. I was, believe you me. But after I got over being mad I realized he was just trying to spare me from any pain for as long as possible. Understand?"

Sarah thought about this. Could Jack really have been trying to protect her? Had he had her best interests in mind all along? Sarah nodded reluctantly. "I think I do." Still, she couldn't turn to Jack for any reliable information.

"Right now you're in the pissed-off stage," Margaret went on. "Once you get back home, you'll have all the time in the world to talk it through."

Clarice brought out their food. A tenderloin sandwich for Margaret and a hamburger and fries for Sarah. "Can I get you ladies anything else right now?"

Margaret held up her glass. "I'll take another one of these."

Sarah looked at her iced tea. "Why not? I'll have what she's having." Clarice picked up their empty glasses and retreated back toward the bar.

They ate in silence for a few minutes, Sarah wolfing down her hamburger. "I'm just so desperate to know what really happened," she said, wiping her mouth with a napkin. "And not just the basics, you know. I know it sounds morbid, but every small detail I learn makes me want to know more. Especially since Jack said he thought he saw his father at the hospital the other day."

"What do you mean, Jack saw his father?" Margaret asked, setting her sandwich back on her plate. A crumb was stuck to the corner of Margaret's glossy lips and Sarah wiped at her own mouth.

"I know he didn't really see him, but the look on Jack's face . . ." Sarah shook her head at the memory. "Part of me is worried about Jack, and part of me is just sick and tired of all the smoke and mirrors."

"Jack's dad back in town?" Margaret pushed her plate away and poked her tongue into the corner of her mouth, catching the crumb. "Now that would be something else." Clarice returned with their drinks and again they fell silent until she was well out of earshot.

"Do you think it's possible?" Sarah asked, taking a deep drink of her Bloody Mary. For the first time she wondered if Jack actually did *see* his dad at the hospital. What if it wasn't just a trick of light or an overactive imagination?

"No," Margaret said quickly. "Why would he come back? That'd be crazy. He would be arrested. No, I'm sure Jack just saw someone who reminded him of his dad."

"Do you believe the case is solved?" Sarah asked.

"Yeah, I think it was John Tierney. I know that Jack didn't do it. No, he was a good, kind little boy. He would never purposely hurt someone."

A pressure eased in Sarah's chest. It was immensely comforting to her to know that Jack's childhood babysitter knew in her heart that Jack couldn't have done this. But still, there were so many unanswered questions. Why had John Tierney murdered his wife and whatever happened to him?

"I hope you're right," Sarah said, reaching for her purse slung over the back of her chair. "It's just that so many strange things have happened in the past few days, I feel like anything is possible."

Margaret leaned toward Sarah and asked conspiratorially, "So what did you find out from the tapes?"

Sarah's meal felt like a rock in her stomach. "That most of the town thought that Jack was guilty. Nearly every single person had an example of Jack arguing with his parents. It wasn't until no one could find his dad that they became suspicious of him." Sarah pressed her fingers to her forehead. She shouldn't have ordered the Bloody Mary; vodka always gave her a headache. "Have you heard the tapes?"

Margaret tipped her glass back and chewed on some ice. "I skimmed through the transcripts quickly before I gave you the envelope, but I didn't actually listen to the tapes," she admitted. "Tough reading, though."

Sarah leaned forward, planting her elbows on the table. "Margaret, I know you've already gone out on a limb for me, but is there any way you can get me more of the case file?" She readied herself for Margaret's refusal. She already had put her job in jeopardy for Sarah.

"I figured that when you sent me the text

saying that you wanted another *recipe* from me that you really meant you wanted more information," Margaret said, pulling her pocketbook from her purse. "This is my treat."

"Oh, no," Sarah protested, reaching for her own billfold.

Margaret placed her hand over Sarah's. "You've had a tough day. Let me."

"Thank you," Sarah said quietly, touched by Margaret's thoughtfulness.

"You might not thank me after you see what's in the trunk of my car. Come on, let's go."

Sarah followed Margaret as she moved through the bar, past patrons who greeted her heartily and teased her good-naturedly. Margaret seemed not to hear but rushed past them without a word. They stepped from the dark restaurant and squinted into the early-evening sunshine. Sarah welcomed the subtle warmth after the chilly, poorly lit interior of the bar. Margaret scurried down the street and around the corner to a green VW Beetle that looked out of place among all the trucks and SUVs parked along the curb.

Margaret glanced around to see if anyone was looking their way, clicked the remote locks and the trunk sprang open. They both bent down to look inside. Margaret pulled away a jacket and revealed a large box. On the side, printed in black block letters was *LYDIA TIERNEY 1985.*

"You said you wanted all the details, well, this is as detailed as you get," Margaret said proudly.

Sarah lifted the cardboard lid. Inside were dozens of file folders, each labeled and dated. "This is the entire case file?" Sarah looked at Margaret. "Really?"

"Not the entire file," Margaret amended. "There's no physical evidence in there. They keep that in the basement under lock and key."

"But still, all these documents. How did you get them?"

"I have my ways," Margaret said cryptically.

"No, really, Margaret," Sarah said with concern. For the first time, Sarah noticed how tired Margaret looked. Her eyes were framed by dark circles and she was pale, though she tried to camouflage her exhaustion with heavy makeup. "You could get in big trouble for this. You could lose your job. Are you sure?"

"I'm sure," Margaret said with feeling. "You only live once, right? Besides, I've seen what Lydia's death has done to my mother.

If there's anything I can do to help my mom, I'll do it. Now, this is the one file that the sheriff keeps in his office. He was down on the jail side talking to Amy so I just went in and grabbed it."

Sarah's eyes widened in alarm. "You broke into the sheriff's office? Oh, my God, Margaret, you could have been caught. I thought you would just go down into some storage area to find it."

"Not with this case file," Margaret said, tapping the lid of the box. "The sheriff keeps it in the closet in his office. He pulls it out once in a while and looks through it."

"But why?" Sarah asked. She itched to pull the lid off the box and start perusing through the contents. "The case is closed. Why would the sheriff care so much?"

Margaret leaned in close to Sarah even though no one was near. "Rumor had it that Sheriff Gilmore and Lydia might have been having an affair. My mom said that was ridiculous, that they were just friends, but you know how people talk."

"No one in the audiotapes mentioned anything about an affair. Everyone interviewed said Lydia and John had a good marriage. Why wouldn't something like an affair come out?" Sarah asked.

"Look at who was interviewing them.

Gilmore." Margaret's eyes shone with excitement. "They wouldn't have said anything, at least not on the record."

"I don't know," Sarah said doubtfully. "It seems a little far-fetched."

A truck crept by and Margaret hurriedly closed the trunk. "I told you my mom was best friends with Lydia, right? She thought something wasn't quite right about the whole thing since the start."

"She doesn't think that John killed her?"

"No, I'm not saying that. She just believes there's a lot more to the story than folks know or are saying. Can you pull your car up and we'll put the box in your trunk?"

Sarah trotted to her car. She still needed to stop by Arthur Newberry's office to pay the retainer; she hoped she hadn't missed him for the day. She climbed inside, checked her phone and found that she had several voice mails from Jack. She didn't even bother to listen to them. She knew she needed to touch base with him, at least let him know where she was, but she was still so angry. She pulled her car up next to Margaret's, stepped out and went around to the other side to open the passenger's-side door.

"You don't want it in the trunk?" Margaret asked.

"This is fine for now. I can't look through

253

it at Dean's or Hal's house. I'll probably have to sit in my car somewhere and go through it."

Margaret hefted the box draped with her jacket from the trunk and transferred it to the passenger's-side seat of Sarah's car. "I'd invite you over to my house, but my mom will be there and it's best if she didn't know what we are up to."

"Thanks again for getting this for me," Sarah said gratefully. "When do you need it back?"

"As soon as possible. What about tomorrow or the next day?" Margaret nibbled on a manicured nail. "God, I can't believe I'm doing this. I must be crazy."

"We can stop — you don't have to . . ." Sarah began.

"No." Margaret shook her head. "I want to. For my mom, for Lydia." Margaret took a deep breath as if to bolster herself and continued. "The sheriff is pretty busy with Amy and the search at Hal's house. So we should be okay until at least then."

"They're still searching Hal's house?" Sarah asked. "I didn't think it would take that long — it's not that big of a home."

"They're searching the outbuildings, too. It looks like they might have found something on the property."

"Evidence?" Sarah asked curiously. Did the sheriff find something that would further incriminate Amy? Exonerate her?

"I don't know," Margaret said, "but from what Tess said, they're going to be there for a while. I'll keep my ears open, though. Do you think you'll be able to go through the whole thing in the next day or two?" Margaret nodded toward the box.

"I'll have to. If I don't find out what happened to Jack's family thirty years ago in the next forty-eight hours, I probably never will."

13

Sarah located the attorney's office, a narrow redbrick building sandwiched between a bakery and a hardware store. An ornate gold sign, engraved with an illustration of a blindfolded Lady Justice, read Arthur L. Newberry, Jr., Attorney at Law.

Sarah, making sure that the evidence box was completely concealed by the jacket, stepped from the car and peeked through the mullioned windows. A grandmotherly woman with tightly curled white hair sat behind a desk reading a novel. Sarah pulled open the door and a bell tinkled, announcing her arrival. The woman looked up from behind thick reading glasses and quickly slid the book into her desk drawer. "Hello, can I help you?" she asked, folding her arthritic fingers behind a nameplate that read Katherine Newberry. Sarah wondered if this was Arthur's mother.

Sarah explained who she was and asked if

256

Arthur was available.

"Arthur is still at the jail meeting with Ms. Quinlan. I don't expect him back until a bit later. Would you like to wait?"

"I'll have to stop back tomorrow morning if he'll be in."

Katherine referred to a large desk calendar. "I have Ms. Quinlan's arraignment down for 9:00 a.m. Will you be able to stop in beforehand?"

Sarah agreed, thanked her and turned to leave when Katherine cleared her throat. "Now there's just the little matter of fees. Mr. Newberry prefers payment up front."

"Of course," Sarah said, digging through her purse for her checkbook. She quickly scribbled out a check for the retainer and handed it to Katherine, who examined it carefully before stowing it into her desk drawer.

"Are you related to Arthur?" Sarah asked, nodding her head toward the nameplate.

"Oh, yes. Arthur is my grandson." Katherine smiled proudly. "He just took over my husband's practice a few months ago after he graduated from law school." Sarah's heart sank a bit and she hoped that what Arthur lacked in lawyerly experience he made up for in hard work and tenacity.

"So you've lived in Penny Gate for a

while?" Sarah asked. If the Newberrys had been here for any length of time, Katherine certainly would have been familiar with Lydia's murder.

"Our whole lives," Katherine said. "Born and bred here."

"Then you might have known my husband's parents? John and Lydia Tierney."

"Of course," Katherine said. "You must be Jack's wife. It's nice to meet you, although these aren't the best of circumstances. I was hoping that Jack would have stopped by himself. I haven't seen that boy in decades."

"You knew Jack, too?" Sarah asked, glancing at the clock on the wall. It was well after 6:00 p.m. Sarah was torn between wanting to hear more about Jack and wanting to dig into the case file.

"Oh, yes," Katherine said with a smile. "Our youngest daughter went to school with Jack. We always liked him. Tragic, what happened to his family. My husband actually represented Jack for a short time during the whole mess." She shook her head. "Poor boy. Imagine being suspected of your mother's murder when all along it was your dad who did it? And now all that's happening with Amy and Julia." Katherine gave a sympathetic click of her tongue.

"Represented Jack?" Sarah repeated, not sure she had heard Katherine correctly. "Was Jack actually arrested?"

"He was arrested but never charged," Katherine assured her. "Julia Quinlan called my husband once she learned the sheriff was focused on Jack as a suspect."

Sarah's stomach flipped. Another lie from Jack. She contemplated getting back into the rental car, driving to the airport and heading back home to Larkspur without a backward glance. But something kept her there. The need to know the entire truth? Love for her husband? She wasn't sure anymore. "Do you have any of that old paperwork?" Sarah asked. "Any notes from when your husband met with Jack?"

Katherine gave her an uncertain look. "Why would you want anything from back then? It was a terrible, terrible time."

Sarah thought fast. "Since coming back to town, lots of memories have been dredged up for Jack and he's been going over things in his mind. Asking a lot of questions, reading a lot of the old news articles." Sarah couldn't believe she was lying so easily to this poor woman.

"I suppose it wouldn't hurt anything," Katherine said more to herself than to Sarah. "I'll just go and see if I can find the file." She rose and disappeared through a doorway in the back of the office and emerged a few moments later with a thin file folder in hand.

"This is all I could dig up," she said, thumbing through the pages. "Like I said. Arthur represented him only for a very short time. Once the sheriff realized that John Tierney had disappeared all the focus went away from Jack. There's just a few pages of handwritten notes here." She handed a file to Sarah. "Here, I made a photocopy for you. Tell Jack to stop in and say hello while he's in town."

"I will and thank you," Sarah said, sliding the folder into her purse. "And I'll be in tomorrow morning at eight to talk with your grandson."

The sun was slowly dipping behind the tree line, tingeing the clouds pink and gold. Daylight was fading fast. Jack had sent her several more texts giving her updates and asking where she was. The sheriff's department was still at Hal's farm. They hadn't finished the search yet. The wake was scheduled for the next evening and the funeral for the following day. He had tried to go and visit Amy at the jail but she was meeting with her attorney at the time. Was something wrong? Please call.

Is something wrong? Sarah began to text. *How about finding out your husband was the main suspect in the murder of his mother and was arrested? You forgot to tell me that part. Yeah, something is wrong.* Sarah exhaled in frustration and then hit Cancel. She thought for a moment and then typed again. *Just have had a lot to think about. I'll be back soon.* At least Jack had made the effort to go see his sister. That was something the Jack she thought she knew would do.

She climbed back into the car and tried to figure out where she could read the case file without interruption. A hotel? That was certainly appealing. She hated the thought of returning to the house where Jack's mother died, hated facing her liar of a husband. In a hotel room she could spread out the entire contents of the box and go through each document thoroughly, take notes and try to fit the pieces of her husband's early life together. Somehow this seemed wrong, though, deserting Jack the night before his aunt's wake. She was hurt and possibly irreparably angry with Jack, but she couldn't completely abandon him, not here, not now. Not yet.

Sarah found herself back on the same stretch of gravel road where she first listened to the audiotapes. She had only seen the one vehicle with the hunters here earlier in the day and hoped that it would be equally deserted now. The sun was dipping below the horizon and she knew she had only a few minutes of daylight left to use as light to read by. She pulled off to the side of the road, put the car into Park, turned on her hazard lights and turned off the ignition. She didn't want to be rear-ended by a car coming up unexpectedly behind her.

Sarah locked the doors, rolled down the windows a few inches and felt a cool light breeze brush across her skin. The road was empty for as far as she could see. A cornfield that had yet to be harvested sat to her right and a meadow filled with long grass and clover sat to her left. No homes rose up in the distance, no silos stood sentry. She was all alone. The only sounds were the rustling of grass and crickets announcing autumn with weary, almost melancholy chirps. She fought the urge to start the car again and turn on the radio just for the noise — she didn't want to miss hearing a car approaching.

Sarah flipped on the overhead light and pulled out the file folder that Katherine Newberry gave her. She skimmed the hand-written notes, learning nothing new. Young Jack maintained his innocence just as he did in his interview with Gilmore.

Next she slid Margaret's jacket from atop the evidence box, removed the lid and pulled out the first file folder.

Inside the musty manila folder she found a thick pile of photographs, bound together by a frayed rubber band, all labeled in black permanent marker with the date, case number and location. The rubber band snapped when she tried to slide it from the stack. She braced for what she was about to see. After hearing the audiotape of Jack's account of the discovery of his mother's body, she knew that the photos were going to be graphic, a harrowing step-by-step visual chronicle of a brutal murder. The first few photos were benign enough. Snapshots of the house, Dean and Celia's house, Jack's childhood home. The photographer documented his journey into the house. The mudroom with an array of shoes and boots neatly lined up against one wall. The kitchen, sun shining incongruously through the window, splashing colorful prisms of light onto the floor. The door to the cellar, slightly ajar, smudged with blood. Jack's fingerprints according to the audiotapes. The steps leading downward into the darkened cellar.

Sarah's fingers stopped. In the distance

she heard the lowing of cattle, a mournful and lonely sound. Her heartbeat quickened and she glanced up, aware of how alone she was. The sun had finally set and except for the car's overhead light she was enveloped in darkness. No stars dotted the sky; there was no sliver of moon, no streetlights. She almost wished she had gone to a hotel. At least there would have been people around. With shaking fingers she continued to thumb through the photos, finally coming to the pictures she dreaded seeing.

The first shot of Lydia's body was taken from above. She was lying faceup on the concrete floor, the lid to the freezer still open, her yellow hair, dark and sticky with blood, fanned out on the floor around her. A piece of fabric obscured the top half of her face, her mouth frozen open in a silent scream.

One hand was outstretched and Sarah wondered if she was trying to protect herself or reaching out for someone, pleading for them to stop. Her dress, the color of lemon drops, was hiked up around her waist, revealing long, pale legs.

The next photos zeroed in on her injuries. The fingers on one hand were bloodied and bent at odd angles, broken, Sarah thought, when Lydia must have tried to ward off the blows. Dark purple bruises bloomed across her arms. Next, the camera focused on Lydia's head wound. A deep gash, four inches long, ran at the edge of her hairline just above her ear, exposing paper-white bone. Sarah had to look away; her stomach flipped dangerously. Who could have inflicted such horrific injuries? Someone very angry or very evil, she thought. Or both. Could Jack have wielded the weapon that did this and then watched his mother die? Not the Jack she knew, the Jack she thought she knew, anyway. But she also would never have believed that Jack could have lied to her so blatantly.

The temperature in the car had dropped and goose bumps erupted along her arms. She reached for Margaret's jacket and threaded her arms through the sleeves, grateful for the warmth. The next photo was a close-up of the fabric covering her eyes, a dish towel embroidered with flowers, already stiff with blood. At first Sarah wondered if perhaps a police officer had placed it over Lydia's face to cover up her gruesome injuries, but quickly realized that wasn't the case. It was part of the crime scene. Jack mentioned on the audiotape that his mother's eyes had been covered with a cloth of some kind. Had Lydia had the towel in her hands when she was attacked and it had fallen across her eyes when she tumbled to the ground? Or had it been placed there by a killer, too ashamed to look into the eyes of the woman he had murdered?

Suddenly nauseous, Sarah dropped the photos onto the seat next to her, and pushed open the car door, nearly tumbling to the ground as she hurried out. She stumbled to the side of the road and bent over, hands on her knees, willing herself not to vomit, but certain she would feel better if she did. She could taste remnants of the hamburger she had eaten earlier in the back her throat. Something scurried near her through the tall grass, causing her heart to skip a beat. On shaky legs, Sarah stood and made her way back to the car. She held on to the door frame, taking deep breaths until the queasiness passed.

Sarah looked at the passenger's-side seat. The photos were strewn across the seat and onto the floor in a jumble. She left them where they lay.

She considered packing up the box, driving directly back to the sheriff's department and handing it over to Margaret. *No,* Sarah told herself. She got back into the car and reached into the box to pull out another folder. This one chronicled the findings of the medical examiner who conducted Lydia's autopsy. Cause of death: blunt force trauma.

Though she wanted to turn away, she was compelled to keep looking at the autopsy photos. Lydia was stretched out upon a metal table, a white sheet pulled up over her chest. Someone had rinsed the blood from her hair and it was slicked back away from her face, now peaceful, the earlier terror smoothed away. Her eyes were closed and except for the ugly gash along her hairline she could have been sleeping.

A close-up of the injury to Lydia's head revealed a curved laceration. Whatever Lydia had been struck with had a rounded, sharp edge.

Since the murder had taken place in 1985, Sarah knew it was a little early for the wide use of DNA testing, but several sets of fingerprints had been found at the scene. Jack's, Amy's, Lydia's and John's fingerprints, identified from his military record. No murder weapon was ever found, but both Amy and Jack in their interviews with the sheriff's department said the cellar had been home to many old farm tools over the years. Something from the cellar could easily have been used as a weapon.

A note from the medical examiner stated

that the injury was consistent with a blow from a heavy object with a curved, sharp edge.

The subsequent files offered little new information, just a rehashing of the scant facts and a jumble of suppositions from the people of Penny Gate who, as the public support of John Tierney faded, shared glimpses of the darker side of their friend and neighbor. *Quiet, kept to himself. Had a bit of a temper. Waved his shotgun around at deer hunters who came on his property without permission.*

The lone ally for John was his sister, Julia. *My brother loved Lydia. He would never hurt her, never do this to his family.*

Sarah picked up the pile of photos from the seat next to her and began to organize them by the small number written on the back of each. Her eye snagged on a familiar image. She took a closer look. A pair of hands. Even without the notation that identified the subject as Jack, she thought she'd know them anywhere. Jack's hands. His knuckles were bruised, fresh lacerations looked raw and painful. The next photo showed the palms of Jack's hands; three half-moon indentations marred each palm. What would cause such marks? *A murder weapon?* Sarah shoved the thought from her mind.

They knew who committed this murder: John Tierney. The only reason he wasn't arrested, tried and convicted was because they couldn't find him. A small voice buzzed in her ear like a pesky insect: Then why had Jack lied to her about everything if he didn't have something to hide?

The final photos showed Jack without a shirt. He was slim and bony chested, large footed and large handed, a boy who hadn't yet grown into himself. No other marks blemished his body, no wounds of any kind. Surely, if he had been Lydia's attacker, she would have fought back, scratched and clawed trying to protect herself. Unless, of course, the attacker was your son, and the blows were unexpected.

Sarah knew that she would never get the graphic images of Lydia from her mind and wondered how Jack could possibly have recovered from finding his mother in that awful state. No wonder he rarely came back to Penny Gate, didn't want Sarah here or his daughters. It made a little more sense now.

Sarah peered into the box. She had breezed through every single piece of paper. There were photocopies of the school attendance records and even the handwritten rosters that the teachers used to mark whether a student was present or absent for a particular class period. Highlighted in yellow on three of the rosters was Jack's name with a capital *A* written beside it. As Jack had stated in his interview he had skipped three of his afternoon classes.

There were copies of phone bills in the months leading up to the murder. The same number was highlighted three times. At the bottom of the page someone had scrawled *Raymond Douglas — known drug dealer.*

Had Jack been using drugs as a teenager? Had his parents found out? Had he skipped school that day in late May and been confronted by his mother? Had he lashed out violently? No, it wasn't enough. Plenty of kids used drugs and didn't murder their mothers. *But plenty of kids did,* a small voice whispered in her ear. She had just heard a news story about a teen from Great Falls who killed both his parents in their beds after they had threatened to send him to a rehab center.

Sarah shook her head in frustration. Why couldn't she just let it go? Jack had lied to her, yes, but it didn't make him a murderer. Besides, the sheriff was confident he knew who the killer was: Jack's father. John Tierney had murdered his wife and taken off. Tragedies like that happened every day. *But how did he get away?* that small, insistent voice asked. According to the sheriff's notes, John's truck was found hidden in the cornfield that separated the Quinlan farm from the Tierney farm. What had Celia said when she was driving Sarah to her home? She could walk straight through the cornfield from her house and it would take you fifteen minutes to get to Hal's. How would John have left town without his truck? Did he have an accomplice? None were mentioned in any of the files.

Sarah returned the last of the files to the box and caught sight of another audiotape at the bottom. She pulled it from the box. She rubbed her eyes and checked the time. It was nine o'clock.

Could the tape wait until the next day? She was so tired. She slid the cassette into the manila envelope that held the other audiotapes. She would listen to it tomorrow.

Though she hated to, she needed to get back to Dean and Celia's house. She had no idea how she was going to explain her extended absence. Could she put on a mask, just like Jack had for all these years? Could she pretend that all was well with her marriage, that she didn't know all the sordid circumstances surrounding Jack's youth and his mother's death? Sarah started the car and pulled onto the winding road that would take her back to her husband, now a stranger. How was she going to casually discuss her day and chat about their daughters with him?

And more importantly, how was she going to crawl into bed tonight with a man she knew was a liar and who could have been capable of so much worse?

14

Sarah pulled down Dean and Celia's lane, past the barn, past the clothesline where Jack's mother once hung the freshly washed sheets, and pulled up in front of the kitchen window where she had surely looked out and watched her children in play. Sarah turned off the ignition and sat staring at the house. The porch light illuminated the declining condition of the home. Sarah recalled the crime-scene photos where there was an array of flowers cascading from pots that hung from the eaves, a stark contrast to the yellow crime tape stretched across the porch.

She hated the thought of going inside, but she was exhausted and she wanted to let Jack know she was done with his lies. She would stay through Julia's funeral, but then she was going back home. She glanced over at the box. She peeled Margaret's jacket from her shoulders and laid it across the box, hooked her purse over her shoulder and stepped from the car. She glanced at the house to make sure know one was looking out a window and quickly transported the box to the rear of the car and closed the trunk with a soft click.

"Sarah?" Jack's voice came from somewhere behind her. She scanned the farmyard and saw Jack and Celia coming her way from the direction of the large barn. They were walking side by side; just a fraction of space separated them. "What's in the box?" Jack asked.

Sarah thought fast. "Just a few items I picked up at the store since we're staying a little longer than planned. I bought a box so we could just mail the things that wouldn't fit in our carry-on bags back home." Jack appeared satisfied with this explanation. "What are you two doing out here in the dark?" she asked. The porch light was too weak for her to clearly examine their faces, but there were no secretive, knowing looks between the two of them. No indication that something clandestine had been going on.

"We were working on the details of Julia's funeral mass," Jack said, "and decided to go for a walk. Are you okay? Where have you been all this time?"

"I was just driving around. Thinking."

Sarah shoved her hands into her pockets. The evening air was cold on her skin and she missed the warmth of Margaret's jacket. "Can I talk to you for a minute?"

"Sure, let's go inside," Jack said, starting for the house.

"Let's walk," Sarah suggested. She wanted to be as far away as possible from the house and out of earshot when she said the things to Jack that needed to be said.

"I'll see you inside," Celia said. "I'll put some coffee on."

The earthy scent of soil and manure rose up from the ground, and the gentle murmur of livestock settling in for the night was somehow comforting as Sarah and Jack walked in silence toward the barns.

From within the house someone flipped a switch and a pair of floodlights affixed to the house came on, bathing the farmyard in a warm light. Sarah wondered why Celia hadn't turned on the same lights for her little walk with Jack. Sarah wished she would turn them off. What she had to say would be easier said in the dark.

"What's going on, Sarah?" Jack asked once they started walking. "I was getting really worried."

Sarah wasn't sure where to begin. "I'm glad you tried to go and see Amy. She's really scared."

"Thanks for getting the attorney lined up." Jack stopped walking. "There's just so much going on with getting ready for the funeral. Dean is sure that Amy did it and it just looks really bad for her and for a minute there . . ."

Sarah glanced back at the house and saw a silhouette in an upstairs window. Too wide and tall to be Celia. It had to be Dean or Hal. She kept walking, wanting to reach the shadows at the edge of the floodlights. "I know that Amy could never have hurt Julia," Jack finished as he jogged to catch up with her.

"Her arraignment is tomorrow morning. I scheduled a meeting at eight with her lawyer. I don't know if Amy did it or not, but she's your sister and I think you should be there," Sarah said, slightly out of breath as they reached the large barn. She leaned her back against the worn, rough boards and looked back toward the house. "You know, Amy thinks that Dean might have been the one to hurt Julia."

"Dean?" Jack laughed, then sobered quickly when he saw that Sarah wasn't joking. "That's crazier than thinking that Amy did it. Dean loves . . . loved his mom." Jack ran a hand over his mouth. "Why would she think that?"

"She said that he was the one who brought a bunch of boxes over to her house, including the one with the bale hook. And —" Sarah hesitated "— the other day I saw Dean grab Celia really hard and he didn't let go until she slapped him."

Jack frowned. "That doesn't sound like Dean. Or Celia. I mean, Dean's always had a bit of a temper, but I always thought the two of them got along fine. Maybe it's just the stress of everything that's been going on."

"I don't know what happened. I just thought you should know what I saw. But that's not why I wanted to talk to you." Sarah stood upright, pushing herself away from the barn with one hand. The sharp bite of weathered wood digging into the palm of her hand caused her to wince. She raised her hand to her face and tried to examine the sliver left behind.

"Did you hurt yourself?" Jack asked, reaching for her hand.

Sarah pulled away. "I'm fine." She tilted her head back and looked up at the night sky. It was black and all encompassing, and she felt as if she was being swallowed up by the night, by this town, by her husband's past.

"Sarah?" Jack asked uncertainly. He sounded scared.

"Right after the funeral I'm going home," she said, trying to keep her voice even and unemotional.

"I don't plan on staying any longer than I have to, either," Jack said.

"I mean it — the minute the funeral is over I'm getting on a plane and going back home to the girls. And when we're home we have to talk about where we go from here. I can't live with a liar, Jack, I just can't." Her voice cracked on the final word. Though she had practiced saying these words the entire way back to Celia's house, it was harder than she thought it would be.

"What? You want me to move out?" Jack asked in surprise.

Sarah straightened her spine as if this simple act could give her the strength to tell him what she had learned. "I told you that I didn't want any more secrets. No more lies."

"But I told you . . ." Jack began.

"Stop it, Jack," Sarah said loudly. "Stop lying!" Sarah's voice echoed across the still night air. A face appeared in the kitchen window. Clearly Celia's. Sarah turned her back to the house and lowered her voice. "In the past few days I learned that your parents did not die in a car accident like

278

you told me."

"Sarah, I explained why . . ."

"Let me speak," Sarah hissed. "I learned that your mother was murdered and your father was the one who murdered her. And I learned that for a time you were the prime suspect. You were arrested, Jack. *Arrested.* How could you keep that from me? Every time I turn around I learn something else that you've lied to me about." Despite the cool night, Sarah felt heat rise to her face as she spoke. From across the farmyard she heard the creak of a screen door. Celia stepped out onto the porch, her slim frame backlit by the porch lights. She seemed to hesitate between coming toward them to find out what was going on and returning inside. "And if that wasn't enough, I learned that your cousin's wife was your girlfriend and that you apparently had a violent temper, got drunk and did drugs." Sarah realized that she was crying and that her voice had once again risen enough that Celia decided that she needed to come see what was happening.

"Sarah, who the hell have you been talking to?" Jack asked angrily.

"Does it really matter?" she asked wearily. "Practically the entire town thought you killed your mother, Jack. I'm sorry such a terrible thing happened to your family and I'm sorry you felt like you needed to lie to me about it. But I'm done. After the funeral I'm leaving."

Celia was coming closer.

"Sarah, you're wrong," Jack said pleadingly. "I promise you, I never would have hurt my mother. Come back inside — we'll talk. You know me. I couldn't do something like that." He wrapped his hand around her arm, pulling her close. She could feel his hot breath on her cheek. "Please, you've got to believe me." His grip tightened, his fingers biting into her wrist. And for the first time she was scared of her husband.

"Let go of me, Jack, or I'll scream," Sarah whispered. Jack dropped her arm.

Celia moved closer, picking up her pace. "Is everything okay?" she called out to them.

"Go tell your old girlfriend that everything's all right," she said bitterly. "I just want to be left alone."

"We're fine," he called back to Celia. "We'll be right in." To Sarah he said, "You're wrong, Sarah. You are completely wrong about me. I shouldn't have lied to you. But I didn't kill my mother. My father did. Or do you think I killed him, too?"

Sarah didn't answer and in not responding she knew that she might have crossed the point of no return. For all intents and purposes, she had just called her husband a murderer or at least someone who could be capable of murder. He turned away from her, shaking his head in disgust, and joined Celia, who had stopped in the center of the yard. *What if you're wrong?* she asked herself as she stood in the dark shadows of the barn and watched the two of them walk back toward the house. *What if you're wrong and you sent him right back into Celia's arms? What if you're wrong and you've lost everything?*

Sarah waited, shivering in the cool air, while Jack and Celia lingered on the front porch. Talking about her, Sarah was sure. What were they saying? Was Jack telling Celia that Sarah was acting crazy, tossing out all these conspiracy theories about how Jack was the one who murdered his mother? Were they laughing at her? Jack seemed genuinely hurt by her accusations. But was he rattled by her anger or just taken aback that she wasn't going to let him get away with his lies anymore?

She watched as they finally went inside the house and followed their movements as lights behind the drawn shades were switched off for the night. First the flood-lights, and then the kitchen and living room lights were extinguished. A few moments passed and then one of the rooms on the second floor darkened. A figure stepped into view from behind another upstairs window. Jack. She would know him anywhere. His tall, angular frame, the slope of his shoulders, the tilt of his head. Once the sight of her husband had brought happiness, a sense of relief. Now the image of him looming above her only brought a sense of trepidation. He remained there for what felt like ages, staring out across the farmyard. She felt his eyes latch on to hers and her heart thundered in her chest and she took three quick steps backward. Sarah knew he really couldn't see her — she was obscured in shadow — but she felt as if he could see right through her, could feel her fear.

Finally, he stepped away from the window and the room went dark. Only one light remained. The weak, cold light emanating from the listing front porch. The crime-scene photos marched mercilessly through her mind. The blood-smeared cellar door, the concrete floor, Lydia's broken fingers, her crushed skull, the cloth draped over her eyes, the pool of blood, Jack's hands. *There's no way,* Sarah shuddered. *There's no way I'm going back in there tonight.*

15

Sarah awoke early the next morning. She blinked rapidly, and when her eyes adjusted to the meager light she found herself on Celia's living room couch, a hand-knit blanket covering her.

She had lasted about twenty minutes standing outside trying to decide where she was going to sleep the night before. She considered sleeping in her car and even in the barn, but the hushed sounds of the night, the ripple of air through the fields, the heavy wing beats and screech of a barn owl drove her inside the house.

She had settled on the couch, not anticipating being able to sleep but grateful when it came. Someone must have laid the blanket over her sleeping form. A kind gesture made ominous because she'd slept so soundly through it.

Stiffly, Sarah swung her legs to the floor and ran a hand through the tangled mess of her hair. She longed for a shower but didn't want to wake anyone up with her movements. She wasn't looking forward to seeing Jack or Celia this morning. Had she overreacted last night? The contents of the case file still swirled around in her head. In the light of day she felt a little silly for being so afraid of Jack. He had never raised a hand to her, never had given her a reason to be physically frightened of him.

Following the scent of coffee, Sarah made her way to the darkened kitchen. Someone had set the automatic coffeemaker and she helped herself to a cup. Sarah checked her watch. It was just before 6:00 a.m. and she knew that the rest of the house would be rising soon.

Sarah had had every intention of making reservations to fly back home to Montana in the next few days, but all the revelations that she uncovered the past few days brought new questions. Sarah's eyes fell to her purse where the unheard audiotape waited. Maybe it would have some answers. Maybe it could provide a tidbit of information that in her mind would absolve Jack or at least help her understand him better. Or, she thought, it could give her even more reason to doubt him.

She needed somewhere private to listen to

the tape. She glanced out the kitchen window and the large barn that the night before had seemed so nefarious now stood benign in the early-morning sunshine. Taking her coffee cup and purse, she stepped outside. The cold air bit at her nose and she longed to go upstairs to grab a sweatshirt but didn't want to risk running into Jack just yet. Dew clung to the grass and her shoes quickly became damp as she walked toward the barn. She fumbled with the tarnished latch and pulled open the door. The interior of the barn was dim and cool, and Sarah rubbed her arms in hopes of warming up. An old barn jacket hung from a wall and Sarah lifted it from the rusty nail and pulled it on. The space was filled with a menagerie of old farm equipment and garden tools. On the walls hung sharp handsaws and corroded tools she couldn't put a name to. A pile of tractor tires and stacks of terra-cotta planters sat in a corner.

Sarah looked around for a place to sit that would provide her privacy as well as give her notice if someone entered the barn. She had no idea how she was going to explain why she was listening to an audiotape using a Walkman circa 1984. She spied a rickety wooden ladder that led up to the hayloft and she decided that would be her best bet.

Carefully she tested the first rung and when it held she slowly made her way upward.

Bits of straw dust plumed around her head and filled her nose, and she bit back a sneeze. The hayloft was empty except for a row of hay bales tied with twine lined up against one wall. The wide rafters above her reminded Sarah of the rib cage of some massive, ancient creature. Cup-shaped swallow nests made of grass, feathers and mud were tucked into crossbeams.

Sarah settled onto one of the bales, and after making sure she could see if anyone climbed up after her, she pulled out the audiotape and Walkman from her purse. She had no idea as to what she was going to hear. It could be another sheriff's department interview with Jack or with some other townsperson. It could be blank. She propped the earphones on her head and pressed Play.

Gilmore: *This is Deputy Sheriff Verne Gilmore. Nine thirty a.m. on June 1, 1985, interviewing, with parent permission, Celia Marie Parker, age fifteen. Celia, just answer my questions as thoroughly as you can. If you don't know the answer to a question just say so. Do you understand?*
Celia: *Yes.*

Sarah's interest was immediately piqued. Of course it made sense that Celia would be interviewed. She was Jack's girlfriend, had most likely spent some time at their home and in the presence of his parents. Gilmore's initial questions to Celia were basic. Her home address, her age, her relationship with Jack. Gilmore then asked Celia about her whereabouts on the day of the murder.

Celia: *I was at school.*

Gilmore: *Did you see Jack Tierney at school on the thirtieth?*

Celia: *Yes. I saw him in the hallway before our first class and then during second period. We have English together. Then we ate lunch in the cafeteria.*

Gilmore: *Was that the last time you saw Jack that day? In the cafeteria?*

Celia: *It was the last time I talked to him. But I saw him in the hallway later in the afternoon.*

Gilmore: *What time was that?*

Celia: *Um . . .it was after sixth period. So at about two o'clock.*

Gilmore: *Two? Are you sure?*

Celia: *I think so. Yes, I'm sure. It was after my anatomy class. I saw him in the hallway.*

Gilmore: *Did you speak to him?*

Celia: *No. He was too far away. I just saw*

him from the back.

Celia's voice shook slightly. Sarah could imagine the nervousness she was feeling. Fifteen years old and your boyfriend is suspected in the murder of his mother. Under the circumstances, Sarah thought that Celia was holding up well.

Gilmore: *Now, Celia, you know that's not true.*

Celia: *No. I saw him. I remember. He was walking down the hallway toward his last class.*

Gilmore: *Maybe you think you saw Jack. He wasn't in school that afternoon. We already know that. Jack already told us he left school around one forty-five.*

Gilmore's voice was gentle. Sarah could almost imagine him leaning forward in his chair toward Celia, his face kind, but his gray eyes sharp and missing nothing.

Celia: *But I did see him. I'm sure I did. I'm not lying.*

Gilmore: *Jack's your boyfriend. I know you want to help him and the best way you can do that is by telling me the truth. Do you understand?*

Celia: *Yes. I think I saw him.*

Gilmore: *But you're not sure?*

Celia: *No. I guess I could have the time wrong.*

Gilmore went on to ask Celia about Jack's relationship with his parents. Did she witness any arguments between them, did Jack ever talk about any fights or disagreements?

Celia: *No. They got along fine.*
The self-assurance had returned to Celia's voice.

Celia: *Jack wouldn't hurt his mom. I know he wouldn't.*
The interview went on in this vein for some time. Gilmore was asking pointed questions about the relationship between Jack and his parents, and Celia was responding that there was nothing wrong. Finally, with a sigh, Gilmore started to bring the questioning to a close.

Gilmore: *Did anything unusual happen that day? Anything at all that made you think twice?*
Celia: *That morning I saw Jack's dad. I was driving to school and I was running late.*
Gilmore: *You have your school permit to drive? What time was this?*
Celia: *Yes. I was driving on Highway 32 toward the high school. It was about eight o'clock.*
Gilmore: *Was he in his vehicle?*

Celia: *No. That's why it was so strange. He was walking along the side of the road. I waved to him. But he didn't see me. I slowed down to see if maybe he needed a ride, but when I looked in my rearview mirror, he was gone. It was like he just disappeared.*

Gilmore: *What do you mean? Did he get a ride with someone else or turn down a different road?*

Celia: *I figured someone else picked him up and took him home.*

Gilmore ended the interview with the direction for Celia to give him a call if she remembered anything else about that day.

Was Celia just a young girl in love trying to protect her boyfriend? She sounded entirely believable. Even her account of seeing Jack in the school hallway when he couldn't have been there, even by his own admission, sounded reasonable, an honest mistake. Would Celia have lied about seeing Jack's father that morning walking along the road? Sarah couldn't see why.

The final interview on the audio recording was Gilmore interviewing Dean. Again, Gilmore first asked all the basic questions and then got down to business. Dean's account of the day matched Jack's. He picked Jack up at the school around one forty-five; they were going to go hang out at the reservoir north of Penny Gate, but Jack was in a bad mood and ended up telling Dean to just take him home. He dropped Jack off in front of his house at about two and then left, going to the reservoir on his own.

Gilmore asked Dean if he was aware of any arguments between Jack and his parents. Dean grew quiet and Gilmore waited him out. The seconds ticked by. Finally Dean began to speak so quietly that Sarah had to turn up the volume on the tape player to hear him.

Dean: *Yeah, Jack and his parents fought. Like all of us do, I guess.*
Gilmore: *Sure, kids argue with folks all the time. What kinds of things did Jack and his folks fight about?*
Dean: (Inaudible.)
Gilmore: *Can you speak up so the tape recorder picks up what you are saying?*
Dean: *Celia. They fought about Celia Parker. They thought they were getting too serious.*
Gilmore: *Were they?*
Dean: *I don't know. I guess so. Jack talked about the two of them running away together sometimes.*
Gilmore: *Did their parents know about this?*
Dean: *I don't know.*
Gilmore: *Come on, Dean. You're Jack's*

cousin. If Jack's going to talk to anyone, it's you. Did his mom find out?

Dean: *Jack's mom knew.*

Gilmore: *How'd she find out?*

Dean: *I think she found some notes between Jack and Celia when she was cleaning Jack's room.*

Gilmore: *Were you there last week when they were arguing or did Jack tell you about it? Say yes or no, so the tape recorder picks up your voice. Were you there?*

Dean: *Yes.*

Gilmore: *When was this? What day?*

Dean: *I'm not sure. About a week ago, I guess.*

Gilmore: *How did she react? Was she angry?*

Dean: *They were yelling. But it was no big deal.*

Gilmore: *So they fought a lot? Jack and his mom?*

Dean: *Maybe. I don't know.*

Gilmore: *They argued. It was no big deal. What did Mrs. Tierney say?*

Dean: *She told him she didn't think that he should see Celia for a while. They were getting too serious. It was interfering with his schoolwork, his work on the farm.*

Gilmore: *What did Jack say?*

Dean: *He told her to mind her own business. To stay out of his room.*

Gilmore: *Those were his exact words?*

Dean: *He said to mind her own effing business and to stay out of his effing room.*

Gilmore: *I bet that didn't go over well.*

Dean: *No, she was mad. Told him not to talk that way in her house and he said, "Fine, I'll leave." She tried to stop him.*

Gilmore: *How did she do that? Did she physically try and keep him from leaving the house?*

Dean: *She grabbed his arm and Jack pulled away and we left.*

Gilmore: *That's it. Nothing else?*

Dean: *That's it.*

Gilmore: *Come on, Dean, what aren't you telling me? We've got pictures of the crime scene. Someone beat your aunt's head in, left her to die on the cellar floor. We need to figure out who did it.*

Dean: *It wasn't Jack.*

Gilmore: *How do you know that? You just got done telling me that they argued. She grabbed Jack's arm. Some of the bruises looked old. About a week old, I'd say. Maybe when Lydia grabbed Jack's arm he grabbed back.*

Dean: *He didn't mean to. He was just trying to get her off him.*

Gilmore: *So he hit her?*

Dean: *No, it was more like he pulled away. Hard. And she fell down. He didn't mean to* *hurt her.*

Gilmore: *She was hurt?*

Dean: *No. I mean, not really. She fell forward, on her hands. Like this. I think she hurt her wrist.*

Gilmore: *What did Jack do? Did he apologize? Did he help her up?*

Dean: (Inaudible.)

Gilmore: *Speak up.*

Dean: *No, he left. We left. She fell . . .*

Gilmore: *She fell or was knocked down?*

Dean: *He didn't mean to knock her down. It was an accident.*

The tape ended and Sarah remained sitting on the bale of hay, trying to make sense out of what Dean had said. Jack and Celia had talked about running away together? To where could two fifteen-year-olds possibly run? And Jack, accident or not, had knocked his mother to the ground and left her there.

Sarah stood and went to the large door that looked over the farm. She stared out at the blue sky that was just beginning to smudge with pearly gray that bled into the landscape. The cornfields were recently harvested, the hay fields newly shorn, the remaining stalks chewed down to jagged nubs, and large barrel-shaped bales of hay sat in wait across the pasture as if anticipating the upcoming winter. Big bluestem lined the ditches and black-eyed Susans bobbed their weighty yellow heads. Her eyes fell on the overgrown, weedy farmyard, the low-slung red barn, the tall silver silo. Such a beautiful landscape, Sarah thought, hiding such an ugly history.

Sarah looked across the fields and could see Hal's farmhouse and outbuildings. Just like Celia had mentioned, the two farms were close, about a fifteen-minute walk through the cornfield. She imagined a young Jack and Amy dashing through the corn, back and forth between home and their aunt and uncle's house.

She wondered if Jack had brought Celia here when they were teenagers, made love in the straw. Sarah could imagine what Celia was like as a teenager. Smart, beautiful and in love with Jack, the boy Celia thought she might marry.

"Sarah," came Jack's voice from down below. "Are you up there?"

Sarah wanted to stay hidden, didn't want to face Jack. Again, she had discovered more secrets. He and Celia had planned to run away together. His mother found out and a week later she was dead?

She wanted to get out of here. She wanted to leave Penny Gate that morning. She wasn't staying for the wake or the funeral.

She was going back home to her children, far away from Jack, far away from here.

"Sarah," Jack called again. Sarah took a deep breath. She would have to come down sometime.

"Coming," Sarah called back. She put the Walkman back into her purse and cautiously climbed down from the hayloft.

"What are you doing out here all by yourself?" Jack asked, examining her face carefully.

"I needed some space to think," she answered, pulling off the barn jacket and replacing it on the hook. "I'm leaving today," she said matter-of-factly. "The first flight out I can get."

"Sarah," Jack said, a note of desperation creeping into his voice.

"No. End of discussion. I'm leaving." She tried to step past him, but he slid in front of her, blocking her way. Her breath constricted in her throat. If she screamed would anyone hear her? Would anyone come running? The house seemed a thousand miles away. "Jack, let me by," she said firmly, trying to keep the panic from her voice.

"I know you're frustrated and confused. I don't want you to go, Sarah." He looked pleadingly into her eyes. "And if I could, I would leave with you, but we can't."

"What do you mean we can't?" Sarah asked in confusion, for a moment forgetting to be afraid.

"The sheriff just called. They found something at Hal's house during the search. Neither one of us is leaving Penny Gate. At least not for a few days."

"What did they find at Hal's?" Sarah asked, thinking about the bloodstains she'd seen on the steps.

"He won't say," Jack said, pushing open the barn door. "He wanted to make sure we both knew that we couldn't leave yet. He had a few more questions for us."

"Why would he have more questions for me?" Sarah asked heatedly. "Jesus, Jack, I did not sign up for this. All I want to do is go home."

"I know, I do, too," Jack said with a raspy voice. Sarah noticed that though freshly showered and shaved, exhaustion pulled Jack's face downward. Sarah wondered if he got any sleep the night before. "The wake's tonight. Will you come?" he asked, looking at her hopefully.

Sarah didn't answer right away. She cringed at the thought of being forced to stay in Penny Gate for even one more day. She was beyond caring what the townspeople would say if she didn't make an appearance, but she did care about Hal and knew he would be hurt and confused if she didn't attend the services. Besides, she needed to return the evidence box to Margaret and she was curious as to what the forensic team discovered at Hal's home. "I'll go," she said, walking toward the house. "But I want you to know I'm doing this for Hal and for Julia. You lied to me one too many times, Jack."

Jack opened up his mouth to protest, but Sarah moved ahead of him toward the house and his words didn't quite reach her ears. Sarah stepped into the house to find Dean and Hal sitting at the kitchen table and Celia washing dishes in the sink.

"Good morning," Hal said, pulling out a chair for Sarah to join them. He was dressed for the day, but his pants were wrinkled and his shirt was untucked; dark circles ringed his eyes. A plate of scrambled eggs sat in front of him, untouched. In just the four days they had been there, he appeared to have lost weight.

Sarah rested her hands on the back of the chair but didn't sit. She felt Celia's covert glances on her back and Sarah wondered if Jack had told her about their argument the night before. "Jack said that the sheriff found something in the search of the house.

Do you have any idea what it is?"

"No idea," Dean said, dropping his silver-ware onto his plate with a loud clatter. "He won't tell us anything more than Dad can't go back into the house yet. They're still processing the scene."

Jack came into the house and leaned against the kitchen counter. "I know it's frustrating, but he'd tell us if he could. Any evidence that can help clear Amy is a good thing."

Dean glowered into his coffee cup.

Celia turned from the kitchen sink and laid one hand on Dean's shoulder as if to calm him. "Julia is being transported back to the funeral home this morning. Someone should be there to greet them."

"I'm meeting with Amy's lawyer at eight," Jack said. Sarah avoided meeting his eyes. She had no intention of going anywhere with him.

"We don't have time for this." Dean frowned.

"Don't have time for what?" Jack challenged. "Don't have time to make sure that my sister, your cousin, has a good lawyer?"

"Hey, man." Dean pushed back from the table, causing Celia to stumble backward. "We're supposed to be planning my mother's funeral. I can't be worrying about Amy right now."

Jack took a step toward Dean. "You know I feel terrible about Julia. I don't know who did this to her, but I know it wasn't Amy. She loved Julia."

Dean stood and Sarah held her breath. "What? Loved her enough to knock her down a flight of stairs?" The room seemed to grow smaller suddenly. Sarah looked to Hal in hopes that he would tell them to knock it off, but he was poking at his eggs with a fork, lost in his own thoughts.

"Dean," Celia warned and reached for his arm, and he shook her off.

"You want to know what I think, Dean?" Jack stepped close. Dean's mouth twitched nervously but he didn't retreat. "I think my sister is in trouble. I think she's sad, scared and totally messed up." Jack jabbed a finger into Dean's chest with each word. "And I think Julia would want us to do whatever we could to make sure she's okay."

Dean knocked Jack's hand away, his face flushed and twisted with anger. "I've spent the past twenty years making sure Amy was okay. Where the hell have you been?"

"Stop," Hal said softly. "Just stop," he repeated more loudly. Glowering, Dean and Jack shifted away from each other. "Julia wouldn't want any of this, I'm sure of that."

"Hal's right," Celia said soothingly. "More than ever, we all need to stick together. It's the only way we're going to get through the next few days. Dean, why don't you and Hal go to the funeral home so someone is there when they come back with Julia, and I'll go with Jack and Sarah to see Amy's attorney."

"Of course you will." Dean glared at Celia.

"What?" Celia challenged. "Do you want to go with Jack?" Dean pressed his lips together but didn't answer.

"I don't think we need three of us to go see the attorney," Sarah said, trying to keep the irritation from her voice. Somehow Celia always seemed to be able to insert herself in Jack's path. "Jack, you and Celia go on ahead. I'll catch up with you later. Excuse me," she said, needing to escape, not caring that her exit was abrupt. The tension and anger in the room was overpowering.

Sarah went upstairs and locked herself in the bathroom, grateful for the quiet. Was Dean jealous of Jack and Celia? In all of this Sarah hadn't thought of Dean and how he felt about Jack and Celia's past relationship. How would it feel to marry your cousin's girlfriend, the girl Jack had plotted to run away with? Did he feel second best? Was he now comparing himself to his younger, fitter, more handsome cousin? Sarah could relate. Celia with her ethereal beauty. She exuded confidence and an elegance that Sarah wished to have. And if Sarah hadn't witnessed that momentary lapse of anger when Celia had struck Dean, she would have thought she was the perfect wife.

Sarah stepped into the shower, turned on the tap and let the steady stream of hot water pour over her. She missed her girls, she missed her home and she missed her own large, beautifully tiled shower that Jack had spent hours constructing for her fortieth birthday gift. Now she stood beneath the meager spray of Celia's showerhead until the hot water ran out.

She took her time dressing and as she was pulling her sweater over her head she caught sight of the closet door, slightly ajar. She thought of the shoe box with Jack's name written on it on the closet's upper shelf. Moving quickly, she pressed the button lock on the bedroom door. She opened the closet door, her eyes flying to the shelf. It was empty. Sarah pushed aside the heavy winter coats and checked the floor. Nothing. Someone had removed the box. Jack. She was sure of it. Had he known that she had come across the box the other day? Was there something inside it that he didn't want her to see? Sarah shut the door in disgust. She quickly riffled through drawers filled with what looked like Celia's old clothes and a tangle of discarded jewelry. No shoe box.

Reluctantly she went downstairs and was glad to see that no one was there, but annoyed that Jack hadn't bothered to say goodbye. He had scrawled a note in his cramped handwriting explaining that he and Celia were going to see Amy's attorney and then would go to the funeral home so they could be there when Julia's remains arrived and finish up with the final funeral arrangements. A sudden surge of alarm flooded through her. The evidence box. She had left it in the trunk of the car. What if Jack and Celia had taken the rental car to see the attorney and for some reason opened the trunk? How would she explain how she came into possession of the documents?

She ran outside and with relief saw that the car was still where she parked it. She had to return the box to Margaret but wasn't quite ready to. She felt that if she just had more time with the documents she could figure out what had happened, understand just why Jack had hidden so much from her. She dug through her purse in search of her keys, opened the trunk and peeked inside just to make sure the box was where she'd left it. She may not be able to hold on to the original documents any longer, but she could make copies of everything in the box if she hurried. Jack and the others would return from the funeral home soon to get ready for the wake, and she didn't want to have to explain her absence.

She looked up the directions to the public library, climbed into the car and sped away from the farm, kicking up bits of gravel and dust, and leaving behind an opaque cloud in her rearview mirror.

Twenty minutes later she turned onto Franklin Street, a wide street lined with mature maples with leaves that had just begun to turn the jeweled tones of fall. By chance she passed the funeral home, a three-story structure painted white and trimmed in black. Such a large building for such a small town. She recognized Hal's truck and pulled directly behind the battered white Ford. Sarah took a deep breath as the unmistakable silhouette of a low-slung black hearse crept slowly past. All of Sarah's self-righteous anger trickled away, leaving her ashamed. There was a real person in that hearse. A wife, a mother, a beloved aunt. Sarah thought back to her own father's funeral. At the time nothing else mattered, no one else mattered. She just wanted her father back, to see his face, to hear his voice one more time.

Sarah thought of the document she had spied in Gilmore's office that mentioned the poison. If sodium fluoroacetate was the true cause of Julia's death, how would Amy get access to it? It was a tightly regulated poison.

She pulled into a parking spot in front of the Sawyer County Public Library and looked through her purse for the thumb drive that she used to back up her Dear Astrid correspondence. If the library was up to twenty-first century standards, it would have a copy machine where she could scan all the documents to her thumb drive.

Unlike many of the buildings in Penny Gate, the library appeared to have been constructed in just the past few years. She stepped from the car and popped the trunk. Careful to make sure that the writing on the side of the cardboard box was hidden, Sarah entered the front entrance. She approached the circulation desk where a young man was bent over a stack of books.

"Hello," Sarah said, and the librarian looked up. He couldn't have been much older than twenty-five but wore a name tag that said Max Malik, Library Director.

"Good morning," Max said warmly. "What can I help you with?"

"Do you have a copy machine where I can scan these papers and transfer them to a thumb drive?" Sarah asked.

Max came out from behind his workstation. "That looks heavy," he said, nodding toward the box. "Can I carry it for you?"

"No, I've got it," Sarah said, pulling the box more tightly to her. Max led her to the copy machine, showed her how to scan a document and save it to her thumb drive, and then how to delete the document from the copy machine's memory.

"That's a big box," Max observed. "What are you copying?"

"My aunt recently passed away," she said, which was technically true. "These are documents related to her estate." She thanked him for his help and waited until he had returned to his desk before opening the box. It was slow, monotonous work. One by one, she pulled each item from the box, made a copy and then returned it to its original place. Periodically, another library patron would need to use the copy machine, so Sarah would step aside and try to wait patiently until they were finished, all the while keeping her eye on the front entrance, sure that Jack or Dean or even the sheriff would walk through the doors.

Three hours and about ninety dollars later, Sarah had scanned all the documents, including the photos and the transcripts of the audiotapes that Margaret had given her. She returned quickly to her car and was just placing the box back into the trunk when a sheriff's car drove slowly past. Sarah made eye contact with the driver, the same deputy who had taken Amy into custody. Sarah gave a half wave and slid the box the rest of the way into the trunk. Had the deputy seen what she was loading into the trunk? Had he been able to read Lydia Tierney's name written on the side of the box?

Sarah climbed into the car and closed her eyes, half expecting that he would turn his vehicle around and order her to open the trunk. When she was certain that he wasn't going to return, she doubled-checked that the thumb drive was tucked safely inside her purse and then pulled out her phone to call Margaret.

"I've been trying to call you," Margaret said by way of greeting. "Where are you?"

Sarah debated whether or not to tell Margaret that she had just scanned the contents of the evidence box that Margaret had stolen for her, but decided against it. She didn't want to cause Margaret any more worry than she already had. "I'm in town," she said vaguely. "What's going on?"

Margaret lowered her voice to a low whisper. "I'm at work, so I can't talk long. Something big has happened at Hal's."

"Jack said that the sheriff's department wasn't finished with their search and that we weren't allowed to go back there just yet. Do you know what's going on?" Sarah glanced at the clock on the console. It was twelve thirty and the wake was set to begin at three. She needed to get back to Celia's house and change.

"No. The sheriff's not saying, but I do know that they called in a state forensic team from Des Moines. They're on the way over there now."

"Why would they need a different forensic team?" Sarah asked, suddenly on alert. They must have found something more than the few droplets of blood that Sarah had seen on the steps. Did it have something to do with the fluoroacetate? "Margaret, do you have access to Julia's case file? I know the medical examiner released her remains back to the family. Is there any mention of the official cause of death?"

Margaret was quiet on the other end.

"I'm sorry," Sarah said in a rush. "I

shouldn't be asking you to do more than you already have."

"No, no. I want to help, I really do," she said, as if trying to convince herself. "Let me think a second. Hold on a minute," Margaret said. "I'll see what I can find out."

Sarah heard Margaret set the receiver down and the click of a keyboard. Had they found the poison at the farm? That wouldn't make sense if Amy had been the one to kill Julia. Wouldn't the poison have been found at her house? Jack had made it sound as if Gilmore wouldn't allow them to leave Penny Gate because of what they had found at Hal's farm.

"Are you still there?" Margaret asked breathlessly a few minutes later.

"I'm here," Sarah said.

"I can't believe it," Margaret said.

"What?" Sarah asked, urging her on but already sure she knew the answer. "What does it say?"

"It was poison. I can't believe Amy would do that."

"The sheriff is sure that it was Amy, then?" Sarah asked, wondering how Jack's meeting with Amy's attorney had gone.

"He must," Margaret said. "He arrested her. She was arraigned this morning. No bail."

That meant that Amy would miss Julia's wake and funeral. As appalling as it was to think that someone would have beaten Julia at the top of the stairs in her own home, it seemed even more horrific that someone would deliberately poison her while she was lying in a hospital bed.

"I've got to go," Margaret said in a hushed tone as if someone had come within earshot of her side of the conversation. "I'll see you at the wake tonight."

Sarah disconnected and began the drive back to Celia's, trying to reconcile the fact that Amy had somehow poisoned Julia while they were at the hospital. Still, it didn't quite make sense. No one, it seemed, except Dean, could provide a reason that Amy would kill her aunt. An argument over Amy's drinking and lost job just didn't seem like it would lead to such violence, but people were killed over much less all the time. Stranger yet was the idea that Amy would go to such lengths to poison Julia. Was Amy afraid that Julia would wake up and identify her as the one who attacked her?

By the time she arrived back at Celia's, the men had returned from making final preparations for the funeral, had changed into their suits and ties, and were just getting ready to leave for the wake. Sarah went upstairs to change and when she came back downstairs, Celia was rushing around, putting together a variety of salads for the funeral dinner.

"Do you want to ride with us?" Jack asked Sarah hopefully. He looked almost boyish or maybe just a little bit lost in his ill-fitting suit and wearing the bewildered expression of someone who had been blindsided by tragedy or had been caught in one too many lies.

Dean looked at his watch impatiently while Hal struggled to button his suit coat across his wide belly with his thick fingers.

"I was hoping Sarah could help me with a few things around here," Celia interjected. "I've got to finish putting together this potato salad for tomorrow and get this cake out of the oven."

"I can stay and help." Sarah reached for the apron that Celia held out for her.

"Okay," Jack answered. Did he look disappointed? Sarah wasn't sure. Maybe he was just nervous that Sarah and Celia would be alone for a length of time. Plenty of opportunity for Sarah to quiz Celia about his past. Maybe Jack didn't want Celia to spill any more of his secrets.

"We'll be there by two forty-five, I promise," Celia said, giving each man a tight hug in turn before they headed out the door.

"Can you mix together the potato salad?" Celia asked, pulling a jar of mayonnaise from the refrigerator and setting it on the counter.

"I thought the Women's Rosary Guild was in charge of the food?" Sarah asked as she opened the lid and stirred the dressing into a bowl of boiled potatoes.

"They are," Celia said, reaching into a cupboard for powdered sugar. "But I like to cook and it helps me keep my mind off things." Tears filled her large eyes. "Except that cooking reminds me of Julia. She loved to help out this way. Julia was always the first one to volunteer to make a salad or bake a cake for a funeral dinner. I remember when Lydia died — I swear, Julia made five pies. Can you believe that? Her sister-in-law is just murdered, her brother accused, and she makes all those pies." Celia went to the oven and turned on the light to peek inside.

"You know," Sarah said as she added mustard to the bowl, "this is the first time someone has actually spoken out loud about what happened to Jack's mom and dad. Why is that?"

Celia twisted a hand towel embroidered with fall leaves between her fingers. "I guess

it's just too hard. You know Hal's genera-
tion — stoic and no-nonsense. Bad things
happen and you need to just put your head
down and forge onward."

Sarah thought about this and had to agree
it was true. Her own parents had a similar
philosophy of life.

"Is it hard living here?" Sarah asked,
changing the subject. "With all that happened, doesn't it ever scare you?"

Celia slid the bowl onto the base of the
electric mixer and turned it on. "You mean
is the house cursed?" she asked over the
whir of the beaters.

"Of course not," Sarah said, and felt her
cheeks redden. "It just must be very strange
living in the home where a murder occurred, especially since you know the family."

"Not really. When Dean and I decided to
move in, we vowed to make new memories
here. Happier ones." She straightened and
glanced at the basement door.

Sarah followed her gaze. She couldn't
imagine living in a home where a murder
took place. "Do you use the basement? I
mean, that's where it happened, right?"

"Actually, we don't go down there much,"
Celia explained. "Nothing but dust, cobwebs and a few boxes of junk. We're just

grateful that Julia let us rent it from her."

"Rent it? Why?"

"Yes, the house has been in the Tierney family forever. When Lydia died and John disappeared, it went to Julia. We've rented the house for the past eighteen years and farmed the land. It's worked out perfectly for us."

Celia walked over to Sarah's side. "Looks good," she said, eyeing the potato salad. She pulled a roll of plastic wrap from a drawer and covered the bowl. "God, I remember that day. It was horrible. My mom came home from work sobbing. When she finally told me what happened I came right here. They wouldn't let me come in. They wouldn't tell me anything. It was an hour before someone told me Jack and Amy were okay, but they wouldn't let me see them."

"When did you finally get to talk to him?" Sarah moved to the sink to wash her hands.

"Not until the next afternoon. He looked terrible." Celia shook her head at the memory. "And he was never the same again."

"What do you mean?" Sarah asked, wiping her hands on a dish towel that Celia had handed to her.

"Before he had been so happy-go-lucky, so funny. And after . . . well, he wasn't. He wouldn't talk to anyone. Went to school, then came home and stayed up in his bed-room."

From what Sarah read in the case file, Jack wasn't particularly a happy-go-lucky kid. On the contrary, he was described as sullen and angry. Was he so different around Celia? Sarah looked down at the dish towel, hand embroidered with leaves of brown, red and yellow thread. Her mind flashed to the image of Lydia lying on the cement floor with a bloody dish towel covering her eyes. "Lydia embroidered that," Celia said. "Pretty, isn't it?" Sarah nodded. "I've got a whole drawer of them, if you'd like to take back a few with you."

"That'd be nice," Sarah managed to say.

Celia looked up at the clock on the wall. Two fifteen. "I should go and get dressed. Will you be all right if I head upstairs for a bit?"

"Go right ahead," Sarah assured her.

Sarah rinsed the dirty dishes in the sink and placed them carefully in the dishwasher, wiped down the counter and looked around the kitchen to see if there was anything else she could tidy up. She looked out the window over the sink, imagining Lydia on that day, doing the same. What was she thinking that morning when she awoke? Did she make a mental list of all the things she had to do that day? Did she stare out this window when she washed the breakfast dishes? Sarah knew from Jack's taped interview that Lydia kissed her children goodbye before they left for school, told them she loved them. How sad, Sarah thought, that she had no idea that would be the last time she saw her children.

Sarah turned from the window and faced the basement door. Slowly she walked toward it, reached up to slide the lock open. She thought back to the crime-scene photos and the picture that showed a freezer standing open. Was Lydia going down there to get a pound of frozen hamburger or a package of pork chops for dinner?

Sarah cocked her head, listening to see if Celia was coming back down the stairs. All was quiet. She put her hand on the doorknob and twisted. The wood frame was warped and she pulled at the knob, but the door wouldn't move. Sarah put one hand on the door frame, planted her feet and gave the knob a tug and it popped open, causing her to stumble backward a few steps before she righted herself.

She kicked off her high heels and slowly approached the top of the steep wooden steps that disappeared into darkness. Sarah felt around for a switch and when she flipped on the light she was plunged back in time. She saw the same rickety handrail, the same wooden steps lined with roof shingles to make them less slippery. The same light-bulb swung from the ceiling.

Sarah took one step downward. She imagined Lydia taking the same step. Was she singing a song? Humming a tune? Or was she hesitant, just like Sarah was now? A feeling of dread slowed her steps. Again, she listened for Celia. How would she explain her descent into the basement? She had no excuse beyond morbid curiosity.

She alighted from the final step and the cement floor was cold and smooth beneath her bare feet. She scanned the room quickly, her eyes landing on a large deep freezer. The same one in the crime-scene photos? She felt a sudden urge to open the freezer, to peer inside just as Lydia had done years before. She took a tentative step forward.

Against one wall were shelves lined with dozens of jars of homemade preserves and pickles. Sarah ran one finger over the lid of one glass jar and came away with a thick layer of dust. She wondered if Celia had done all the jarring or if they were relics of the life Lydia had left behind. In a far corner of the large room were a stack of boxes and an array of what looked to be old farm and garden equipment.

Sarah felt a light tickle across her knuckles and she glanced down just as she saw the spindly legs of a daddy longlegs skitter across her hand and she frantically shook it away. Sarah's elbow struck one of the glass jars and it shattered against the concrete floor. Sarah leaped back to avoid the splatter and the acrid smell of pickle juice filled the air. Quickly, she began picking up the shards of glass and deposited them into a small garbage can next to the freezer. Using an oily rag left on a bottom shelf she wiped up as much of the pickle juice that she could. As she scrubbed she thought of Lydia and the puddle of blood that lay beneath her broken skull. In the dim light, Sarah's eyes swept the floor, searching for some remnant that Lydia had died here. Was that dark spot over there a stain where the blood pooled? Someone must have cleaned it up. Was it someone from the sheriff's department or perhaps a family member? Was it Julia?

"Sarah?" Celia called from somewhere within the house.

Sarah rose to her feet, tossed the rag into the garbage can and quickly hurried up the steps and back into the kitchen; she closed the basement door and slid the lock into place as quietly as possible. She stepped back into her high heels and moved to the sink where she ran her hands beneath the tap, trying to wash away the smell of dill and vinegar from her skin and wondered if Lydia's killer did the same? Had they stood in this exact spot, trying to scour away the bright red blood and its coppery cloying scent?

"Sarah?" Celia called again, this time from the living room. "Are you ready to go?"

"Ready," Sarah called back, trying to keep her voice light and casual, her eyes darting toward the cellar door. Silly, she told herself. There was nothing down there anymore. Nothing to be afraid of.

16

Sarah and Celia drove separately, Sarah in the rental and Celia in Hal's truck. Hal was hopeful that the sheriff would be finished searching the property and he would be able to go back home after the funeral. They arrived at the funeral home, a large Victorian structure, half an hour early, but already the townspeople of Penny Gate and the surrounding area were gathering. Sarah spotted Jack and Dean standing outside talking to a small group of mourners. As soon as Jack saw her, he came to her side.

"I'm so glad you're here," he whispered. He looked terrible. His eyes were bloodshot and his skin was sallow. The clothes that Sarah had bought for him to wear didn't quite fit. The shirt cuffs were too long and the hem of his pants hung to the floor, the fabric pooling around his ankles.

"Did you get a chance to talk to Amy today?" she asked.

"Just for a few minutes." He adjusted the knot in his tie. "She insists she has no idea where the bale hook came from, says that Dean was the one who brought it over in a box filled with other things."

"Do you believe her?" Sarah asked, resisting the urge to help him with his tie. A small gesture she would have gladly performed just a few days before. Now she could barely look at him.

"I want to," he said as they entered through a side door where the funeral director was waiting to escort them to the viewing room. "But right now everything's pointing to Amy." Situated throughout the room were dozens of pictures of Julia. Pictures of her as a baby in her baptism dress, as a child in a First Communion dress, as a young woman in her wedding dress. There were pictures of Julia with Hal and Dean through the years. Jack paused in front of one of the pictures and lingered for a long moment.

Once he moved on Sarah lagged behind to get a better look. It was a picture of Julia with Jack's mother, their arms linked, beaming smiles on their faces. It looked as if it was taken at a family celebration, a birthday or graduation, maybe. They looked content, as if all was perfect in their worlds. Unexpectedly, there were also several pictures of Amy with Julia. Generous, Sarah thought, since Amy was sitting in jail for Julia's murder. She was sure that Celia had a hand in making sure that Amy was included.

The casket Hal had chosen for Julia was a simple stained cherrywood casket, hand-made in Dubuque. He had chosen a closed casket for Julia due to her many injuries. "I just wish I could see her one more time," he kept saying over and over to anyone who would listen.

"I'm sure the funeral director can arrange that for you," Sarah said, trying to console him. "I bet they do that all the time."

The funeral director lined them just to the right of the casket that was surrounded with dozens of bouquets of flowers sent by friends and family: irises and roses, mums, ferns, potted plants and a small tree to plant in Julia's memory.

Soon Sarah was shaking hands and accepting hugs from complete strangers who all had one thing in common: they had adored Julia. *Such a sweet soul,* one elderly woman said, holding on to Sarah's hand for a long time. *A good, good woman,* said another.

The line seemed to stretch on forever. It extended the length of the large viewing room and snaked out a door and around a corner. Sarah felt a hand on her arm and she turned back to see Margaret, dressed all in black and accompanied by a woman with the same stalwart stature and red hair, who Sarah assumed was Margaret's mother.

"Jack Tierney," Margaret said softly. "Is that really you? I haven't seen you since you were a boy."

Jack squinted, trying to put a name to the face. "It's Margaret McDowell," Margaret said. "Now Margaret Dooley. You don't remember me? I babysat you and Amy."

"Of course," Jack said, "Of course I remember you and your mother." Jack turned to the elderly woman and embraced her. "Vivienne, it's so good to see you again."

"Jack." The woman's lips trembled with emotion. "I miss your mother every single day."

"I miss her, too." Jack blinked back the moisture that was collecting in his eyes. "Vivienne, Margaret, this is my wife, Sarah," he said, clearing his throat.

Sarah extended her hand in greeting. "Margaret and I met the other day. Good to see you again," she said, trying to keep her voice casual.

"I've got kids now," Jack said, pulling out

his phone. "Elizabeth and Emma. They're freshmen in college." Jack showed her his screensaver, a picture of the girls standing on the shore of Larkspur Lake.

"Beautiful." Vivienne smiled. "They have Lydia's smile, I think."

Sarah stepped out of line to get a bottle of water from the small room where the family kept their personal belongings. Margaret followed close behind.

"I have the box in the trunk of the car," Sarah said quietly, unscrewing the lid from the bottle of water and taking a drink.

"I can get it after the wake," Margaret said.

"I've just got to figure out a way to get away from the others," Sarah said, taking a sip of her water.

"You could tell them you offered to help me take some of the food for the funeral over to the church basement," Margaret suggested.

"That should work," Sarah said, glad to know that she would be getting rid of the box soon. "Did you hear anything more about what's going on at Hal's?"

"Just that the crime-scene team from Des Moines brought a dog with them," Margaret explained.

"A dog? Like a drug dog or search dog?"

Sarah asked, taken aback. "Why would they do that?"

Margaret shrugged. "I don't know. The sheriff didn't say. He's been trying to keep everything hush-hush so the newspaper doesn't find out."

Vivienne and Jack were still talking when Sarah stepped back into the receiving line. "So good to see you, Jackie," Vivienne said, placing a gnarled hand on his cheek.

Jack smiled. "No one's called me that in years."

Vivienne turned to Sarah. "Nice to meet you, Sarah. You take good care of this boy."

Sarah nodded but couldn't bring herself to answer out loud.

Margaret and Vivienne reiterated their condolences and moved onward with the promise of seeing them at the funeral the next day.

Twenty minutes later, just as Hal was shaking hands with the last guest, Sheriff Gilmore walked in with a deputy that Sarah didn't recognize.

"Hal, boys, I can't say how sorry I am about Julia. She was a fine woman."

Hal nodded, his eyes welling with tears. "We appreciate that, Verne. Thank you."

"Everything finally squared away at Dad's?" Dean asked stiffly. "Did you get what you needed?"

"Well, that's one of the reasons we're here."

"Can we go back to the house?" Hal asked. "Can't you talk to us there?"

"That just isn't going to be possible right now." Gilmore's face was unreadable, but Sarah sensed that something was terribly wrong. Why else would the sheriff show up at the funeral home on the eve of Julia's funeral?

"Let's take a seat," Gilmore suggested.

"Just spit it out," Dean said impatiently. "Can't you see how tired my dad is?"

Celia put a hand on Dean's arm. "Shhh," she chided. "Let's sit down. Your dad has been standing for over five hours."

Gilmore sat and cleared his throat. "In the course of searching your house, Hal, we made an unexpected discovery."

"What kind of discovery?" Dean asked shortly.

"First of all, you know that we found items in Amy's house that were suspicious. Initial findings from the medical examiner confirm that the blood on the bale hook is the same blood type as Julia's. That and some other evidence led us to arrest Amy. She was arraigned this morning."

"What other kind of evidence?" Dean asked.

"We did a luminol test for blood on the steps," Gilmore began.

"But we know that Julia fell down the stairs. Doesn't it make sense that there'd be blood?" Celia rose from her seat and stood behind Hal, placing a hand on his shoulder.

"We found some on the steps, of course, but that's not where we found the concentration of blood," Gilmore went on. "It appears that Julia was attacked at the top of the stairs. The luminol test showed significant blood splatter and that someone tried to clean it up. The medical examiner also gave an official cause in Julia's death."

Sarah glanced around at the small group. Everyone looked expectantly at the sheriff. Only she seemed to know what was coming next.

"Julia was poisoned at the hospital in the hours around the time of her death," Gilmore said. He watched their faces carefully and Sarah made a point to widen her eyes as if she was learning this information for the first time.

"Poisoned?" Hal asked in disbelief. "You think Amy poisoned Julia?"

"Of course he does," Dean said angrily. "Who else could it have been?"

"I can't believe this," Jack snapped. He leaned forward in his chair toward Dean. "Amy loved your mom. There's got to be another explanation."

"Like what?" Dean asked. "A bale hook with my mom's blood on it was found in Amy's house. I don't need any more proof that she did it."

"That's funny, Dean," Jack said, his voice tight with anger, "because Amy thinks *you* did it and planted the bale hook in her house."

Dean stood, looming largely over Jack.

"Sit down, Dean," the sheriff said sharply, and Dean halfheartedly complied. "Hal, right now, it looks like Amy bludgeoned and poisoned Julia. We don't know why yet, but we are going to do our best to find out.

"And I'm afraid I have more bad news." Gilmore pressed his lips together grimly. "We didn't just find drops of blood on the stairs. We found remains. In an old cistern. We found a body."

Gilmore was met with stunned silence.

"A body?" Celia was the first to speak. "Whose body?" she asked incredulously.

"That we don't know. It's too soon to tell. It could have been there for quite a while or placed there recently."

"What does that mean?" Dean pressed.

"A week, a month, a year? That old cistern hasn't been used for years and years," Dean continued. "Since before I was born. I remember moving the cover when I was a kid and my mom giving me hell for it."

"It's an old farm," Hal added. "Julia and I moved there nearly fifty years ago and it was a century farm then. Bought it in an auction."

Gilmore nodded. "The old Larsen farm."

"Any Larsens around anymore?" Jack asked.

"Not for years," Celia said. "Remember that nutty old lady who lived on Grover Street. She was a Larsen."

"Vera Larsen," Hal recalled. "That's who lived there before we did. Died back in '69 or '70. Had to been a hundred years old."

"When you say remains, do you mean a body, bones, what?" Dean asked.

"I'm not able to share that just yet," Gilmore said.

"Is Hal in danger? I mean, could whoever killed Julia have killed the person you found?" Jack asked.

"I don't have any reason to believe Hal's safety is at risk. We turned the remains and other items over to a forensic specialist who will try and figure out when and how the person died. Hopefully she'll be able to identify who it was."

"What other items?" Jack asked.

"Looks like some clothing. We're still hoping to find some form of identification."

"Do the remains belong to a man or a woman?" Sarah asked. "Do you think it has anything to do with what happened to Julia?"

"That question certainly comes to mind, but we just don't know. We didn't want to get too close and disturb the remains. We don't know if it's male or female. We'll leave that to the experts," the sheriff said.

Sarah had been watching him carefully. Though he portrayed himself as a reluctant interloper delivering more bad news to the family, she also knew that the timing was calculated. Gilmore wanted to share the news of the body on the property when they were at their most vulnerable and he could gauge their reactions.

She also knew Gilmore was being less than forthcoming. He most likely knew exactly what was inside that cistern along with bones.

"This couldn't wait?" Celia spoke up. "You had to come to the funeral home? This time should be about the family and remembering Julia."

Jack slid Celia a grateful look.

"Just trying to do my job, Celia. We'll try to be respectful of your privacy the next day or so, but we will need to talk with each one of you."

Sarah wasn't ready to let the coincidence of Julia's murder and the discovery in the cistern go just yet. "What made you think to look in the cistern?" she asked. "It's a long way from where Julia fell."

"I don't have any more information to share with you at this time." Gilmore looked levelly at Sarah. "But if you think you might know something that might be helpful, you know how to get ahold of me."

Gilmore rose and stood next to Hal. "Hal, I'm so sorry about all this. Celia is right, you should be able to lay Julia to rest in peace, but we haven't had a murder in Penny Gate in twenty-five years. Now in the past week we have Julia's murder and possibly another."

Jack's face was difficult to read, but Sarah thought she caught a wisp of something. Worry, guilt?

"When can I go home?" Hal asked. He looked up beseechingly at Gilmore. "I really just want to go home."

Gilmore looked down at Hal for a long moment and then spoke. "That's not possible right now. The property is a crime scene and will remain so at least until tomorrow. Stay away until I give you the okay to return. Again, sorry to bother you folks tonight," Gilmore said, "but I wanted you to hear the current updates directly from me."

In turn, Gilmore shook everyone's hand, including Sarah's. The look he gave her was implacable, but still she felt he was trying to communicate something to her through the tight grip he had on her hand. *Be careful,* it seemed to say. Or maybe she was projecting her own fears.

"What the hell is going on?" Dean asked once the sheriff and his deputies had left. "A body?" Dean turned to his father. "Do you have any idea who could have been buried there?"

Hal shook his head numbly.

"We should get you back to the house," Celia said with concern. "Hal, you have to get some rest."

Sarah was struck by Jack's gentle ministrations as he helped his uncle to his feet. "Try not to think about what's happening back at the house right now," he told him. "Look at all the people who came tonight. I think the whole town showed up."

As a group they moved outside and all Sarah could think about were the remains found at Hal's farm. She had so many questions, but the sheriff had cut her off, not willing or able to give them any details.

"Sarah," a voice said from behind them, and Sarah and Jack turned to see Margaret sitting on a bench, brightened by a streetlamp just outside the funeral home.

"I told Margaret I'd help her take the desserts she made to the church for the funeral tomorrow," Sarah explained.

"I really appreciate Sarah's help with this," Margaret said. "My mom was going to, but her back's been bothering her."

"Can I help?" Jack offered.

"No, I can do it," Sarah said. "You should go with Hal. He seems really shaken up."

"Okay, see you back at Dean's." Jack leaned in to kiss Sarah, but she turned her face and his lips landed near her ear. He tried to mask his hurt at her rebuff with a smile directed at Margaret. "Thanks for helping with the funeral dinner. I know it's a big job."

"Glad to do it," Margaret assured him.

Sarah watched as her husband climbed into the truck next to Hal. He didn't even glance back at her.

"What was that all about?" Margaret asked, seeing the strained interaction between Sarah and Jack.

"It's a long story." Sarah dropped down onto the bench, the cold from the wrought iron seeping through her dress. "And besides, all hell just broke loose. Did you know they found a *dead body* at Hal's?"

Margaret's eyes widened. "A body? Who is it?"

"They don't know or aren't saying."

Sarah followed Margaret to Saint Finnian's. When they arrived, Margaret pulled out a key to the church and together they unloaded the desserts that the Women's Rosary Guild had made for Julia's funeral dinner.

Back in the parking lot, Sarah opened the trunk of her car and the two of them stared down at the box.

"So did you get all your questions answered?" Margaret asked.

Sarah shook her head. "Somehow I've ended up with more questions than answers. I don't know what it is. But there's something that just doesn't seem right."

"Do you want me to take a look? Maybe I'll notice something you missed."

"Sure," Sarah said, shining her cell phone light over the box.

Margaret removed the lid, and thumbed through the contents until she came across the stack of photos. Slowly, she began flicking through the pictures, examining each carefully. "I'm just not sure what I should be looking for."

"Wait," Sarah said. "What's that?" Together they looked at the photograph of Lydia on her back, one arm outstretched, a bloody cloth covering her eyes, her mouth contorted into a frozen scream.

Revulsion skittered across Margaret's face but she continued to inspect the photo. "What is it? What do you see?"

"What does that look like to you?" Sarah pointed to a shiny glint of silver on the floor next to Lydia.

"Maybe a coin or a piece of jewelry." She looked up at Sarah. "Is that what you're thinking?"

"Yes. It's a little hard to see, but it looks like a bracelet charm to me."

Sarah turned the photo and took note of the number written on the back. "I'm not sure yet. But the other day at the hospital, Amy was carrying around a silver charm similar to this."

Margaret shrugged. "Maybe it belonged to her mother, a kind of memento."

"No." Sarah shook her head. "Amy said she found it on the floor next to Julia when she discovered her at the bottom of the stairs. She thought it belonged to her."

"That is a little odd," Margaret conceded, "but a lot of people wear bracelets with charms on them."

"It's more than odd," Sarah insisted. "Two women from the same family, both bludgeoned, both dead, and now both with a silver charm found near them. Look." She tapped the photo. "Lydia isn't wearing a bracelet or jewelry of any kind. Where's the broken bracelet?"

"Maybe John took it after he killed her," Margaret offered.

"But that doesn't explain the charm that Amy found. Margaret, it can't be a coincidence. It just can't."

"But John killed Lydia and all the evidence for Julia's death points to Amy. Amy was only eleven when her mother was murdered, so what, you think that *John* killed Lydia and then came back and killed Julia? That's impossible."

"Is it?" Sarah asked, thinking of Jack's purported sighting of his father at the hospital. Maybe he really did see him there. "I've got to talk to Amy. I need to ask her about the charm she found."

"That's impossible," Margaret said. "At least at this time of night. It will have to wait until tomorrow during visiting hours."

"I don't want to wait that long. I'm going

to Amy's," she said suddenly. "Do you want to come with me?"

"To Amy's house? Why?" Margaret asked.

Sarah hefted the box from her trunk and transferred it to the trunk of Margaret's car. "I want to see if I can find that charm in her house. Compare it to the one in the crime-scene photo."

"How are you going to get in?" Margaret's brows knit together in dismay. "You're not going to break in, are you?"

"Not if I don't have to, but I could use a lookout." She looked at Margaret hopefully.

"That isn't a good idea. Just wait until morning. Nothing bad is going to happen between now and then," Margaret said firmly as she made her way to the front of the car, then stopped abruptly. Something had caught her attention, and she rose on her toes to get a better look. "What's that?" she asked.

"What?" Sarah peered into the darkness, but saw nothing.

"That." Margaret pointed to an object tucked beneath the windshield wiper on Sarah's car.

Sarah leaned forward and squinted. "I don't know. Hold on a sec." She moved to the front of the car and lifted the wiper, retrieving the item from beneath. "It's a watch," she said, handing it to Margaret. "At least, part of one."

Margaret shone her cell phone light on the object. It was the face of a watch attached to half of a grimy stainless-steel band. It was a Seiko with a silver face and black hands with the day of the week and the date where the Roman numeral III should have been. "God, my dad used to have a watch like this."

Sarah leaned toward her. "My dad did, too. I bet every father from the '70s had a similar one. Why would someone put an old, broken watch on my car?"

Margaret shrugged and handed the watch back to Sarah. "Maybe someone found it on the ground by your car and thought it belonged to you. You didn't notice it on the drive from the funeral home?"

"No." Sarah shook her head. "I'm sure I would have seen it. Someone must have put it there when we were down in the church basement." Sarah eyed the parking lot. The street was obscured by a row of honey locust trees. Was someone watching from behind a lacy veil of leaves? It was dark and completely deserted except for their two cars. Behind the church lay the cemetery with its wrought-iron fence gate and acres of smooth ivory headstones rising from the earth. "It's pitch-black out here. How would someone even see the watch on the ground?"

Margaret inched more closely to Sarah and looked around warily. "And why would anyone be walking through the parking lot at this time of night? Maybe we should call the sheriff."

"And say what? Someone put an old watch on my car? There's nothing criminal in that." Sarah strained her eyes, trying to take in her surroundings to see if anyone was skulking nearby. "Compared with what he's dealing with right now, this is nothing. Besides, won't he wonder why the two of us are out here alone in a deserted parking lot?"

"We'd just tell him the truth, that we were delivering food for the funeral. But it still creeps me out," Margaret said, drawing her jacket more closely around herself. "Where are you heading to now?"

"I guess I should go back to Dean's."

"Well, text me when you get back to the house, so I know you got there safely. And go straight to Dean's," Margaret ordered, pointing a red-tipped fingernail at her. "I'll see you at the funeral tomorrow."

"See you," Sarah said. "And thanks for all your help, Margaret." Sarah quickly climbed into her car, locked the doors, tucked the watch into her purse and made sure that Margaret got into her car safely. Though Sarah had been avoiding going back to the house and didn't look forward to the tension that was sure to greet her there, she was curious to learn more about the remains in the cistern. It seemed, Sarah thought fearfully, that every time she went back to that house another secret was uncovered, another crack in her marriage appeared.

17

She turned on her phone after having silenced it for the wake and immediately it buzzed. It was Gabe, her editor.

"Sarah," Gabe said shortly.

Sarah was startled by his sharp tone. "What's wrong?"

"I tried to call you, sent you emails and texted you. I was getting worried."

"I had my phone turned off. I've been at Julia's wake," Sarah explained as she watched Margaret pull away from the parking lot. "Were you able to find out where the emails are coming from?"

"No, not yet. I've got one of our tech guys checking on it. But I did a little digging."

"What kind of digging?" Sarah asked.

"After you told me about Jack not telling you how his mom really died, I checked it out. I have a contact at the Cedar City *Gazette,* Burt Wenstrup, who did an in-depth exposé on the murder back in the day."

"I read his articles. I found them online."

"I called Burt yesterday. He runs the newsroom now but has never forgotten this case. He had lots of theories about what really happened to Lydia Tierney, but most of what he learned was small-town gossip and couldn't be corroborated. So of course he only wrote the facts, but he's never been fully satisfied with the outcome."

"No one's satisfied with the outcome," Sarah said. "Is there a way you can send me his notes electronically?"

"Yeah, but let me give you the highlights. Burt talked to a lot of people. Only a few could come up with names of anyone who may have wanted to kill Lydia Tierney and the last person on the list was her husband.

"Burt interviewed just about everyone in Penny Gate. Jack's uncle Hal is in here, so is a Deputy Sheriff Gilmore and his wife, Delia. The priest, the coroner, even the mayor."

"Wow, that is really thorough," Sarah said, impressed. The case file didn't have that many interviews.

"Burt is a great reporter. He really knows how to get people to talk to him, trust him. He could also be the most ethical journalist

I've met. He never included something in an article just because it was shocking or would sell papers. He could get to the heart of a story, but made sure that he included facts, not idle gossip."

"So Burt doesn't think that Jack's dad did it?"

"Like I said, most folks were shocked that John Tierney was the main suspect. At first, some thought it was a crazed drifter, though no one reported any strangers in the area around that time. Then they discovered John had disappeared and the general consensus was that he had to be the one who did it."

"Listen, Gabe," she said, putting the call on speakerphone, shifting the car into gear and pulling out of the parking lot and into the road. "I know that Jack was a suspect at one point. I heard the taped interview Gilmore had with him. Nothing in this file could be worse than listening to that."

Still, Gabe hesitated before speaking. "Several people that Burt interviewed mentioned Jack as a possible suspect. At fifteen he was getting into all kinds of trouble. He hung out with an older crowd, was running around town, drinking and raising hell. A few people, though, said that Jack could be pretty aggressive. Got into quite a few bang-up fights at school." Before today she would have said that this didn't sound like Jack at all. "There was one person who told Burt that Jack had once even struck Lydia."

"I heard about that," Sarah said softly. "Is there anything else?"

Gabe didn't answer. "There's more, but I think you should probably just read Burt's notes."

"Gabe," Sarah said impatiently, "just tell me."

Gabe expelled a long breath. "Burt had a source that said Jack threatened to kill his parents. Over some girl. Said if they didn't leave them alone, he was going to kill them."

"Who? Who said that?" Sarah demanded.

"It was Jack's aunt. Julia Quinlan."

"I'm having a hard time believing Julia would say that about Jack," Sarah said as she left Penny Gate and turned onto the quiet rural highway. "Why would she take him into her home, if she thought he was capable of violence, of hitting his own mother, let alone murdering her?"

"She never *actually* said she thought Jack was the murderer," Gabe pointed out. "Just that he had a temper, that she had seen it a time or two."

"Still, why would she bring this up to a

reporter of all people? I didn't see anything about this in any of the police reports I looked through."

"She made Burt promise to keep everything she said about Jack off the record. That the boy had been through too much, but she wanted someone to know what had happened just in case."

"In case what?" Sarah asked. She tried to keep her eyes focused on the road in front of her, but something caught her eye in the rearview window. "That makes no sense whatsoever," Sarah finally said. "Unless Julia thought there might be some other evidence to show that Jack could have . . ." She couldn't bring herself to say the words.

"Sarah, I'm so sorry. I thought I was helping. I didn't mean to upset you or suggest that I think Jack had anything to do with his mother's death. I just thought you would want all the information."

"Thank you," she said, her eyes still flicking back and forth from the quiet country road to the rearview mirror. "I'm the one who called you. I asked for your help and I appreciate it. I just can't believe Julia would ever have allowed him to move into her home if she thought he was a murderer."

"You could be right. Besides, whoever wanted Lydia Tierney dead had been planning it for quite a while," Gabe said. "It wasn't just a heat-of-the-moment murder."

"What do you mean?" Sarah asked. All along she had thought that Lydia's murder was due to an angry interaction that ended violently, and now Gabe was telling her otherwise.

Suddenly, from behind her, a vehicle appeared. Its headlights shone brightly through the rear window, causing her to squint against the light. "Gabe, I've got to go."

"What's wrong?" Sarah could hear the worry in his voice.

"There's a pickup truck behind me driving really close," Sarah said, twisting in her seat to get a better look. The headlights were blinding. "Gabe." Sarah's voice rose in alarm.

"Just let him pass you," Gabe urged. "Pull over to the side and let him pass."

"I can't," Sarah said, gripping the steering wheel more tightly. "There's nowhere to pull over, and if I go any slower, he's going to ram into me. I'm hanging up." Sarah disconnected.

The vehicle crept closer and Sarah revved the engine and the car leaped forward with a roar. The truck followed suit, tapping the back bumper. Sarah screamed and overcorrected, causing the car to veer across the centerline. Her phone began buzzing incessantly. Gabe, she knew, calling her back. She struggled to get control and managed to pull back to the right side of the road. Again, the truck surged forward, this time crashing into her bumper, and then tore past her. Sarah screamed again, losing control of the steering, and the car careened off the road and bucked down a small embankment, plunging into a cornfield that had yet to be harvested. The sky above her disappeared and all Sarah could see were cornstalks whipping wildly against the windshield with a rapid *thunk, thunk.* She frantically pressed her foot down and the screech of the brakes filled her ears and her body strained against her seat belt as the car came to an abrupt stop.

Then all was still. Stunned, Sarah mentally checked her body for injuries. She was numb. Slowly she moved her neck, looking side to side. Sarah then tried to lift her arms. Pain pulsed through her right shoulder and she groaned, clenching her teeth against the pain. *What the hell just happened?* she asked herself. *Someone just ran me off the goddamn road,* she thought. But who? Why? Why would anyone want to hurt her?

She felt the passenger seat for her phone but couldn't find it. Was it safe to get out of the car? The truck had flown past her as she left the road but that didn't mean whoever was driving wasn't waiting for her up there somewhere. Sarah unclicked her seat belt and, with effort, pushed open the car door. Sarah winced at the pain in her shoulder as she stepped out onto the even soil.

Sarah reached back into the car and rooted around until she found her cell. She steadied herself against the open car door and dialed 9-1-1. A man's voice answered and with a trembling voice she explained that her car had been run off Highway 32 somewhere south of Penny Gate, and no, she didn't need an ambulance but a police officer would be helpful.

"Jesus, Sarah," Gabe said when she called him back. "Are you okay?"

"A truck just ran me off the road," Sarah said as she picked her way through the corn, trying to follow the path created by the car. "I'm okay, though. Just stay on the line with me until the police arrive."

Though it seemed that she had traveled much farther, the road was only about a hundred yards from where the car was stranded. Sandpaper-rough stalks of corn brushed against her arms, her high heels sinking into the earth. Sarah thought of the two hunters she met on the gravel road. Had they somehow tracked her down and been the ones to send her into the cornfield? Sarah held her sore right arm close to her body as she tripped through the tall grass that ran along the side of the highway. By the time she reached the asphalt, she was breathing heavily and sweating despite the chill in the air.

With the sprawling fields behind her and the wide-open road in front of her, Sarah felt too exposed. She stepped back into the shadows of the field, afraid that whoever was driving the truck might come back, but fearful of what might be lurking in the shadows of the corn.

Gabe maintained a steady stream of chatter, trying to calm her nerves, but Sarah could only respond briefly, her attention drawn to each rustle of leaves, to every movement caught in the corner of her eye. It was with relief when fifteen minutes later she saw the flashing lights of a sheriff's car approaching.

The deputy pulled up to the side of the road, stepped from his vehicle and approached Sarah cautiously. He was heavyset and middle-aged and he walked toward her sluggishly, as if dragging his own weight.

"He's here, Gabe. I'll call you later," Sarah said, and then hung up.

"Are you the one who called in the accident?" the deputy asked.

"Yes, thank God you're here. Someone ran me off the road," Sarah said frantically. "They came out of nowhere. My car's down there." He shone his flashlight in the direction that Sarah was pointing, illuminating the flattened corn that disappeared into the darkness.

"Are you okay? Are you sure you don't need an ambulance?"

Sarah rotated her shoulder; it ached, but she didn't think anything was broken or torn. "No, I'm fine, but I think someone did this to me on purpose."

"Why don't you take a seat in here," the deputy invited, walking her back to his car and opening the back door, "get you warmed up."

She gave her statement to the deputy, though she didn't have much to offer. She couldn't give him a description of the vehicle that had run her off the road, except that it was probably a pickup truck, and couldn't describe the driver. "Uh-huh," the deputy said in a way that Sarah was sure meant that he didn't quite believe her version of events.

"Have you been drinking tonight, ma'am?" he asked.

"No, not at all. I just came from a wake," Sarah insisted.

"Do you have any idea who would want to run you off the road?" he asked, looking down at her over the top of his glasses.

Sarah thought about telling him the truth. That she had been secretly investigating the murder of her mother-in-law and had found a connection, thin as it might be, between that murder and the death of Julia Quinlan. And now someone had just tried to kill her. The deputy would think she was out of her mind. No, she needed to wrap her head around all of it before she dared to utter her suspicions out loud to someone besides Margaret or Gabe.

The deputy looked at her expectantly.

"No." She shook her head. "I don't know who would do this."

"Maybe just some kids out joyriding or someone who had one too many drinks tonight," the deputy said congenially. "But without a description of the truck or a license plate number, it will be pretty tough to find them. How far back do you think your car is?" he asked, nodding toward the field.

"Not far," Sarah said. She needed to call

someone. If the deputy couldn't retrieve the car, someone would probably need to come get her. Jack came to mind first. Funny, she thought, even with all the suspicions and distrust, he was still the first person she thought of calling in an emergency. "Can I call my husband?" Sarah asked. "He'll be worried that I'm not back yet."

"Go right ahead. You stay here and I'll go see if I can drive your car out. Hopefully we won't need a tow truck." Sarah handed the deputy her car keys and he shut the door, locking her in the back of his car.

Sarah watched as the deputy was swallowed up into the cornfield. A fist of anxiety planted itself firmly in her chest. What if whoever ran her off the road was still nearby? What if the deputy didn't come back out? She made three attempts at reaching Jack with no luck. In frustration she left him a message. "Jack, please call me. I've been in an accident. I'm fine. I'm not hurt, but I need you to call me. Please, it's urgent."

Relief poured through her when the deputy finally emerged from the field and managed to maneuver her car through the ditch and back up onto the road. He stepped from the vehicle, circled the car, examining it for damage, and snapped a few pictures using a digital camera that he pulled from his car.

He opened the car door, releasing Sarah from the confines of the backseat, and handed her the keys. "Looks like you got quite a bit of damage to your back bumper, but it drives just fine. I doubt there was much if any damage to the truck that did this to you, though. I'll call the farmer whose field this belongs to, let him know that a few ears of corn won't make it to harvest."

"Thank you," Sarah said, slowly easing herself from the backseat. Her shoulder twinged painfully.

"Where are you headed?" the deputy asked. "I'll follow you and make sure you get to where you're going okay."

"Thanks. I can't seem to contact my husband . . ." Sarah's shoulder throbbed and tears pricked at her eyes. Maybe she was hurt more than she thought. "I'm staying at Dean and Celia Quinlan's home."

"I know just where that is. Go ahead and I'll follow you." The deputy watched as Sarah got into her car and then pulled onto the road behind her.

When they arrived at the house, Sarah thanked the deputy and walked up the porch steps to the front door. She turned and waved to let him know that she would be okay. He lifted his hand in return and waited until she was safely inside and then rumbled away.

Sarah pushed open the front door and quietly shut it behind her. She followed the soft voices coming from the kitchen but stopped short, remaining unseen in the darkened hallway to listen.

"Is everything okay between you and Sarah?" Celia asked, her voice filled with concern. "She seems really uncomfortable being here."

"She's had a lot come at her in the past few days," Jack said, his voice laced with exhaustion. "I think she just wants to go home."

"But you're the one whose aunt died," Celia protested. "It's your sister who's in trouble. You're the one who has had to come home to the last place in the world you want to be." Celia's voice sounded indistinct, loose.

Sarah felt white-hot anger rise in her chest. She couldn't believe that Jack and Celia were sitting in the kitchen talking about her. She waited for Jack to come to her defense. To say that of course Sarah was uncomfortable and tense staying in the home where his mother was murdered and his former girlfriend now lived. He remained silent.

"Do you remember the time when things were so bad at my house?" Celia asked. "We were, like, fourteen and my dad was out of control. I called you, crying, and you took your dad's truck without asking and picked me up."

Jack gave a low chuckle. "Yeah, we only got as far as Storm Lake before the highway patrolman stopped us. Our parents were pissed."

"Do you ever wonder what would have happened," Celia asked, "if we would have kept on driving?"

Sarah stepped from the shadows of the hallway, not wanting to hear Jack's response, not wanting to hear him say that he wished things had turned out differently between him and Celia.

She found Jack and Celia sitting side by side at the kitchen table, heads close together, a bottle of vodka set on the table between them.

They both looked up, startled, when they heard her.

"Sarah," Celia said a little too loudly, and Jack shushed her. "Sorry," she giggled. "Sarah." She lowered her voice. "Come join us. We're just having a drink to celebrate the end of this god-awful day."

"No, thanks," Sarah said, trying to make sense of the scene in front of her.

"Oh, come on," Celia urged. "It's Grey Goose and cranberry juice, Jack's favorite." She was right, Sarah thought, cringing. It was his favorite drink. "Remember back in high school," Celia said, her face only inches from Jack's, her hand resting on his arm. "You would steal your dad's vodka and I would smuggle cranberry juice out of my house."

"Just a second, Celia," Jack said, standing and going to Sarah's side. "Sarah, are you okay?"

"Where's Dean?" Sarah asked. "Where's Hal?"

"Sarah," Jack said again, studying her carefully. "What happened to your arm?"

"I was in a car accident," Sarah said, her voice cracking. "I've been trying to reach you for almost an hour. You wouldn't answer your phone."

Jack's hand flew to his back pocket and he pulled out his phone and looked at the display. "Jesus, I'm sorry. What happened? Are you okay?"

"Sit here," Celia said, rising from her seat unsteadily and then sitting back down. "Are you hurt?"

Sarah ignored Celia and looked to Jack. "My shoulder hurts."

"Can you lift it?" Jack asked.

Sarah slowly lifted her arm and nodded.

"Was it a deer?" Celia asked, her words slightly slurred. "Lots of deer running across the roads this time of year."

"It wasn't a deer," Sarah said sharply, looking at Celia. "Are you drunk?"

Celia choked back a laugh. "Maybe." She pinched her thumb and index finger together. "Just a little bit, though."

"What happened?" Jack asked.

"I was driving here from the church. A truck came flying up behind me and hit my bumper." Sarah shivered at the memory of seeing the glaring headlights of the truck bearing down on her. "I went off the road and into a ditch. Ended up in a cornfield."

Jack hurried into the living room and reappeared with a throw blanket and wrapped it gently around her shoulders. "Jesus. What happened to the other guy? Did he stop? How did you get home?"

Sarah shrugged the blanket away, irritated by Jack's ministrations. "He didn't stop. I called the sheriff's department. I could drive the car, but it's got a little damage."

Jack tenderly brushed her hair behind her ears. "Don't worry about that right now.

Do you need to go to the hospital?"

"I'm fine. Jack, I tried to get ahold of you for an hour and I find you sitting here drinking. We have to talk." She glanced at Celia and stopped. Sarah knew how crazy she'd sound if she started talking about the case files, the photos and silver charms. "When did you get here? I mean, after the wake, did you come straight here?" Sarah asked. Could it have been Jack who had run her off the road? Had he discovered that she was digging into his past? He definitely had access to a truck.

"Yeah, we came right back to the house. Hal went right to bed and Dean's somewhere around here," Jack explained.

"I swung by the store and picked up a few things," Celia said, holding up the bottle of vodka as Jack handed Sarah his glass of Grey Goose and cranberry juice.

"Are you sure you're okay?" he asked. "Here, drink this."

"Do you think that's a good idea?" Celia asked. "What if she has a head injury?"

"I don't have a head injury." Sarah snatched the glass from Jack. She took one unsure sip and then drained the rest.

"Sarah, why don't you go on upstairs and rest and I'll clean up here," Celia suggested.

"I'm fine," Sarah said. "I don't want to

interrupt your party." She stressed the word *party* with disdain and instantly regretted it. She didn't want to give them the satisfaction.

"We were just going over the details of Julia's estate," Jack murmured. "Nothing that can't wait until later." Jack guided her, his hand on the small of her back, slowly and soundlessly up the steps.

Once in the bedroom she kicked off her high heels and Jack helped her out of her dress, a seam ripping as he lifted it over her head. Tenderly, he helped her put on a pair of sweatpants and a T-shirt, pulled back the covers and led her to the bed.

From below, the sound of Celia's laugh floated through the house and then quieted as if she was trying to stifle her giggles. Sarah didn't think she was trying very hard. Jack shook his head good-naturedly. "She's had one too many, I think."

"Jack, I need to talk to you. It's important."

"Hold on." Sarah watched as he left the bedroom and came back a few minutes later carrying a glass of water and a medicine bottle. "Here, take two of these."

Sarah struggled to sit up. "What is it?"

"Hydrocodone. It was in Julia's medicine cabinet. It will help with the pain." Sarah

359

looked down at the pills. She knew she shouldn't take them. She had so much to think about, so many details to sift through, but the throbbing in her shoulder had intensified. Against her better judgment Sarah swallowed the pills.

"We really need to talk. There are some things I need to ask you about . . ."

"Don't worry about it tonight, Sar. Get some rest." He kissed her softly on the forehead. "We'll talk tomorrow." Sarah closed her eyes, willing sleep to wash over her. Jack sat next to her on the bed for several minutes, before quietly leaving the room.

Tomorrow. Tomorrow after the funeral, after the sheriff questioned her for the last time, she planned to leave Penny Gate. She should have never come here. It was poisonous. But now she didn't know if she could leave just yet. She had so many more questions. First chance she had, she would go to Sheriff Gilmore, confess that she'd heard the audiotapes, had looked at the crimescene photos, the charms. Every bit of it.

The pills were slowly working their magic and the pain in Sarah's shoulder eased; her eyes grew heavy and the horrors of the day began to fade away. She lay awake for as long as she could, trying to make sense of it all, but drifted off to sleep, missing pieces of the strange puzzle hovering just beyond her reach.

18

The following morning brought a fine, cool mist, but the forecast called for a sunny afternoon; hopefully the rain would pass by the time they made their way to the cemetery for the interment. Sarah awoke from a dreamless sleep, her shoulder aching and her head heavy from the hydrocodone and vodka.

It was a lovely church, small but ornate with jewel-colored stained-glass windows that depicted mournful saints who looked down on walnut-stained pews.

Sarah found herself standing in front of Celia and the two regarded each other cautiously. Celia wore a simple black sheath dress and heels, and her mass of curly hair was tamed into artful waves that framed her pale face. Celia was the first to speak. "I'm sorry about last night," she said, looking down at her shoes. "Yesterday was just awful and I had a little bit too much to drink.

I was rude."

"I think we're all feeling on edge," Sarah said, though Celia's affection toward Jack the night before still irked her. "Let's just chalk it up to a bad day."

"Thanks," Celia said with relief.

Sarah pulled her phone from her purse to turn it off before she entered the nave and saw that she had a text from Gabe. Call me! it read. She knew she didn't have time to have a conversation with him before the funeral began and reluctantly began to shut her phone down when another text from Gabe appeared. Emails are coming from Penny Gate!

Sarah's heart skipped a beat. The emails were coming from Penny Gate? Impossible, she thought.

"They're getting ready to start," Jack said, and she startled. With fumbling fingers she shut down her phone.

The pews had filled quickly and the ushers had to set out some folding chairs along the side aisles for everyone to have a seat. "Julia would have been pleased," Hal whispered as they took their places in the vestibule.

The town of Penny Gate had come out in full force to lay Julia to rest. The haunting violin music began as they started the long, solemn walk down the aisle behind the casket and pallbearers.

Sarah tried to wrap her head around Gabe's text. The emails were coming from Penny Gate. She had thought they were just the crazy ramblings of some fan of the Dear Astrid column. Everyday fodder for someone in her line of work.

But the origin of the messages changed everything. Surely it wasn't a coincidence that three emails from the same sender were coming from her husband's hometown, a place she just happened to be visiting. Out of the corner of her eyes she studied the crowd and recognized a few of the mourners. Sheriff Gilmore and several of the deputies, Amy's next-door neighbor. Margaret Dooley and her mother were there. Margaret gave her a small wave and an encouraging smile. As they stepped into the front pew Sarah felt her chest constrict. Any one of them could have sent her those emails. But who? And more important, why?

Sarah collected her thoughts. The emails were addressed to Astrid. Could the lunatic who sent those emails have known that Sarah was the real person behind the advice column's persona? Could they have been targeting her? But that was impossible. No one in Penny Gate knew that Sarah wrote for the column.

No one, that is, except Jack.

Sarah tried to catch her breath, but panic had filled her lungs. Was Jack sending her the emails? But why? It didn't make any sense.

Sarah robotically went through the motions of the mass. She stood when those around her stood and sat when those around her sat. She desperately wanted to excuse herself to the bathroom so she could look at the emails on her phone, but they were sitting in the front pew and she couldn't steal away without drawing curious stares. Her mind pirouetted uncontrollably, trying to remember exactly what the emails had said. Something about strawberries and blood pulsing and a yellow dress. Sarah thought back to the crime-scene photos. Immediately a close-up of Lydia's crushed skull, her mouth wide and gaping and the bloody cloth over her eyes filled Sarah's head. She tried to pull back on the image, tried to focus on the items in the photographs that weren't so prominent. The open freezer, a plastic package lying on the floor just beyond Lydia's reach. Strawberries? Possibly — there was so much blood congealing on the floor it was difficult to be sure. Sarah nearly gasped out loud and covered her mouth as if concealing a cough. Jack's mother, barefoot, lying on her back and wearing a cotton dress, butterscotch yellow beneath rivulets of blood.

Next to her Celia was weeping softly and clutching Dean's hand. Hal had his head down and his eyes shut as if in prayer. She looked over at Jack, his face inscrutable. Had he always been so difficult to read?

Think, she told herself. Who else knew she was Astrid? Her mother and sister. Gabe, of course. A few others at the *Messenger*. Gabe's administrative assistant, Maura, who had worked there longer than most, someone in payroll most likely. Penny Gate was only a three-hour flight from Montana. Theoretically, someone from the newspaper could have flown here and sent the emails. She wanted to believe it was possible, but she knew that made absolutely no sense. No matter which way she played it out in her mind, there was only one explanation: it had to be Jack.

The priest's sonorous voice filled the church. "Julia Quinlan was born and raised in Penny Gate," he said. "Julia lived a simple life. She cherished her church, her home, her son, her husband and gave much to those around her but asked for so little in return. She was the consummate farmer's wife."

She glanced over at Jack, but he kept his head down, his eyes half-shut, immersed in all the memories that this town brought back to him. Sarah tried to refocus on the eulogy, but had difficulty concentrating on what the priest was saying.

It was the final song, "Amazing Grace," that brought the congregation from tears to weeping. They processed out behind the casket, the air thick with the cloying scent of incense.

After Julia's burial they walked through the cemetery back to the church where the Women's Rosary Guild had prepared a feast.

Their plates were filled to capacity and they sat at the table reserved for family members. Sarah's mind swirled with questions. She was eager to step out and call Gabe to get more details about where the emails had come from. She wanted to dig back into the documents she had scanned onto the thumb drive to see how many more details from Lydia's murder matched the emails.

Sarah picked at her food, mindful of all the eyes watching them. Jack, for his part, managed to make small talk with everyone at the table, but Sarah could tell it wasn't easy for him. She wondered how many people gathered there knew that Julia's death was now officially a murder investigation and that a set of remains had been found on the Quinlan property. Probably everyone. Sarah knew how word traveled in small towns.

Sarah excused herself to use the restroom but instead stepped outside to get her bearings and call Gabe about the emails.

Her mind kept returning to Jack. If anything, he was more fanatical about their privacy than Sarah. He made sure their home phone number was unlisted; he periodically checked the girls' social-media accounts to make sure no crazies were in contact with them; he locked all of their personal information in a fireproof safe. He had a shotgun and a handgun that he kept locked safely away, though he hadn't hunted since he was a kid and Larkspur was a very safe, sleepy town. Jack was the one who wanted Sarah to give up her job writing as Dear Astrid after she had received frightening letters in the past.

Jack could have told his family she was Astrid, though Sarah would be surprised if he had done so. He had only seen them a handful of times over the years, talked to them sporadically. Jack didn't tell Amy anything personal about their life. It was as if their happiness, their success, made Amy even more sour about the difficulties she faced — the failed relationships, the substance abuse, her run-ins with the law. Amy would be the very last person he would tell that Sarah wrote the Dear Astrid column. If Jack told anyone it would have been his aunt Julia and she certainly hadn't told anyone.

Gabe picked up on the first ring. "Sarah, did you get my texts?" His voice was taut and anxious. "The emails that you wanted me to check on, they're coming from Penny Gate."

"I got them. Julia's funeral was starting and I couldn't get away until now. Are you sure? Could it be a mistake?" she asked.

"It's no mistake. Those emails are coming from Penny Gate. According to our tech guy, at least one of them came from the public library server."

"The library?" Sarah thought back to the other day when she had been at the library scanning the documents from the case file. Had the person who sent the emails been hiding behind the stacks, watching her every move? "How does he know it came from the library?"

"He tracked down the IP address, which

is connected to a computer at the library in Penny Gate."

"What about the other two emails? Where did they come from?" Sarah asked.

"Gary thinks that they most likely originated from a prepaid burner phone."

Sarah shook her head warily. "This makes no sense at all, Gabe."

"It doesn't matter if it makes sense, Sarah," Gabe said impatiently. "It's too odd of a coincidence. I think you need to go to the police. Tonight. Now."

"No one here knows I'm Astrid," she managed to say. "No one except Jack."

"Sarah, you know I'm no alarmist. We get bizarre emails at the paper all the time. But these I think you need to worry about. Whoever is sending you these messages knows exactly who you are and where you're at."

She thought back to the night before and the watch left behind on her car. What did it mean? And the truck that ran her off the road. Now she was sure it wasn't someone who had too much to drink or an accident. Someone purposely sent her into that cornfield. Were they trying to kill her or just send her a message to stop digging into Lydia's death?

"Sarah, this isn't a game. You could really

be in danger."

"I'm beginning to think you're right." Sarah told him about the body in the cistern and described finding the watch on her windshield.

"This is hitting too close to home. I think you need to get out of there."

"Believe me, I can't wait to get out of this town," Sarah assured him.

"Who do you think sent them?" Gabe asked.

"I really have no idea. The only clue we have is that it's someone from Penny Gate, and seeing as I know only a total of about five people from here, I guess it would have to be one of them. The easy answer would be Amy, Jack's sister."

"You can't think of anyone else?" Gabe prodded.

"No," Sarah said hesitantly.

"Seriously, Sarah, you need to go to the sheriff about this."

"Don't worry, I'll talk to someone. I'll call you later," she said before hanging up.

She made her way back into the church basement and from across the room Sarah could see Jack sitting at one of the long folding tables, her purse sitting on the chair next to him. She watched as he reached into her purse, rooted around, pulled out a package

371

of tissues, then dug a little deeper. A quizzical expression appeared on his face as he looked down at the secondary items he retrieved from her purse. Sarah craned her neck to see what he was looking at but it was too small. She wove her way between tables and past townspeople who offered their condolences. Sarah paused to thank them but her eyes never left her husband's face. When she was just a few steps away she recognized what was in has hand: the watch that was left beneath her windshield wiper the night before.

Jack peered down at the watch face, his eyes narrowed, his forehead furrowed. He flipped it over, brought it close to his face and lowered it again.

"Jack?" Sarah asked.

He looked up at her, his eyes filled with tears. "Where did you get this?" he asked, his voice raspy.

"Why? What's wrong?"

"Where did you get this?" Jack said loudly. The chatter around them stopped and Sarah felt a roomful of eyes on them.

"It was on the windshield. Last night after the wake. Someone put it on my windshield." She sat down next to Jack and gradually the murmurs of conversation resumed.

"This watch," he said. His eyes were wide, his face ashen. "It belonged to my dad."

19

"Your dad?" Sarah asked. "How do you know?"

"I just know. He had it forever and he never took it off. He had it on that day."

"Are you certain?" Sarah asked.

"Can you picture your dad's hands?"

Sarah could. She didn't even need to close her eyes to remember her father's hands. They were tanned and rough from the elements and hard work, but slim and graceful, too, like a musician's. She could also clearly see the Zenith watch he wore on his left wrist with its golden numbers and face clouded with condensation that had somehow gotten beneath the glass. She nodded.

"I can, too," Jack said earnestly. "Sometimes I can't remember his face, but I remember his hands." He looked at her with fear and something else. Was it hope? "Maybe my dad put it there?"

"You need to give this to the sheriff,"

Sarah told him. "What if he's the one who hurt Julia?"

"I don't believe it." Jack shook his head.

"What've you got there, Jack?" Sheriff Gilmore asked. He seemed to have sneaked up on them from out of nowhere.

Jack's fingers closed tightly around the watch. "Jack," Sarah prodded. "Show him." Jack slowly unfurled his fingers to reveal the object. "I found it on my windshield last night. I put it in my purse, then got in the accident and forgot about it. Jack just found it."

Gilmore held out his hand and after a long pause Jack laid the watch in his outstretched palm. "Who do you think it belongs to?" Gilmore asked, turning it around in his fingers.

"I think it belonged to my dad," Jack replied, his voice shaking with emotion.

"You both need to come to the sheriff's office." Gilmore's lips flattened into a grim line beneath his mustache.

"Now? Why?" Jack asked in surprise. "We can't leave in the middle of my aunt's funeral dinner."

"Yes, Jack, now. Your mother was murdered, your aunt was murdered, a body was found on your uncle's property and someone placed this watch on your wife's windshield. A watch that you seem pretty certain belonged to your dad."

Jack rubbed a hand over his face and nodded.

Jack and Sarah said a quick goodbye to Hal, Dean and Celia, and told them they would see them back at the house in a little while. Gilmore allowed Jack and Sarah to drive separately to the sheriff's department. Wordlessly, Jack passed the car keys to Sarah with shaking fingers.

"Jack," Sarah said as soon as they were in the car, "what's going on?"

"I don't know," he said, and Sarah almost believed him. They drove in silence to the sheriff's office, both lost in their own thoughts.

When they arrived at the station, the sheriff escorted them into the waiting area.

"Sarah, come on back with me," he said, and Sarah looked pleadingly at Jack.

"It's okay," he said. "I'll be right here waiting."

Sarah followed the sheriff down the hallway to his office. "Now, tell me how you got this watch." He pulled the watch, now safely ensconced within a plastic bag, from his pocket.

"There isn't much more to it than what I told you over at the church. After the wake last night, Margaret Dooley and I dropped off a bunch of desserts in the church basement. When I came back out to my car, Margaret noticed the watch on my windshield."

"You didn't think that was strange?"

Sarah raised her eyebrows. "Honestly, nothing much surprises me about this place anymore. But yes, I did think it was a little bit odd. I put the watch in my purse and forgot about it."

Gilmore rubbed his chin. "You didn't notice anyone hanging around the church or the parking lot? Anything suspicious at all?"

"No, nothing." Sarah shrugged. "I know I'm not much help, but I can count on one hand the people I know in Penny Gate. I didn't notice anything unusual."

"Well, someone certainly knows who you are," Gilmore said, setting the watch on a stack of file folders atop his desk. "You were run off the road last night. My deputy made it sound like you thought you were purposely targeted. Is that what you think?"

Sarah thought about the blinding headlights and how the truck came out of nowhere. "Last night it sure seemed that way. In the light of day it doesn't seem quite as ominous," Sarah said. "But now I don't know. It could have been a drunk driver."

"We'll keep looking into it," the sheriff promised. "Officially, the Lydia Tierney murder investigation is closed. But now we have a watch, purportedly belonging to John Tierney, and you were run off the road after someone placed it on your windshield. Raises some questions, am I right?" Gilmore asked.

"But that makes sense if John Tierney was the murderer. He comes back, kills his own sister — you have to admit the two cases bear some striking similarity. Maybe he leaves the watch on my car, sends . . ." Sarah stopped abruptly.

Gilmore looked at her curiously. "Sends what?" he asked.

Sarah wasn't quite ready to share the emails with Gilmore. Not just yet. "Sends Jack back into this nightmare."

"I have to agree with you on a few points, Sarah. There are similarities between Lydia's and Julia's deaths, but I don't believe that John Tierney committed either of them." He pointed to the Baggie on his desk. "And I think that watch, where it's been for the past thirty years and your husband just might hold all the answers."

"Now you think Jack killed both his mom and dad?" Sarah asked.

"Come on now, Sarah." Gilmore stood and walked to the closet. "Don't tell me it hasn't crossed your mind. Just the other day you were standing here asking me if you could take a look at Lydia's case file." He placed his hand on the doorknob and Sarah held her breath. Had Margaret had time to return the box to its original spot?

Gilmore opened the closet door, reached up to the top shelf and pulled down a box and set it gently on top of his desk. It was labeled LYDIA TIERNEY 1985. Sarah tried to conceal her relief, trying not to think about what would have happened if the box hadn't been there. "Now I have two active murder cases to investigate. I'm afraid you and Jack won't be leaving Penny Gate just yet." He walked to his office door and waited for Sarah to join him.

Numbly, Sarah walked back to the lobby, Gilmore at her elbow. Jack stood when he saw them. "Jack, come on back," Gilmore said, and Jack looked at Sarah warily.

"I'll wait here," Sarah said.

"Oh, I wouldn't wait," Gilmore said. "This could take a while."

"Why's that?" Jack asked. "I don't know any more than I've already told you."

"The thing is, Jack," Gilmore said. "The watch left on Sarah's car? It looks like it goes with those remains found on your uncle's farm."

Jack blankly stared at Gilmore for a moment and then realization spread across his face.

"What do you mean?" Sarah asked, still not comprehending. "What's the watch have to do with what you found in the cistern?"

"We found a wallet." Gilmore's voice was grave. "We still have to wait for the test results, but we believe the bones in the cistern belong to your dad."

"What?" Jack said, blanching. "That's impossible. He killed my mom. He ran away years ago."

Gilmore shook his head. "It doesn't quite look that way anymore, Jack. It looks like we're back to square one again."

Jack turned to Sarah. "Go ahead. I'll call you when I'm finished here," Jack urged.

"Jack," Sarah said in exasperation. "I already know that you were the first suspect in your mother's murder. You don't have to hide that from me anymore." To the sheriff she said, "That's what you mean by square one, isn't it?"

"I'm afraid so," Gilmore said almost apologetically.

Jack turned to Sarah with desperation in his eyes. "I didn't do this," he said. "I promise you. Please call Art Newberry for me. He can help clear this up. Sarah, you have to believe me." His voice was earnest, pleading.

Sarah knew the words that Jack wanted her to say. That she believed him, that she knew there was no way he could have killed his parents. But she couldn't. "I'll call Arthur," was all she could manage.

Sarah walked out of the sheriff's office without a backward glance. He did it, she said to herself. He killed his mother in the cellar of their home, and he killed his father and dumped him in an old cistern. How was she going to tell Elizabeth and Emma?

She checked her watch. Two thirty. She pulled out her phone and made the call that Jack asked her to. Most likely the last thing she would ever willingly do on his behalf again.

20

Sarah drove directly to the library. If Jack was the one who had been sending her the emails, maybe there would be some record of him using one of the library computers.

The young library director was standing behind the checkout counter. "You're back," he said. "Do you have some more scanning that you need to do?"

Sarah shook her head. "Not this time. I was wondering if you have any computers for public use."

"Of course," the man said as he stepped from behind the counter. He led her past a cozy children's section where a small boy sat on his mother's lap reading a book, his pudgy fingers struggling to flip the pages. There was a wall of DVDs and a table where two elderly men were playing chess. Tucked away in the back of the library was a room that housed three circular workstations. Each held four computers. None were being used at the moment.

"Do I need to have a library card or sign a sheet or something?" Sarah asked as she pulled out a chair.

"No," the man said, shaking his head. "If a visitor wants to check out a laptop, then yes. But the desktops are first come, first served. Once in a while I have to kick someone off who feels the need to spend six hours binge watching videos."

"So you have no way of keeping track of who's working on a particular computer at a certain time?"

"We have everything on safety mode if that's what you mean. Kids can't access dangerous sites. We have employees cruise through here to keep an eye on things. Are you worried about your kids?"

"What if someone sent an anonymous email from one of these computers? Is there a way to find out who sent it?"

"That's a bit beyond my expertise," the man said. "I'm sure someone could figure it out. But anyone can set up an email address."

Sarah thought about this for a moment. "What about cameras?" She looked around the room in search of any sign of a security system.

He cocked his head. "Who did you say

you were again?"

Sarah laughed self-consciously. "You must think these questions are odd. My daughter received some weird anonymous emails. I'm trying to figure out a way to find out who sent them."

"Can't you call the police?"

"Just being an overprotective mom. But just in case, what about security cameras? Do most libraries have them?"

The man shrugged. "I guess it depends. We have cameras at the entrances."

"What about this man?" she asked, pulling out her phone and showing him a picture of Jack. It was one of her favorites of him. He was sitting in one of their Adirondack chairs next to the lake, a soft, easy smile on his face. "Have you seen him in here the past few days?"

"Is he the one you think was sending the emails to your daughter?" He peered closely at the photo. "No," he said almost regretfully. "I haven't. But he could have come in when I wasn't working or I might have missed seeing him."

Sarah thanked Max and took a few minutes to wander around the stacks of books. She wasn't sure why she lingered. Whoever was sending those emails might have left a trail somewhere.

On a whim Sarah sat back down at one of the computers and navigated to her and Jack's online banking site. She logged in and skimmed through Jack's credit card purchases over the past month. There was nothing to indicate that he had bought a burner phone, but that didn't mean anything. He could have paid for one in cash.

She sat staring at the computer screen for several minutes, trying to figure out what to do next. Finally, she typed the word *Seller85* into the search engine. Sarah clicked on the first link that appeared and it took her to an online auction site and Seller85's profile page. Immediately a series of pictures of items for sale popped up. Sarah scrolled through the items. The first picture showed an old brass-and-iron water pump.

The next photograph showed an object that looked similar to a wrench and was described as a "primitive iron tool for notching the ears of pigs and hogs. Measures about ten inches long and has a patina of age and old red paint." There were dozens of more pictures of items that Seller85 had for sale: a set of dishes made of pink Depression glass, a primitive-looking Pennsylvania Dutch wooden trunk hand painted with vines, strawberries and other flowers. Sarah clicked on the image and zoomed in to get a closer look. It was a lovely piece. Nothing on the page seemed nefarious.

Next, Sarah phoned Margaret Dooley. She didn't know who she could trust in Penny Gate, but Margaret was the closest thing to a friend she had here.

"Sarah," Margaret said when she picked up the phone. "What happened? You and Jack left the dinner so quickly we didn't even get to talk. I heard that the sheriff asked you to go to the station."

In a low whisper Sarah gave Margaret a condensed version of the events that had happened since they parted ways in the church parking lot the night before: the car accident, John Tierney's remains in the cistern, the emails she was receiving, the strange photos on the online auction site. On the other end Margaret went quiet. "Margaret, are you still there?"

"The body in the cistern is John Tierney's?" she asked in disbelief.

"That's what the sheriff said." Sarah twisted around in her chair to make sure no one could overhear her. "Margaret, what if Jack is the murderer? What am I going to do?"

"Are you still at the library?" Margaret asked.

"Yes." She checked the clock on the wall. It was nearing four o'clock.

"I'll be right there," she said in a rush, and disconnected.

Sarah returned her attention to the computer screen. The profile had been created the year before and didn't offer any other contact information for Seller85 than through the auction site. No city or state was listed, no phone number. There was no way to know if this was the same Seller85 as the one who was sending her the emails.

Her phone pinged, announcing a new text message. Sarah glanced down at the screen and her heart stopped. See how they run? it read, and there was an attachment. Before Sarah could click on it, another text came through.

You can't catch me.

The person sending her the cryptic emails also knew her cell phone number.

With dread Sarah clicked on the attachment and a photo appeared. It took a moment for Sarah to realize what she was seeing: an elderly woman, her leg bent at an odd angle, lying on her back at the bottom of a familiar-looking staircase.

It was Julia.

Covering her eyes was some kind of cloth, soaked in blood.

Goose bumps erupted on her arms. Whoever had done this had taken a photo of their handiwork. Sarah's stomach roiled. She quickly rang the sheriff's office to ask if Jack Quinlan was still meeting with the sheriff and the voice on the other end of the line said she couldn't share that information with her.

For all the lies and secrets Jack had told her, he appeared to have all his faculties. Wouldn't someone capable of murdering his parents and covering it up for decades be insane, show some signs of being unbalanced? Yes, Sarah thought, unless, of course, he was a psychopath.

Had she been living with a psychopath all these years? Had she slept in the same bed and bore the children of a cold-blooded killer?

Fifteen minutes later, Margaret rushed in. Her skin seemed ashen, nearly stark white against her heavy makeup. She slid into the seat next to Sarah, and before she could even say hello, Sarah proceeded to show her everything.

"Sarah, you have to go to the sheriff with all of this," Margaret said after they had reviewed the photo and the emails. "This is too dangerous. You could get hurt."

"I know you're right," Sarah said, still shaken by the image of Julia at the bottom of the steps. "I just need to figure out what to hand over to the sheriff."

"You have to give him everything," Margaret urged. "And don't worry about me," she added. "We're in this together. You didn't make me do anything I didn't want to."

Margaret's eyes darted around the library. Only one other patron was nearby. "I started thinking about what you said earlier about the silver charm that Amy said belonged to Julia and the one in the picture next to Lydia's body. This is the most horrible thing I think I've ever seen," she whispered as she pushed a small envelope across the table. "It's only a photocopy, but I figured it might help."

Sarah carefully opened the envelope and pulled out the piece of paper. Even though it was a photocopy of a photograph, the detail was frighteningly explicit. Sarah stared down at the autopsy photo, not one from thirty years earlier, but from earlier that week. A close-up of the catastrophic wound to Julia's skull. "Where did you get this?" Sarah asked.

"It was surprisingly easy," Margaret admitted.

Sarah clicked through the documents on her thumb drive until she found Lydia's autopsy photos. The two women's head wounds were somewhat similar.

"But there's no way Amy could have killed her mother — she was only eleven at the time. Besides, she's still in jail and couldn't have just sent me the text with the picture of Julia. The only person I can think of would be Jack."

"But wait," Margaret said, shaking her head back and forth. "You and Jack weren't even in town when Julia was hurt. There's no way he could have done it."

Sarah sat back in her chair, dumbfounded. "Oh, my God, you're right." She allowed herself a small moment of relief. "But that just means we're no closer to knowing who did. And what about Julia's autopsy report that said her cause of death was poisoning? Remember?"

"But Jack couldn't have been the one to hit her, so why would he poison her? Unless —" Margaret's eyes widened "— Jack and Amy planned it together."

"But why?" Sarah asked, running her fingers through her hair in frustration. "I just can't wrap my head around all of this.

Somehow Lydia's and Julia's deaths and these emails have to be connected."

Sarah thought back to what the priest had said earlier at the funeral. That Julia was the consummate farmer's wife.

A chill ran through Sarah. *The consummate farmer's wife.* Those words seemed to fit Jack's mother, as well. She was active in her church and her community. By most accounts she was an attentive mother and wife. What did the emails say? *Three blind mice, two blind mice, one blind mouse. See how they run.* How did the nursery rhyme go? She thought back to when the girls were little, the way they giggled over the silly lyrics. Wasn't there mention of a farmer's wife?

Lydia Tierney, farmer's wife. Dead.

Julia Quinlan, farmer's wife. Dead.

Both women had cloths covering their eyes — blind mice.

Sarah thought of Celia — beautiful, capable. The perfect farmer's wife. A cold sweat erupted on her skin.

One blind mouse.

She needed to get to Celia. Sarah quickly ejected the thumb drive and handed it to Margaret. "Can you hold on to this for me?"

"Sure, where are you going?" Margaret asked in confusion.

"Back to Dean and Celia's," Sarah said,

gathering up her things.

"Whoever is doing this is insane and for some reason he's trying to pull you into it. Sarah, you have to go to the sheriff," Margaret urged.

"I will, I promise. I'll talk to him tonight. I just want to check on a few things."

"Okay," Margaret said anxiously. "But if you don't call me in an hour I'm calling the sheriff."

Sarah nodded and paused to give Margaret a quick hug. "I'll be fine. I feel like we're so close to figuring it all out."

"But I don't want you to die trying," Margaret whispered in Sarah's ear before releasing her. "Whoever is doing this has already killed two people, possibly three. I don't want you to be next."

"No way." Sarah gave her a reassuring smile. "I'm the farthest thing away from a farmer's wife. It's Celia I'm worried about. Besides, I've got a pretty hard head and if they try I'll take them down with me."

21

On the drive over to Dean and Celia's house, Sarah debated as to what to do next. She had tried and tried to get ahold of Celia, but with no luck. It was after seven thirty and Sarah hadn't heard from Jack and wondered if the sheriff was still interviewing him or maybe had even arrested him.

She checked her phone again for a message or a missed call from him. Nothing. Where are you? she texted him and waited for a response. When none came, she called. The phone rang several times before going to his voice mail and she hung up without leaving a message.

She pulled up in front of the house, hoping to see Celia's car, but no other vehicles were in sight. The porch light gleamed brightly, but the rest of the house was dark.

Sarah pushed open the car door and stepped out into the cold night air. No movement or sound came from the shorn fields, but she felt as if she was being watched and hurried up the steps to the front door. She rapped on the door and waited, not expecting anyone to answer. Turning, she shivered and peered into the darkness. The silo stood sentinel straight, overlooking the farmyard. The door of the large barn was open, like a wide gaping mouth in the center of the property.

She was always amazed by how places had their own unique scents. In the fall, their home on Larkspur Lake smelled of mountain air and the spicy clove-like perfume of golden currant, and here, the unique dusty odor of recently harvested corn mixed with the sweet smell of alfalfa settled in her nose. Sarah cocked her head to listen. The inky night sky was pricked with starlight, but strangely the air was still and void of sound. No rustle of leaves from the treetops, no gentle murmurs from the cattle across the road, no dogs yipping, no earnest clucking from the hens. It was too quiet.

Sarah turned back toward the front door and knocked again. She knew that Celia would most likely think she was crazy, but it was better to be safe. Sarah needed her to know what she had learned.

She tried Jack again. Maybe she should call Arthur Newberry. Surely if Gilmore had arrested Jack, someone would have contacted her. But would anyone call her if he had been released? That was what she really feared. That she was too late. That the sheriff let Jack free and then he came here to finish what he started. In exasperation she pressed her back to the front door and sank to the porch floor. She tried Celia's number again but the phone rang and rang. The faint trill of a ringtone seeped from behind the door. Sarah lowered the phone and rotated her head so that her ear was pressed against the scuffed wood. The ringing stopped. Shifting to her knees she pressed redial and listened. Again, the sound of Celia's distinctive ringtone came from inside the house. She disconnected the call and the shrill ringing ceased.

If Celia was gone, why was her phone in the house? Sarah rose and knocked soundly on the door. "Celia," she called. "Celia, it's Sarah!" Maybe something had already happened to her. Sarah pounded on the door. "Celia, are you in there?" Panic flooded her voice. She turned the knob, shoved the unlocked door open and stumbled into the house.

The house was dimly lit and quiet. A low fire burned in the fireplace. Sarah's eyes fell to an end table near the front door where a cell phone rested. Celia's phone. "Celia?" she called out uncertainly. No response. Three more steps would take her past the foyer. To the right would be the steps leading upstairs. To the left, the kitchen and the steps leading to the cellar.

Sarah took a deep breath, heart pounding, hand on her phone just in case she needed to dial 9-1-1. She stepped forward and looked to the right. She exhaled in relief. No body at the bottom of the steps.

She turned to the left, toward the kitchen, toward the cellar door, but stopped. She mentally kicked herself for being so spooked. Maybe Celia had been here but had to leave unexpectedly. Maybe the sheriff gave them permission to return to Hal's house and Celia had inadvertently left her phone behind. She couldn't bring herself to step into the kitchen, fearful of what she might find. Should she wait for Celia to return, or leave? Leave, she decided. Get into the car, call the sheriff, let them investigate.

Before turning to go her eyes swept the large open room. Everything seemed neatly in its place. The kitchen table was empty except for an expertly arranged glass jar of dried hydrangeas. An open bottle of wine and two glasses sat on the kitchen counter, and a red sweater lay in a puddle on the floor. Sarah's eyes narrowed. Such a small thing, but in the short time she'd known Celia, dirty dishes and clothing left in the middle of the kitchen seemed incongruous. She walked over, bent down and lifted the sweater from the ground, and a black lace bra fluttered to the floor.

This is ridiculous, Sarah thought. Celia was probably upstairs with Dean, and Sarah had just barged into their home while they were obviously otherwise occupied.

She just needed to be done with this, drive over to the sheriff's department and tell him everything she had learned. She turned to head back out into the chilly night.

"Sarah?" a voice asked from behind her. Startled, Sarah turned and her phone tumbled from her hand, clattered and slid across the wood floor, coming to rest beneath the barn-board coffee table.

"Jesus, Celia," Sarah cried. "You scared me."

Celia was standing halfway up the staircase that led to the second floor, staring in confusion down at Sarah. "You scared *me,*" she said, clutching the railing. Celia cast a quick glance behind her shoulder, then walked the rest of the way down the steps and moved past Sarah to close the front door. "It's freezing. What are you doing here? Is everything okay?"

"I knocked, but no one answered," Sarah tried to explain. Celia looked at her dubiously and even to her own ears it sounded suspect. "I was worried about you."

"Why didn't you just come in?" Celia asked. There was no anger or accusation in her voice, just confusion, but still Sarah reddened with embarrassment.

"I'm sorry, I thought . . ." Sarah stopped. She didn't know what she thought anymore. "I'm sorry," she repeated. "But I really need to talk to you." Celia cast another look behind her and up the stairs. Sarah followed her gaze.

"Where's Dean?" Sarah asked.

"He went with Hal back to his house. The sheriff said Hal could go home now. Dean is going to spend the night there with him tonight. He's just so devastated, Dean didn't want him there alone." Celia drew the oversize flannel shirt she was wearing more tightly around herself. Her legs were bare.

Another thought had wheeled into her brain. Maybe Jack wasn't at the sheriff's department any longer. Had he come here? To do what? Had Sarah had it all wrong, and Celia and Jack were having an affair?

"Are you alone?"

"Yes, of course," Celia said. "Why?"

Sarah slipped past Celia and took the steps two at a time.

"Sarah, what's going on? Where are you going?" Celia followed close behind but Sarah kept moving, checking each room. "What are you doing? What are you looking for?"

Sarah ignored her and moved toward the master bedroom. She flung open the door. The room was empty. A candle burned on a bedside table. One side of the queen-size bed was rumpled. A book lay open, spine up, atop the comforter. Sarah paused briefly and then stalked over to the closet, opened the door. Nothing but precisely hung blouses and trousers and shoes lined up neatly on the floor. Sarah pressed the heels of her hands against her eyes and gave a sharp bark of laughter.

She felt Celia come up behind her. "Are you okay? What's the matter?"

Sarah turned to face her, cheeks high with color. What could she say to Celia? That she thought Jack was there to murder her and then after seeing the pile of clothing thought that maybe the two of them were having an affair? "Nothing," Sarah said, flushed with embarrassment. "Nothing's wrong. Just a stupid misunderstanding."

"Let me get dressed," Celia said. "We'll go downstairs and talk." Celia pulled on a pair of jeans and stepped into her shoes before leading Sarah downstairs to the kitchen.

"I think you're in danger," Sarah said, going to the kitchen window to peer outside. All was still. She turned back to Celia.

"Danger?" Celia said, laughing. She saw the distress on Sarah's face and her smile fell away. "Why? You're starting to scare me."

"I think someone is killing the women in Jack's family."

"That's not news, Sarah. Everyone knows that John Tierney killed his wife. As for Julia —" she shook her head regretfully "— as hard as it is to come to terms with, I think it was Amy."

"But why?" Sarah asked. "What possible reason would she have for killing her aunt? It doesn't make sense. Ever since I arrived in Penny Gate I've been getting strange emails. Cryptic messages referencing Lydia's and Julia's murders. Amy's been in jail and there's no way she could have sent them. I just got another one with a photo. The sender quoted the rhyme 'Three Blind Mice.' Here let me show you." Sarah patted her pocket for her phone. It wasn't there.

"You know how crazy this sounds," Celia said. She went to the coffeemaker and poured them each a cup of coffee. She was beginning to sound impatient and Sarah knew she was losing her.

"The emails started out with three blind mice, then when Julia died I got one that said two blind mice and then one with one blind mouse." Sarah raised her hand to her face. "And the photo shows Julia at the bottom of the steps. Both Lydia and Julia were found with something covering their eyes. They're the blind mice."

Celia carried her mug to the kitchen counter. "I just don't buy it. It sounds insane."

"Celia, someone just sent me a picture of Julia just after she was hit over the head and pushed down the stairs. Do you know where Jack has been all afternoon?" Sarah went to Celia's side, ready to shake her in frustration. "At the sheriff's department. I found an old broken watch on my windshield last night and Jack is sure that it belonged to his father."

Celia turned to Sarah. "You think Jack's dad put the watch there?"

"Not anymore. Gilmore says that the body in the cistern belongs to Jack's dad."

"Jack's dad? But *he's* the one who killed Lydia and ran away."

"No, that's not the way it happened," Sarah said. She went to the back door and flipped the lock. "Keep your doors locked. You're not safe."

Celia shivered and crossed her arms across her chest. "What do you mean?"

"You're the last farmer's wife."

"Oh, my God." Celia brought her hands up to her mouth as if in prayer and began pacing around the kitchen.

Celia abruptly stopped walking. "But who? Who would do this?"

"For a while I thought maybe it was Jack, but now I'm not so sure. He couldn't have been the one to hurt Julia. We weren't even in Penny Gate when it happened."

"Jack?" Celia said doubtfully. "None of this makes any sense at all. Why would Jack hurt Julia?"

"Maybe Amy and Jack planned it together? I don't know. I know it sounds ridiculous when I say it out loud. The only thing I can think of is that maybe Julia found out that Jack had something to do with Lydia's death and Amy was trying to protect him. We came back to Penny Gate and he finished the job. And now that his dad's body has been found, it looks even worse for him."

"I just don't believe it," Celia said.

"Come on, Celia, even you tried to give him an alibi back then, when you told Gilmore that you had seen Jack at school at around the time of the murder. For a minute you even doubted him."

"How do you know all this?" Celia asked warily. She slowly backed away from Sarah as if she was afraid of her.

Sarah shook her head. "It doesn't matter, but I know. And I also know that Julia didn't actually die from her head injuries. She was poisoned."

"Listen to yourself, Sarah. Beatings and poisoning, three blind mice. It sounds insane. You honestly believe that Jack is a murderer?"

Sarah struggled to speak. "Yeah, I do," she finally said.

Remarkably, Celia didn't react with the shock or indignation that Sarah expected. She just looked immensely sad. "What else did the emails say?" Celia leaned against the counter in resignation.

Sarah scanned her memory for the details. "They talked about a beautiful spring morning, laundry on the line, a yellow dress. Something about iron, cold and hard."

"Iron? Like something made of metal?"

"I know, it doesn't make sense. I think

that maybe it could have been the murder weapon."

Celia's eyes went wide. "I have to show you something." Celia went to the basement door and slid open the lock.

"What? What is it?"

"Someone left it on our front step." Celia pulled on the doorknob but it wouldn't open. "I came home last week and found it. I asked Dean about it and he said he had no idea what it was, but said something like, 'It sure would make a good murder weapon, though, wouldn't it?' " Celia yanked on the knob again and the door popped open. She flipped the switch on the wall and started the slow descent.

Sarah followed close behind. Her thoughts went to a fifteen-year-old Jack making this same trek down the stairs. "Celia, slow down. What is it?" With each step downward the temperature seemed to drop. The air was cool and damp. The air smelled vaguely of mildew.

The basement was immersed in darkness. The only light came from the top of the stairs. Next to her, Sarah heard Celia fumbling for something and then the click. Immediately they were bathed in the weak light of a naked bulb hanging from the unfinished ceiling.

Sarah flashed back to the crime-scene photos. She thought of Jack standing in this exact same spot and finding his mother wearing a sunny-yellow dress, lying on the concrete floor, arm outstretched, a bag of half-thawed strawberries just out of her reach, a bloodied dish towel covering her eyes.

"Sarah, here," Celia said, and Sarah dragged her eyes from the cracked cement floor to where Celia was pointing to a dark corner of the basement.

Sarah stared at the foot-long wrench-like tool made of cast iron. Though she wanted to erase the images from Lydia's autopsy photos, they kept flashing through her mind. Compared to the crime-scene pictures, while gruesome and bloody, the autopsy photos were more clinical but just as horrific.

"Don't touch that," Sarah ordered.

Celia pulled her hands back as if burned. "Why?"

"Because I think this could be the murder weapon." Sarah's heart was thumping in her chest.

"What do we do?" Celia asked, now seeming more panicked. "Oh, my God, do you think it was Dean? Do you think Dean did all this?"

"I don't know." Sarah patted her pocket for her phone to call the police. "Dammit, I dropped my phone upstairs."

"I don't have mine, either," Celia said.

Sarah turned on her heel and in three long strides was at the foot of the stairs when something caught her eye. Her eyes shifted to a large wooden trunk intricately painted with strawberries and vines and flowers. The hair on the back of Sarah's neck stood up. Sitting on the trunk was a box filled with hand sickles and corn knives. Something clicked in her mind. Exactly the same items that were in the photos on Seller85's auction site. Something was wrong. Very wrong. Seller85. Cellar 1985.

Behind her Celia spoke.

"What did you say?" Sarah asked. She slowly inched toward the stairs, lifted one foot onto the first step, laid one hand on the rickety railing.

"See how they run," Celia whispered.

From the corner of her eye, Sarah saw a flash of movement, felt the searing pain of metal on bone and then nothing.

22

With effort, Sarah opened one eye and found herself on her back, staring up at the unfinished basement ceiling. Pain throbbed through her skull and a wave of nausea swept over her. Celia's beautiful face appeared in her field of vision, staring down at her, a bemused expression on her face.

"Why?" Sarah managed to say, blood pooling in her mouth.

"It took you long enough to put the pieces together, Sarah. I thought for sure you were going to go back home to Montana without figuring it out."

Sarah struggled to sit up, her elbows digging into the rough concrete.

"Oh, no, stay put, Sarah," Celia ordered. "I don't want to have to hit you again."

Sarah willed herself to stay conscious, but the blessed escape of sleep kept pulling her one functional eye shut. *Think of Elizabeth, think of Emma,* she told herself. "Why?"

Sarah asked again.

Celia knelt down next to her, careful to avoid the blood that had trickled onto the floor. *"Why, why, why,"* she mocked. Sarah's eyes glanced toward the door. "Aw, waiting for your Jackie boy to come save you? You can scream if you like, but no one will hear you. Nobody heard Lydia, you know. She screamed and cried like a scared little baby."

Tears slid down Sarah's cheeks. "Jack was always such a simple boy," Celia said. "He won't know what to think when he gets here."

"What about Dean? Where is he?" Sarah asked as her eyes searched the room for something, anything, to use as a weapon. The shelves of preserves in glass jars, a rake standing in a corner. Both too far away.

"Dean isn't an issue." Celia's eyes gleamed dangerously. Had Celia killed him, too? Sarah wondered. And what about Hal?

"But I still don't understand," Sarah said, watching Celia swing the metal tool almost casually at her side. "Why did you kill Lydia?"

"Lydia was a nuisance. Stupid bitch tried to keep us apart and when I realized that Jack was never going to stand up to his parents I saw him for what he really was. A weak little boy. And that's when I truly saw

John for the first time." Celia's face grew thoughtful. "I loved him. But I knew he would never leave her. So Lydia had to go." She shrugged as if it was only rational. "I grabbed the nearest thing I could find." Celia held up the notching tool. "I hit her and she kept looking at me as if asking, *Why?* So I hit her again and again but she kept staring at me." Celia smiled at the memory.

"So you put the cloth over her face," Sarah finished for her.

Celia pulled her cell phone from her jeans pocket and examined the screen. "The sheriff released Jack. Not enough evidence to hold him. Yet," she added. She typed quickly. "He'll be here any minute."

Sarah could scarcely believe what she was hearing. Celia had been in love with Jack's father all along? "You were having an affair with Jack's dad?" Sarah asked.

A shadow of irritation swept across Celia's face. "I thought he would be happy that Lydia was gone. We could finally be together," Celia said, shaking her head with regret. "But it didn't work out that way." Celia set her face into a little pout that would have been charming on her in any other situation. "I told him what I'd done. What I'd done for *him* and he went crazy.

He pushed me away. He was so angry. He wanted to go to her and I knew I had to stop him. He was going to tell." Tears gleamed in her eyes. "It could have been so perfect."

"So you killed him and pushed him into the cistern," Sarah filled in. All these years everyone thought that Jack's dad had murdered his wife and run away. It was all a lie.

"And Julia? You're the one who hit her? Pushed her down the stairs? I still don't understand." Sarah's head screamed with pain. A slow river of blood slid down the side of her face.

"I made a mistake. It broke and all the charms rolled across the floor. I thought I got all the pieces but I missed one.

"Julia found the bracelet last week when she was helping me pack up some things for Goodwill. I had it hidden in a drawer beneath some old clothes. She kept asking me questions and wouldn't stop." Celia's voice rose to a high mimicking cadence. *Those charms look just like the one that was found with Lydia when she died.*"

"So you beat Julia over the head and pushed her down the stairs so she couldn't tell anyone. But why leave another charm at her side?"

"Shhh." Celia put a finger to her lips. "I

think he's coming." Celia cocked her head toward the stairs. Heavy footfalls echoed above them.

"Celia?" Sarah was at once relieved and terrified to hear the muffled sound of Jack's familiar voice. She choked back a sob. He wasn't guilty of any of this. He kept secrets, yes, but after twenty years of marriage, how could she have thought that he was capable of such horrific acts?

"Get up," Celia gritted into her ear.

"I can't," Sarah cried. "My head." She touched her temple and when she pulled her hand away blood dripped through her fingers.

"Get up," Celia said again, grabbing Sarah's sore arm, her clawlike fingers gripping into the soft flesh above her elbow. Sarah gasped in pain but managed to shift first to her knees and, with Celia's prodding, to her feet. Another wave of nausea swept over her and her stomach clenched violently.

"Celia?" Jack called again.

"Down here!" Celia responded, her voice suddenly frantic and pained.

I'm bigger than she is, Sarah told herself. *I'm stronger.* But her limbs felt heavy. She wobbled dizzily and leaned against the freezer to keep from falling over. Jack's steps came closer. Sarah looked upward. He was in the kitchen now.

Sarah wanted to call out to Jack. "Run," she tried to shout, but it came out too softly. He couldn't hear her.

"Shut up," Celia snapped, striking her in the face with the palm of her hand. "Down here," Celia cried loudly. "Jack, I need your help!"

Sarah could hear Jack's pace quicken as he descended, the wooden stairs creaking with each footstep. Celia left her side for a brief moment but returned carrying a long, slim object. Black spots appeared before Sarah's eyes and her fingertips tingled. A shotgun. She moaned in terror. By pure determination, she remained upright. She wasn't going to lose consciousness and give Celia the easy way out. If Celia was going to kill her, Sarah was going to force Celia to look her in the eye.

"Is everything okay?" he asked as he cleared the final step and turned the corner. "Where's Sarah?"

"She's here," Celia said, and pulled the trigger.

23

The acrid smell of gunpowder filled Sarah's nose and her ears rang with the power of the blast. A hazy smoke filled the room and it was a few seconds before Sarah realized she was staring at her husband's crumpled form resting against the opposite wall. A red stain bloomed against his white shirt and his face was a mask of pain and disbelief.

"Sarah?" he mouthed silently.

Sarah fell to her knees. The concrete bit into her skin, but she barely felt the pain. Sarah cried, "Oh, my God, Jack! Jack!" Jack fell forward, his head striking the floor with a sickening thud.

Celia continued talking as if nothing happened. "After I took care of his parents, I thought that Jack and I would go back to the way things were."

"You're crazy," Sarah murmured, struggling to stand.

"You ruined everything," Celia said, her voice filled with rage and disdain. "You started digging into things. I saw how you and Margaret were off whispering whenever you got the chance. I saw you snooping around Jack's old room, looking in drawers. You were *this* close to finding the bracelet. I got to wondering why you were so careful to lock your car all the time, even out here in the country. No one does that, unless they are trying to hide something. So I took a little peek in your trunk and saw the evidence box." Celia's eyes burned with anger. "You couldn't just let things go."

"But there was nothing in the box that pointed to you," Sarah tried to explain. "You don't have to do this."

"You're a little whore and if it weren't for you, Jack would be with me. He loves me, you know." Celia scowled as if the words were bitter on her tongue. "We belong to-gether."

"You're delusional," Sarah said. She was weak with blood loss and exhaustion.

"Shhh," Celia hushed with her finger pressed to her lips. She looked at Jack, who appeared to be unconscious, blood seeping out from beneath him in a black puddle. "He's sleeping, you'll wake him up."

Sarah knew that if she didn't get to a

phone, Jack would bleed to death and she would be next. She needed to keep Celia talking. "You framed Amy. You put the bloody bale hook in the box."

"Well, aren't you the little Sherlock Holmes?" Celia said in mock approval. "I had no idea that Amy found the charm I put next to Julia. That was just my little inside joke."

Sarah felt nauseous. "But if you shoot both Jack and me, the police will know that someone else did it."

Celia laughed. "Do you think I'm that stupid?" she mused. "I won't be the one they think shot Jack. He lured you down here and attacked you. You grabbed the gun from the corner and shot him trying to protect yourself," Celia said with a smirk. "But sadly, you will die from your head injuries." Celia gave an exaggerated sigh. "Coincidentally caused by the same weapon used to kill Lydia." With her free hand she pointed to the notching tool. "And poor, poor Celia will be found unconscious at the bottom of the stairs, a witness to it all."

"But how are you going to explain Julia's head injury. Jack wasn't even in town when she was hurt. And it was the poison that killed her, not the blow to the head."

"You're pretty smart for someone so

dumb." Celia tapped Sarah's temple, causing her to cry out in pain. "There's still Amy. Amy hit Julia and Jack poisoned her. The two siblings were in it together. I've already hid the poison and the burner phone in Jack's suitcase. Gilmore will find them and all the loose ends will be tidied up."

"You're insane," Sarah whispered. "No one will believe you." Out of the corner of her eye she saw Jack's fingers move. He was still alive. He managed to lift his head slightly and made eye contact with Sarah.

"I've fooled everyone for the past thirty years, haven't I? Why would this time be any different?" Celia rested the shotgun on her shoulder and turned toward where Jack lay. Suddenly, Jack's hand shot out and he grabbed Celia's ankle, causing her to stumble to her knees, and the shotgun clattered to the ground.

Without thinking, Sarah lunged for the barrel, her fingers wrapping around the cool metal. At the same time Celia reached for the stock of the shotgun and for a moment they were locked in an absurd game of tug-of-war with Sarah acutely aware that Celia's fingers were just inches from the trigger.

Sarah loosened her grip on the shotgun and the momentum forced the butt to strike

Celia squarely in the mouth. Celia cried out in rage as blood spurted from her lips and she yanked back on the rifle, pulling it from Sarah's bloody hands. Breathing heavily, Celia planted her feet and once again hefted the shotgun to her shoulder, taking aim.

Helplessly, Sarah tried to meet Jack's eyes, but he had moved from her line of vision. She had so much she wanted to say to him — that she loved him, loved their life together, that she was sorry she had ever thought the very worst of him — and now she would never get the chance. She screwed her eyes shut, not wanting Celia's face to be the last image she would see in life. The blast of the shotgun rattled her teeth and all the air was thrust from her chest.

Unable to move, Sarah stared up at the ceiling, the naked lightbulb swaying lazily above her in hypnotic circles. The world around her became void of sound; a strange, not unpleasant warmth slid down her neck and darkness closed in around her.

24

Sarah woke to the sound of a familiar voice. She tried to move her right arm but found she couldn't. She lifted her left hand and found IV tubing trailing up to a bag holding clear liquid. She gingerly touched her temple and felt a thick layer of gauze. She was in a hospital. She was alive.

"Jack," she managed to croak.

A figure stepped into her line of vision and Margaret Dooley's plump, pleasant face leaned over her.

"She's awake," Margaret reported to someone that Sarah couldn't see. Margaret's voice sounded hollow and far away. She turned back to Sarah and murmured something that Sarah couldn't understand.

"I can't hear you," Sarah said. Her lips were chapped. Her mouth was dry.

"From the shotgun blasts," Sheriff Gilmore said loudly, stepping into view. "It's just temporary. It should improve in time."

"Jack?" Sarah asked again.

"In surgery," Margaret said. "He's going to be okay," she added quickly.

Sarah closed her eyes and breathed out a sigh of relief. He was going to be okay. Jack had been innocent all along. It was Celia who had brought so much pain and loss to the family, and Jack was just another one of her victims.

"I'll go get you some water," Margaret said, and left the room.

Gilmore pulled up a chair next to the left side of Sarah's bed where she could see him with her uninjured eye. "That's going to take some time to figure out."

"Is she dead?"

"Yes."

"I tried to get the gun away from her, but it must have gone off." Gilmore looked down at her with his cool, unreadable gaze. Sarah knew she should have felt relief or even regret for nearly taking the life of another human being. But she didn't. She felt nothing.

"You didn't shoot Celia," Gilmore said. He rubbed his chin and for the first time Sarah noticed the gray stubble on his chin, the deep grooves of exhaustion that lined his eyes. "Jack was able to get the shotgun away from her and hit her with it. She was knocked to the floor and struck her head on the concrete. She died during surgery."

Margaret stepped back into the room with a plastic cup filled with ice water in her hand. She came to Sarah's bedside, pressed the control on the bed to slowly raise Sarah's head and held the cup while Sarah took a small sip from the straw. The cold water felt good on her throat. Margaret set the cup down and pulled up a chair next to Gilmore. "After we met at the library, you never called me like you said you were going to. I tried to get ahold of you and you didn't answer. Finally, I called the sheriff, told him that you were planning on going to Celia and Dean's."

"You owe Margaret here your life," Gilmore said seriously. "It took some convincing, but Margaret is persistent. She told me how you thought the three blind mice from the emails were the farmers' wives. John and Lydia, Hal and Julia, Dean and Celia."

Sarah nodded, pain coursed through her head and she gave a small cry.

"Do you want me to call a nurse?" Margaret asked in alarm.

"No, no, I'm fine," Sarah insisted. She knew the pain medication would cause her to become sleepy and she wanted to know what had really happened.

"Well," Margaret went on, "after you left the library I realized that Celia wasn't the final farmer's wife. You were."

"Me?" Sarah gave a small laugh. "I'm not a farmer's wife."

"That's where you're wrong," Gilmore said, taking up the story. "Technically, the farm belongs to Jack and Amy. Dean and Celia just rented the house and the land from Julia."

"But Celia wasn't ever a suspect," Sarah recalled. "She was only, what? Fifteen or sixteen years old?"

"A very disturbed fifteen-year-old," Gilmore said.

Sarah thought a moment. "Celia put the watch on my windshield to make everyone think that John was back."

"Or to make everyone think that Jack put it there, or Amy. She didn't care as long as it didn't point back to her. Remember, Jack was our number-one suspect for a time and Amy, well, Amy's had a troubled past."

"All along she was the one sending me the emails." Sarah gave a small laugh. "Some investigative reporter I am."

"Don't feel too badly. Celia was living right here in town for decades and I didn't know what she was capable of, either."

"She lured me down to the cellar to make it look like Jack attacked me and I shot him in self-defense."

"That way both you and Jack are dead, out of the way." Gilmore stood. "By the way, when you get a chance, you should call that newspaper man from Montana. He's pretty worried about you. He's called here about ten times in the past twenty-four hours."

Sarah remembered one of her last conversations with Gabe. "He told me something about Lydia's murder not being a spur-of-the-minute killing — that it was planned. How did he know that?"

Gilmore crossed his arms in front of his chest. "There were traces of rat poison in Lydia's system. Not enough to kill her. At the time we thought John had first tried to poison her and then ended up bludgeoning her to death when that didn't work. Obviously we were wrong. She was slowly being poisoned just like Julia — three blind mice," Gilmore said grimly.

Sarah thought of Elizabeth and Emma and tried to sit up. "What about the girls? Did anyone call Elizabeth and Emma? Do they know that we're going to be okay?"

"I hope you don't mind," Margaret said almost shyly. "I called them and told them what happened. I told them you both are going to be just fine."

"Thank you," Sarah said with relief.

"You talk to your girls now and then get some sleep," Gilmore said. "I'll stop back in a few hours." Sarah watched as Gilmore's tall, lanky frame retreated.

"I should have gone to the sheriff the minute I got the first email," Sarah said hoarsely.

Margaret patted her hand. "Sarah, if you hadn't been so persistent, no one would have known what really happened to Lydia and John. No one would have known what happened to Julia."

Sarah clutched at Margaret's hand. "I can't thank you enough, Margaret. If you hadn't called the sheriff, everything would have turned out so differently. The girls would be planning our funerals right now."

Margaret returned the squeeze. "I'm glad I could help. And by the way, I told the sheriff all about how I helped get you the case files."

Sarah cringed. "I'm so sorry, Margaret," she said apologetically.

"Don't worry," Margaret said. "I still have my job. The sheriff couldn't fire the woman who helped solve three murders, now, could he?"

"Margaret," Sarah said before releasing

Margaret's hands. "What about Amy? Is she out of jail?"

Margaret smiled. "She sure is. In fact, she's sitting out in the waiting room right now." She stood to leave. "I'll go get an update on Jack, and you go ahead and call those girls of yours."

EPILOGUE

Yellow and crimson leaves swept around their ankles and crunched beneath their feet as they followed the large procession from the grave site. The cool late-September air bit at Sarah's nose and she pulled her coat more tightly about her, the hazy afternoon sun already waning into evening. To her left, Elizabeth and Emma walked along beside her in respectful silence while Hal, Dean and Amy lagged a few steps behind. Next to her, Jack reached for her hand and squeezed her fingers tightly.

They were moving slowly, Jack because his arm was still encased in a cast and sling from the gunshot wound to his shoulder, and Sarah from the injury to her head. She had concealed her shorn head and zipper-like scar with a hat that Emma and Elizabeth assured her was stylish. They thought it would have been a modestly attended funeral, just what remained of Jack's small family, but it appeared as if the entire population of Penny Gate had come out to lay John Tierney's remains to rest next to his wife's after thirty years of being apart. Sheriff Gilmore and his daughter came, as did Margaret Dooley and her mother.

In the church basement, the women of Penny Gate once again had a feast prepared. Unlike Julia's funeral and dinner, this one had almost a celebratory feel. Amy had been released from jail and John Tierney's name had been cleared and a thirty-year-old mystery had been solved.

Margaret Dooley was next to Sarah chatting companionably when Jack stood and went to the front of the room. Elizabeth and Emma looked at their mom questioningly, and Sarah shrugged her shoulders. Jack held up a hand and cleared his throat. Gradually, the chatter in the room ceased.

"Thank you for being here today," Jack began, his voice soft, difficult to hear. "It means a lot to our family that you all are here to support us." His voice gained strength as he went on. "We all know what brought us together today, though we most likely will never completely understand why these terrible things happened to my family. But they didn't just happen to me, or to Hal or Dean, or Sarah. Or Amy. It happened to Penny Gate. To all of us. It changed the fabric of who we are, as a town, and a community and as people.

"There is so much that I've forgotten over the years about my life before my mother and father were taken away, but now, I'm slowly starting to remember, allowing myself to remember."

Jack's eyes found Sarah in the crowd. He was looking directly at her. Speaking directly to her. "My mother, Lydia Tierney, was a good mom. She was the kind of mom who made ice rinks in barns, made waffles for supper, and made Amy and me feel like we were the most important people in the world."

Jack's voice became thick with emotion, his eyes grew shiny, but still he held Sarah's gaze. "My father was a farmer. He taught me to farm . . ." he began.

Once the last of the townspeople slowly left the funeral, Gilmore, dressed in a suit and tie rather than his sheriff's uniform, approached. "Nice eulogy, Jack," he commented. "Your mom and dad would be proud of you."

"Thanks," Jack said a bit warily, as if he couldn't quite believe that the sheriff thought he was completely innocent in the deaths of his parents and aunt, even though all the evidence pointed to Celia alone. Celia's death, while a relief, also left a wake of misery and so many unanswered questions. The sheriff's department was still sifting through Celia's computer and personal papers, trying to find any additional insights into her twisted mind.

"So you're all settled in at Hal's?" the sheriff asked Dean. After the bloodbath in the cellar, Dean and Amy had moved in with Hal.

"Amy was right," Dean told them, "about our home being a house of horrors. I don't want to ever set foot in there again. But I should have known," Dean lamented. "She was my wife. How could I have not known?"

Jack embraced his cousin. "It's not your fault. We were all fooled by Celia for a very long time."

"She had all of us doubting one another," Amy said quietly. "She had Dean thinking I was the one who killed Julia and had me believing it was Dean." She turned to Sarah. "If you hadn't pushed so hard to find out what happened, I would still be in jail and probably would be for the rest of my life." She struggled to hold back her tears. "Thank you."

"I wish you could stay longer," Hal said longingly.

"We'll be back," Sarah promised. "And you can all come see us anytime you'd like. You would love Montana."

Hal turned to Jack. "I guess you'll want to change your name back to Tierney now that you know the truth about your dad."

"No." Jack shook his head, his eyes welling with tears. "I'm proud to be a Quinlan and I couldn't have asked for a better man to step in to be a father to me and Amy."

Hal reached up and laid a hand on his nephew's cheek and reached for Amy's hand. "Julia loved you like you were her own children, and I do, too."

"I know," Jack managed to say while Amy wept into her uncle's shoulder.

Sarah thought she could never love a place more than she loved their small home in Larkspur. Once back home, she spent countless hours, bundled up warmly, sitting on their back patio overlooking the lake and surrounded by mountains. She would watch as Winkin, their dog, trotted down the wooden steps to the end of the burnished brown deck and paced back and forth, scanning the water in search of a flicker of movement — a water bug skating across the surface, a duck not yet ready to head south wading nearby and, if he was especially lucky, a largemouth bass.

For the past few weeks, as they healed, Sarah and Jack moved cautiously around each other. Both were deeply bruised physically and emotionally. Elizabeth and Emma were overly attentive, calling two or three times per day, and Sarah's mother came over every single day. So many times, Sarah would catch Jack looking at her, and she could see the words ready to spill from his lips. What would he say? Would he be angry at her for not telling him about the emails right away? For digging through his mother's crime-scene evidence? For not trusting him?

Or would he apologize for not being forthright about his history? Would he beg for her forgiveness for leading her blindly into a town filled with secrets, to a disturbed woman intent on eliminating her?

For a while Sarah never gave him the chance. Every time he seemed ready to speak about the events in Penny Gate, she would look away or change the subject or retreat to the patio or her bedroom. Sarah didn't know if their marriage would be able to withstand all that had happened. Jack wasn't a murderer, but he also wasn't the man she thought she married. As a teen he had pushed his mother down and threatened his parents. He had lied to her in countless ways, and she didn't know if she'd ever be able to trust him again.

Jack came to her on a late-October afternoon. She was sitting on an old stump at the edge of the lake, looking out onto the smooth water, trying not to think about the damp, dark cellar, of cobwebs and of a lone lightbulb swaying overhead.

He knelt down in front of her and laid his head on her lap. "I loved you the minute I met you," he murmured. Sarah sat very still, her hands hanging loosely at her sides. "I wanted to tell you about what happened to my mom and dad. What I thought happened to them, but I was so afraid." He lifted his face from her lap and looked up at her. "I wanted a chance at having a family. A real family. I was afraid that if I told you about how my mom died, about how I was a suspect, about my dad, I thought you would run the other way. I knew if I didn't make a family with you, I never would, and I wanted that so, so badly. You and the girls have given me what Celia stole from me. Please forgive me, Sarah, please. I couldn't stand it if I lost my family all over again."

Tentatively, Sarah lifted one hand and lightly brushed his hair from his forehead with her fingers and nodded. "You haven't lost us," she whispered. "We're right here."

ACKNOWLEDGMENTS

An immeasurable amount of gratitude goes to my editor, Erika Imranyi. Her eye for detail, never-ending patience, collaborative nature and humor have made her a joy to work with. Thanks also to Liz Stein for her insights.

Thank you to Marianne Merola and Henry Thayer for all the behind-the-scenes support and encouragement.

Special thanks goes to my early readers — Jane and Meredith Augspurger, Lenora Williams and Ann Schober. Your input and encouragement was priceless. Thanks also to Mark Dalsing, who patiently fielded my questions about law enforcement.

Much gratitude goes to my parents, Milton and Patricia Schmida, and my five siblings. I love you all.

Finally, thank you to Scott, Alex, Anna and Grace for your support and faith in me — love always.

ABOUT THE AUTHOR

Heather Gudenkauf is the *New York Times* and *USA Today* bestselling author of *The Weight of Silence* and *These Things Hidden*. She lives in Iowa with her husband, three children, and a very spoiled German Shorthaired Pointer named Lolo. In her free time Heather enjoys spending time with her family, reading, hiking, and running. She is currently working on her next novel.